Acclaim for

"A beautiful story—poignant and heartwarming, filled with delightful characters and intense emotion. Chapel Springs is a place anyone would love to call home."

—RAEANNE THAYNE, *NEW YORK TIMES* BESTSELLING AUTHOR (FOR *THE WISHING SEASON*)

"No one can write a story that grips the heart like Denise Hunter . . . If you like Karen Kingsbury or Nicholas Sparks, this is an author you'll love."

—COLLEEN COBLE, *USA TODAY* BESTSELLING AUTHOR OF THE HOPE BEACH SERIES

"Denise Hunter knows how to warm up an inspirational romance with sizzling chemistry."

—KRISTIN BILLERBECK, BESTSELLING AUTHOR OF *WHAT A GIRL WANTS* (ON *DANCING WITH FIREFLIES*)

"Romance lovers will . . . fall for this gentleman who places his beloved's needs before his own as faith guides him."

—*BOOKLIST* (ON *DANCING WITH FIREFLIES*)

"Hunter's latest Chapel Springs Romance is a lovely story of lost and found, with a heroine struggling to accept that trusting God doesn't make life perfect—without loss or sorrow—but can bring great joy. The hero's love for her and willingness to lose her to save her is quite moving."

—*RT BOOK REVIEWS*, 4-STAR REVIEW (FOR *BAREFOOT SUMMER*)

"*The Trouble with Cowboys* is a fast, fun, and touching read with the added draw of a first kiss that is sure to make my Top 5 Fictional Kisses of 2012. So saddle up, ladies: We have a winner!"

—USATODAY.COM

The Wishing Season

Other Novels by Denise Hunter

The Chapel Springs Romance Series

Barefoot Summer
Dancing with Fireflies
The Wishing Season
Married 'til Monday
A December Bride

The Big Sky Romance Series

A Cowboy's Touch
The Accidental Bride
The Trouble with Cowboys

Nantucket Love Stories

Driftwood Lane
Seaside Letters
The Convenient Groom
Surrender Bay

Sweetwater Gap

Novellas included in *Smitten, Secretly Smitten,*
and *Smitten Book Club*

The Wishing Season

A CHAPEL SPRINGS ROMANCE

DENISE HUNTER

THOMAS NELSON
Since 1798

NASHVILLE   MEXICO CITY   RIO DE JANEIRO

Published in Nashville, Tennessee, by Thomas Nelson. Thomas Nelson is a registered trademark of HarperCollins Christian Publishing, Inc.

Thomas Nelson titles may be purchased in bulk for educational, business, fund-raising, or sales promotional use. For information, please e-mail SpecialMarkets@ThomasNelson.com.

Scripture from THE HOLY BIBLE, NEW INTERNATIONAL VERSION ®, NIV®. Copyright © 1973, 1978, 1984, 2011 by Biblica, Inc. ® Used by permission. All rights reserved worldwide.

Publisher's Note: This novel is a work of fiction. Names, characters, places, and incidents are either products of the author's imagination or used fictitiously. All characters are fictional, and any similarity to people living or dead is purely coincidental.

Library of Congress Cataloging-in-Publication Data

Hunter, Denise, 1968-
 The Wishing Season : a Chapel Springs Romance / Denise Hunter.
  pages cm. -- (A Chapel Springs romance)
 ISBN 978-1-4016-8704-5 (pbk.)
1. Christian fiction. 2. Love stories. I. Title.
PS3608.U5925W57 2014
813'.6--dc23

2014023770

Printed in the United States of America

14 15 16 17 18 19 RRD 6 5 4 3 2 1

In loving memory of Diann Hunt

You taught me by example, you inspired me with your beautiful spirit, you made me laugh until I cried. But most of all you loved me, just as I am. I'm so grateful God brought you into my life. You will forever be in my heart.

"She is clothed with strength and dignity;
she can laugh at the days to come."
Proverbs 31:25

Patricia "Diann" Hunt

August 2, 1955–November 29, 2013

Chapter One

PJ MᴄKɪɴʟᴇʏ ᴡᴀs ᴀʟᴍᴏsᴛ ʀᴇᴀᴅʏ ᴛᴏ ᴄᴀʟʟ ɪᴛ ᴀ ɴɪɢʜᴛ when she heard the sound. She paused in her bed, hand stilling over her tablet.

Slam.

It was probably just the wind. Or the old furnace or a loose shutter. She'd been in the rental less than a week, wasn't familiar with its sounds. She needed to chill. She was always freaking out over nothing.

She saved the changes she'd just made to her marketing plan. It was almost perfect. Just two more days. She took a breath, her nose filling with the savory aroma of the fettuccine carbonara she'd made hours before. Next time she'd try it with pancetta instead of bacon for a less smoky flavor. Maybe a touch less Parmesan and a splash of white wine.

Thud.

The sound was close. On the porch. She swung her feet to the floor. Not a 911 emergency yet, but she'd feel better with her cell in her hands. Unfortunately, she'd left it charging in the kitchen. Her heart pumped wildly.

Stop freaking, PJ.

This was Chapel Springs, not Indianapolis. But she was used

to living on campus surrounded by dozens of students, not alone. Much less set back off the road in the woods.

Clunk.

Her heart raced. That one was even closer. At the front door. She reminded herself to breathe.

She had to get to her phone, never mind the curtainless picture window or her flimsy tank and boxers. It was definitely 911 time. What good would hiding do if someone were breaking in? She eased off her mattress and tiptoed across the room.

Please, God . . . I know it's been awhile, but—

The doorknob rattled as she reached the living room. She sucked in a breath, her eyes darting to the door. The light from her bedroom shone into the darkened room, gleaming off the brass knob.

It turned.

Her breath became shallow. *Think, PJ!* She grabbed the first thing she saw: a French violet in a sturdy clay pot. She darted to the back side of the door, lifting the planter overhead just as the door cracked open.

Her breath froze in her lungs. Her fingers curled around the pot. The door flew open, banging against her bare toes and bouncing back into the body that stumbled in. A man. Tall and broad.

She went up on tiptoes, aimed for his head, and came down with the pot as hard as she could. The clay broke apart in her hands as a squeak escaped her throat.

The man grunted, swaying in the doorway. *Please oh please oh please!* He dropped to the floor with a heavy thud.

"Omigosh, omigosh." PJ danced in place, her hands trembling, her legs quaking with adrenaline. She flipped on the light, ready to grab another weapon.

But the man didn't stir. She hopped over him and went for her phone. She tapped in 911 and reported the break-in to Nancy Lee, who promised she'd send Sheriff Simmons right over. But PJ knew what that meant. The sheriff moved at a snail's pace, and she had a dangerous criminal facedown on her living room floor. A criminal who could wake any second.

Ryan. He could get here faster. She speed-dialed her brother and filled him in with a series of disjointed sentences.

"Lock yourself in your room and take your phone with you," he said. "I'll be there in three."

She hung up, staring at the still lump on the floor, scowling. Not even a week on her own and already needing her family's help.

The man wore jeans and a dark T-shirt. She wondered why he didn't have a jacket to ward off the May chill. Maybe hardened criminals didn't get cold. He had short dark hair and thick arms, one thrown out behind him, the other curling up toward his head. She squinted at something on the floor. Blood?

She tiptoed back into the room, her heart racing. It was blood, she saw as she neared. Matting his dark hair, pooling on the wood floor at an alarming rate.

Omigosh, I killed him.

No way was she checking his pulse. She just hoped he wasn't bleeding out on her floor. A knot was already forming on his forehead, but it was the top of his head that was bleeding.

Thank God Ryan was on his way. He was a volunteer firefighter, an EMT. Should she stanch the blood flow? But what if he woke up? She moved away from the man, staying by the open front door as if that would get her brother there sooner.

A couple minutes later she heard the hum of an engine and

3

the crunch of gravel. Ryan or the sheriff. She was putting her money on her brother.

A car door slammed, and soon Ryan barged through the open doorway.

He took in the sight on her floor, then shot her a look. "I told you to lock yourself in your room."

"He was bleeding."

She neared the man, feeling braver now that her brother was here. She nudged his back with her foot until he rolled over.

"Mister? Hey, mister?" His chest rose and fell. "He's breathing. Thank God."

Ryan knelt down, taking his pulse, checking his wound.

Her eyes roamed the man's face. It was a nice face. Tom Brady nice, with a sturdy jawline and long dark lashes that fanned the tops of his cheeks. A sheen of sweat covered his forehead. He didn't look like a criminal, that was for sure.

Like you've seen so many of them?

"Get a towel and apply pressure to his head," Ryan said.

She followed his orders, kneeling down and placing the towel on the man's head.

"What'd you hit him with?"

She gestured to the shattered remains of the pot and clumps of flowers and soil. "Mom and Dad's welcome home planter. So much for that."

"Yeah, well, not like it stood a chance anyway."

She shot him a look as he began treating the wound.

A minute later he frowned, setting his hand on the guy's forehead. "He's burning up."

"What does that mean?"

Ryan's eyes flickered up. "It means he's sick."

"But why would a sick man break into my house?"

Ryan looked around, picked something shiny off the floor, and held it up. A key. "Maybe he wasn't breaking in."

Her eyes fell on something else she hadn't noticed before. A small gray duffel bag that had fallen between the coffee table and couch. "Look."

Ryan's eyes followed hers. "Looks like your burglar may not be a burglar after all."

Chapter Two

COLE EVANS WOKE TO PAIN THROBBING IN HIS HEAD. Chills racked his body, and he huddled into the warmth. A voice chattered nearby. Water dripped, then something cool settled on his forehead.

Where was he? He fought through the fuzz in his head, tried to pry his eyes open. A bird chirped somewhere. More chatter. A woman's voice, pleasant, lilting. He was dreaming. Then he heard the sound of singing. Bad singing.

He couldn't even dream right.

"Cole? Hey, Cole. Wake up."

Cole fought the pull of oblivion and strained toward the dream. Toward a heavenly sweet flower scent. Pain accompanied the reach. He moaned.

"So you are alive. You going to open your eyes? 'Cause I have to go to work, and I'm not nuts about the idea of leaving you here alone all day again."

He fought the battle with his eyelids and won. A brown-haired angel leaned over him. Doe eyes, silken hair. Pretty lips, the lower one thick, almost buckling in the center.

"Thank God. I was afraid I killed you."

He wet his lips. "Where am I?" His throat was as dry as sawdust.

"Here you go." She held a straw to his lips, and he drank deeply. "You seem more alert this time. Doc Lewis checked you out. You're pretty sick. Well, plus I kind of konked you on the head." Ice rattled in the jug as she set it down.

He dropped his head to the pillow and closed his eyes a second, breathing like he'd just gone twelve rounds.

"You have a concussion. Sorry about that." She winced as she bent over his head, lifting something. She smelled like flowers and sunshine. He inhaled deeply.

Lines furrowed on her forehead. "Oooh, that looks bad."

He let his eyes drop shut for a long second. "Where am I again?"

"You don't remember? You broke into my house. Well, except you had a key, and when you came around you said you'd rented the house? I guess there was some kind of mix-up, so technically you weren't breaking in. And it's not actually my house, but I'm renting it for the summer. This is my pool house—only I don't really have a pool, so I guess it's more like a garden shed.

"Anyway, I'm PJ McKinley. I already know who you are— Cole Evans. My brother looked through your wallet. Sorry, but he was kind of freaked about me taking care of you and asked Sheriff Simmons to run a background check—don't worry, you're clean. Otherwise we wouldn't have let you stay, but the doctor said you needed to stay put, and you said you had nowhere to go—do you remember any of this?"

Had he thought the voice pleasant? It was too loud and saying too many words. He scanned the tiny room, sparsely furnished, windows on every wall, letting in too much light. He groaned.

"You probably have a headache, right?" Susie Sunshine reached for something beside the table, and pills rattled in a bottle. She dropped them into his hand, still rambling about her house.

He raised his head for another sip of water and then lay back, letting his eyes fall shut. He thought back to his last memory. Driving toward Chapel Springs, Indiana, his body aching like it would the morning after a strenuous workout. His mind foggy, his stomach woozy.

Chapel Springs. The contest. The presentation. His eyes snapped open. "What day is it?"

"Wednesday."

He'd lost a day. Where was his stuff? He struggled to sit up.

She set a hand against his chest. "Whoa, whoa. Where you going?"

He swung his jean-clad legs over the edge of the bed and felt the room spin. "Where's my stuff?"

"Listen, you're really sick. You need to lie back down."

He scanned the room, his eyes settling on his gray duffel on the sofa. He stood, blinking against the wave of dizziness, and crossed the small room.

"You shouldn't be up. You have a concussion, and you're sick."

He unzipped his duffel and riffled through until he found the folder. Only then did his racing heart begin to settle. He wavered, rocking back on his heels.

"That's it. Back to bed." Her hand wrapped around his bicep and tugged fruitlessly.

"What time is it?"

"Morning. I mean it, back to bed."

He let her tug him toward the bed, her hands cool on his heated skin. He clutched the folder in his hands. He had a lot to do before tonight. And somehow he had to think through the fog in his brain.

"I left some food over there. You've got to be hungry. My mom's going to stop by and check on you a couple times like she did yesterday. I have to leave the door unlocked 'cause I lost the key—long story."

He sank onto the flimsy mattress, blinking against the dizziness. She felt his forehead, then gave him a long look as if trying to figure him out. "Your temp is down. That's good." Her eyes darted down his chest, lingering a moment before returning to his face.

Something pulled in his stomach at the look in her eyes.

"Anyway . . . are you going to be okay, 'cause I'm going to be late for work. It's not much, but it's all I've got for the time being, and I can't get fired or I'll lose my house. And I'd never hear the end of that." She muttered the last part.

"I'm fine." Or would be when he had all his papers in order and his brain in gear. And quiet. That would help too.

"So, water here, pills, food over there. I won't be back until late tonight, but you're welcome to stay until you're better since I, you know, konked you on the head."

He leaned back against the pillows, waiting for the dizziness to pass.

She turned at the door, her straight hair flipping around her shoulders. Her eyes narrowed as she pointed her finger at him. "Stay in bed."

He would. For a while anyway. "Yes, ma'am."

And then she was gone, taking her sweet flower smell and rambling chatter with her.

PJ slipped through the door of Grandma's Attic and scanned the antique store, waiting for her eyes to adjust from the bright May sunlight. Her workday had sped by. There'd been a steady flow of customers at Fiona's Fudge Shoppe, and her arms ached from working fudge on the marble slab.

The familiar smell of old treasures filled her nose as she walked into the store. She'd spent many summer afternoons here as a child, playing in armoires and breaking things.

"PJ!" Her mom crossed the room, a feather duster in her hand, and squeezed PJ's arm. With her blue eyes and winning smile, Joanne McKinley was still a beautiful woman. "Don't you look like a savvy businesswoman. That red is stunning on you."

"I can't believe it's time. I'm so nervous."

"Relax. These people have known you all your life."

"That's what I'm afraid of. They remember me running up the church aisle in my diaper, picketing Lonnie Terrell's lemonade stand, and a hundred other foolish antics."

Mom's eyes smiled. "Well, you always were a handful."

PJ pulled at her skirt.

"You look beautiful, and you're completely prepared. Relax and let your passion shine through."

A text came in and PJ checked her screen. "Kayla. Wishing me good luck." Kayla was her roommate from college.

"Did you tell her about your dangerous intruder?" Mom's lips twitched.

"I'm telling you, he busted through the door like a wrecking ball. Scared the tar out of me. How was he this afternoon?"

"Better. Fever's down. He's alert, as you said. Polite, though not very talkative."

"Yeah, I kind of got that."

"He kind of has the looks of Tom Brady," Mom said, "though it galls me to say so."

"I know, right?" This was Colts territory, after all. The Patriots were on their love-to-hate list. PJ covered her mouth as a sneeze built and escaped. Another one followed. "Great. I'm probably getting the flu. That's what I get for tending a sick stranger." She sneezed again.

Mom waved the feather duster. "Or your dust allergies are flaring up again."

"Oh. Yeah, that's possible." PJ tugged at her skirt again. "Is this too short?"

"Not at all. You're just used to wearing pants. Hold your chin up and look them in the eyes. You've got a great plan for the Wishing House, and they'll see that."

"Yeah, but my competition probably does too."

"You've got the hometown advantage. Mrs. Simmons loves you, and she knows you want what's best for Chapel Springs."

"That's true."

Mom walked to the front and flipped the Closed sign on the door. She checked her watch. "Well, I have a young man to check on, and you have an important interview to get to." She opened the door.

PJ slipped by her, turning on the sidewalk. "Wish me luck."

"Even better—I'll pray for you."

Oh yeah. That too. "Thanks, Mom."

Chapter Three

PJ PULLED TO THE CURB AND GOT OUT OF HER 2002 MONTE Carlo, her eyes taking in the Wishing House. Over a century old, it was a sprawling historical just outside of town on Main Street. A stone retaining wall separated the property from the sidewalk and ended at a set of cracked cement steps leading up to the lawn. A handful of ancient oaks towered over the well-manicured yard and immaculate flower garden.

Her eyes moved over the two-story house itself: white built-in bays, a wide front porch, gingerbread molding that crawled along the high eaves. It was a veritable mansion. The perfect place for her bed-and-breakfast slash restaurant.

She'd never be able to afford a place like this, not if she worked twenty years at Fiona's Fudge Shoppe. *And please, Lord— that can't happen.*

With trembling legs, she crossed the yard, climbed the concrete steps to the porch, and pressed the doorbell.

Evangeline Wishing Simmons appeared a moment later on the other side of the screen door. Her short stature gave PJ a bird's-eye view of her short silver hair and frail frame. She was lively and spry for a woman in her mideighties and had been known for an antic or two of her own.

"PJ, come right in." Her voice crackled with age. "You look beautiful."

"Thank you. I hope I'm not too early."

"Not at all." She poked her wire-rim glasses into place. "Almost everyone's here. We'll get started once the other candidate arrives."

The house smelled of lemon Pledge and old money. A brass chandelier half the size of PJ's car dangled overhead on a brass chain, its light fractured by a thousand crystal pendants.

PJ followed Mrs. Simmons down a short hall and into the grand sitting room where the sound of quiet chatter echoed through the nearly empty house. It had been cleared out in anticipation of Mrs. Simmons's move to Colorado to live near her kids and grandkids. She could've just sold her family home like a normal person, but "normal" was a word no one used to describe Evangeline Simmons.

The formerly elegant room was an open space, with high white walls and age-worn wood floors. A table stretched across the back of the room. On its far side, facing her, sat a handful of people she'd known all her life. Mrs. Simmons's Persian cat, Snowball, sat in the center, her white tail flicking regally.

PJ greeted the panel, set down her laptop, and sat at the end of the table next to Mrs. Simmons. The advisory panel would help determine the outcome of the final round, though PJ suspected that the only "advice" that mattered would be Mrs. Simmons's own.

Cappy Winters was on the other side of Mrs. Simmons. He owned the local pizzeria. Beside him was Carl Dewitt, owner of Dewitt's Marina, where her brother-in-law Beckett worked part time. Janet Lewis was last. She was on the board of tourism.

PJ had to convince them her plan was the best for Chapel Springs. She hadn't gotten a bachelor's degree to work at a fudge shop. This was her shot, and she was going to win, regardless of what her siblings thought. Maybe she was the baby of the family, but she was still capable of big things. Not that they'd ever come out and say otherwise.

As she opened her laptop to her PowerPoint presentation, the doorbell rang. Mrs. Simmons went to answer the door, and Snowball leapt from the table and pranced silently across the floor in her wake. The cat turned in the doorway and gave the panel a pretentious look before continuing on her way.

PJ heard voices in the foyer, then footsteps. Mrs. Simmons appeared in the doorway, followed by a man. PJ's lips parted, and a small squeak escaped.

The man moved more easily than PJ remembered. He was immaculate in a black suit, crisp white shirt, and satiny red tie. His jaw was smooth-shaven, his hair neatly groomed.

"Panel and PJ," Mrs. Simmons said, stopping in front of the table, "please meet our second candidate, Cole Evans."

Chapter Four

COLE SCANNED THE GROUP, A POLITE SMILE IN PLACE UNTIL he came to the end of the table. Even with the lingering fog of illness, even with her professional updo and careful makeup and starchy red suit, he recognized her.

Her mouth was open, her eyes startled. He looked away, refocusing, and took a seat at the opposite end of the table, setting his presentation pieces on the floor. He felt woozy as he straightened. His head hammered. The pain pills hardly took the edge off.

His fever was gone, with the worst of the aches, but his head was still fuzzy. *Please, God. You have to help me out here. I need this. The kids need this.*

"We drew straws before you arrived," Mrs. Simmons said after she'd introduced everyone. "PJ, you're first."

"Thank you, Mrs. Simmons." Susie Sunshine smiled widely at the group and took a moment to set up her laptop. A minute later a photo of Mrs. Simmons's mansion flashed on the screen at the front of the room.

The easels he'd requested stood beside the screen. He looked at the three handmade posters at his feet and shifted in his chair.

PJ began her presentation. She wanted to open the Wishing House B & B with a fine-dining restaurant called The Grille. It was clever, giving the place Mrs. Simmons's family name. The elderly woman would like that. He wished he'd thought of it.

PJ outlined her qualifications, starting with a bachelor's degree in culinary arts and hospitality and management, then immediately focused on ways her business would benefit the community. Her eyes brightened as she spoke, her enthusiasm pouring through her words and body language.

She showed slide after slide delineating potential income and increased revenue for the town. She had graphics showing the town's lack of lodging for tourists and how her restaurant would draw people from neighboring communities and offer jobs to locals.

When she finished her closing speech, the panel was all smiles. They applauded as she disconnected her laptop and took a seat at the other end of the table.

"That was wonderful, PJ. Just wonderful," Mrs. Simmons said. "Cole, dear, whenever you're ready."

"Yes, ma'am." His eyes drifted to PJ.

She lifted her chin a notch and raised a delicate brow in challenge.

Game on, Sunshine.

PJ's leg bounced under the table as Cole stepped to the front of the room. He set three white boards on the easels, back sides out, and turned toward the group.

"As you know, my name is Cole Evans. I have one goal in life, and that's why I'm here." His voice was deep and quiet, but sure. It somehow made the room hum with energy.

PJ knotted her fists in her lap. He didn't seem so sick now. There was no frog in his throat, no sweat on his brow. She couldn't believe she'd been nursing her adversary back to health. Putting him up in her garden shed because she'd felt guilty about whacking him on the head.

She jerked her mind back to Cole and his presentation. He was talking about the foster homes he'd been in. He flipped the first board over. It was covered with photos of children.

"These are the faces of foster children. I know all of them because, at one time or another, I was in a foster home with them. Some of them have lost both parents. Others have parents who are drug-addicted or in jail or otherwise unable to care for them. Most are too old to be adopted, so they end up in foster care for the rest of their childhood. Sometimes the foster homes are pretty good. Sometimes not."

PJ felt a stab of pain and glanced at the panel. Mrs. Simmons dabbed at her eyes.

"When you're in foster care and you turn eighteen, that's the end of the line. We call it 'aging out.' You have to leave your foster home—the only home you have. Most have no family to turn to. In Indiana you receive minimal financial support. You're in the middle of your senior year in high school. You have no transportation, no means of supporting yourself, and no idea where to go or how to take care of yourself."

PJ's heart sank. Both for the situations he was describing and for the way this was going. But something like this was going to cost a fortune. It wasn't a moneymaker; it was a money pit. And it wouldn't benefit the community—something that mattered to Mrs. Simmons.

Cole flipped over another board, revealing neatly drawn

graphs. "When youth age out without a permanent family, the statistics show that 12 to 30 percent of them struggle with homelessness and 40 to 63 percent don't finish high school. Between 25 and 55 percent are unemployed, and only 38 percent of those who get jobs are still employed a year later. In addition, 40 to 60 percent of the young women become pregnant within twelve to eighteen months."

A sniffle down the table drew her attention. Janet Lewis blinked rapidly. The knot in PJ's stomach tightened.

When he finished with that board, he flipped over the third. More charts and graphs. PJ read the neat print, and her heart sank. Funding! He already had funding.

He spoke quietly about the commitments he'd already secured. He'd worked up potential costs based on a transitional house in Florida.

Finally he wrapped it up. "Eighteen-year-olds are still kids. They need a place of transition. A place where they can belong and have support and stability while they finish high school and learn a trade or put themselves through college. They need to learn how to work, how to support themselves, how to budget for a household, and so many other things.

"When I saw the ad online for this contest, I knew this was the place to start. It's my dream to open up Crossroads, a transitional home for post–foster care children. I hope you'll give me the opportunity to help these kids. Thank you."

PJ looked down at the table, her heart in her throat. This hadn't gone well at all. Even she was ready to open her doors to these kids.

But one of the criteria for this contest was community benefit. Cole had barely brushed over it because there wasn't a benefit. It would be a not-for-profit. A constant financial drain. Not to mention a bunch of rowdy teenagers running through the Wishing family parlors. That couldn't be what the woman had in mind for her beloved home.

"Thank you, Cole," Mrs. Simmons said. "I'd like to talk to my panel for a few minutes, if you two would please step into the foyer."

"Certainly." PJ stood and walked to the doorway, her heels clacking against the floor.

Once they were in the hall, Cole pulled the pocket door closed behind them, leaving them alone.

Shoulders back, she met his gaze. "Nicely done."

"You too."

"You look a lot better. Almost like you're not sick anymore at all."

He looked at her a long time. His eyes were the color of tree moss. But there were slivers of gold in there too. And brown, the shade of molten caramel. She fought against their pull and found herself on the losing end. She finally wrenched her eyes away.

"What's that supposed to mean?"

"Nothing. Just saying."

"I didn't know you were the other candidate."

"Of course you didn't. How could you?" Her heart was beating a million miles an hour. What was wrong with her?

"Then what's your point?"

"No point. There's no point at all." Except that she'd nursed her opponent back to health so he could come and steal her dream away.

He was looking at her still, and this did nothing to slow her heart rate.

But there was something fishy. Had there really been a mix-up with her rental? Maybe he'd known all along who she was. Maybe he'd snooped through her things while she'd been at work. This was his dream too. Who knew what lengths he'd go to?

"How did you end up with a key for my house again?"

He looked at her for another long second. "I rented the house until Friday."

"I rented it through July."

He held eye contact. "All the same, it's true."

She turned her body toward him and crossed her arms. "I know the Tacketts personally. I've had the place booked since last fall. Mrs. Tackett is a friend of my family's. She gave me a great rate."

He shrugged. "I booked it a month ago when I found out I was a finalist."

"How'd you get the key?"

"It was under the plant on the porch, just where he told me it'd be, Susie."

"Sus—it's PJ. And I'll be calling Mrs. Tackett about this."

"Do that."

"And I hope you've packed your things, because my garden shed is officially closed." She tipped her chin up and set her jaw.

They did battle with their eyes. It was an unfair fight.

The door slid open, and still she couldn't break free from the weird hold he had on her.

Someone cleared her throat.

PJ swung her head toward Mrs. Simmons.

The woman's penciled brows drew together as she looked between PJ and Cole. "Everything okay, dearies?"

PJ's eyes bounced off Cole as he straightened.

"Yes, ma'am," he said.

"Just peachy."

Mrs. Simmons took them both in for a long second. "Well then. I've come to tell you that you've made our job incredibly difficult. The panel is split, and that means the ball is in my court. I'm afraid I'm going to need a couple days to think this over."

PJ felt her stomach slide down to her squished toes. Stupid heels. Nevertheless, she patted Mrs. Simmons's slight shoulder. "Of course. It's a big decision."

"I'll call you both when I've made up my mind. Fair enough?"

Cole gave a nod. "Yes, ma'am."

"Thank you, Mrs. Simmons."

"You'll hear from me by Friday."

Chapter Five

TALK ABOUT NO ROOM IN THE INN. PJ HADN'T BEEN KID-
ding about the town being short on lodging. This was apparently
the first week of the farmers market, and there wasn't a spare bed
in the whole town. It was late, his head was banging, and he was
ready to call it a day.

He drove until he found a darkened lot near the back of a
park and pulled in. Across the way the marina lights twinkled
over the river. A roll of thunder rattled the windows of his truck.
A minute later the downpour started.

Feeling the drain of the day, he bundled up his duffel bag
and laid it against the window to cushion his head. He thought
back to the presentation. It had gone well. He'd left nothing on
the field.

But neither had PJ. Her plan made better business sense.
He could see that. It all depended on whether Mrs. Simmons
decided with her head or her heart. And he didn't know her well
enough to make that call. All he could do was wait.

He shifted, trying to stretch his legs in the tight space.
The rain pounding the roof was almost deafening. He hoped it
wouldn't keep up. Lightning flashed in the sky over the river, and
another crack of thunder sounded. The smell of rain permeated
his truck.

He thought of the nice warm bed where he'd spent the past two nights, remembered that PJ had left the shed unlocked. He wasn't even tempted. No wonder the house had come so cheap. It was occupied—with a chatty, weapon-wielding crazy lady.

He'd better get his money back. He punched up the duffel and resituated, taking the strain off the knot on his head.

His phone buzzed, and he grappled for it in the dark. Lizzy.

"Hey Lizzy-Lou. You should be in bed."

"Like I could sleep without hearing how it went."

"It went fine. Won't have any answers till Friday, though."

"Friday! That's forever."

He smiled at her impatience, imagining her poking her wire-rim glasses into place. "It's only two days. Is everything okay there?"

"I guess."

Lizzy had joined his foster home when she was three. She'd reminded him of his sister, Noelle, with her fragile frame and haunted blue eyes. Her baby-fine brown hair had grown long over the years, pulling the curls out to a gentle wave. He'd taken her under his wing from the beginning, and he loved her like a sister. They'd remained close even after he moved out on his own.

"Is school all right?"

"I guess so. It's almost over, thank God."

An ex-boyfriend had started rumors about her last year, and she'd had a lot of male attention ever since—the wrong kind. The girls at school had turned on her, and it had become a real mess. He wished Greg and Becky, her foster parents, would talk to the principal or something. Cole was counting the days until Lizzy turned eighteen next April. She was working hard to graduate early. He hoped to God he'd have a place for her to go. She was young and so vulnerable.

He heard a noise on her end.

"I better go," she whispered. "I'm supposed to be in bed."

"I'll call you Friday. Tell Greg and Becky I said hi."

He put his phone in his pocket so he'd feel it, just in case she needed him. If that old boyfriend was giving her trouble again, Cole was going to hunt him down and teach him a lesson.

Just eleven more months and she'd be out of foster care. Greg and Becky would make room for a younger kid. They had good hearts. But Lizzy was way too naïve to be on her own.

Please, God. I need that house. Not just for Lizzy but for the other kids. There are so many. He felt small and incapable of the monumental task. One kid at a time, he reminded himself.

He sank down in the seat and nestled against his duffel bag again. Thunder cracked. He was never going to get any sleep.

Chapter Six

PJ CLIMBED THE STEPS OF THE COACHLIGHT COFFEEHOUSE, her heart knocking against her ribs. She barely noticed the beauty of the brick Victorian building or the wide, cozy porch bustling with late-afternoon customers.

When she entered the shop she drew a deep breath, the robust smell of coffee filling her nostrils. A quick scan of the crowded room turned up no Mrs. Simmons or Cole Evans. She was early but hadn't been able to help herself. She wanted to kr w, wanted to know *now*. She hadn't been able to decipher a single hint from her brief phone call with Mrs. Simmons. Was it a good sign they were meeting here instead of at the house? Or did it just indicate a sudden caffeine craving?

PJ ordered an Americano with heavy cream and carried it to a four-top along the side brick wall. Across the room Daniel Dawson seemed to be in the middle of a business meeting. He was the town's mayor and, more importantly, her new brother-in-law.

He caught her eye and nodded in greeting.

The bell over the door tinkled as it swung open. Cole Evans filled the frame. His form was silhouetted, emphasizing his broad shoulders and narrow waist. This wasn't the weak, injured man she'd left in her shed. This man oozed raw male energy. She wondered where he'd come from. If he had a girlfriend waiting somewhere.

She shook the thought away, reminding herself who he was. That his love life was none of her business. That after today he'd be gone. *Please, God.*

She felt, rather than saw, his eyes find her. Something inside her hummed.

He approached the table, his movements slow and purposeful. The wood floor creaked under his feet, audible even above the chatter.

He reached for the nearest chair. "May I?"

"Of course." PJ leaned back in her own chair, needing some space.

His knee brushed hers under the table. She shifted away and took a sip of her coffee.

"Mrs. Simmons not here yet?" he asked.

"I should warn you, she generally runs late."

"What's another ten minutes?"

She looked him in the face for the first time since he'd arrived. He seemed weary, despite his stoic expression. She wondered where he'd been staying. She'd half expected him to remain in her garden shed, despite her withdrawn invitation. He did have a concussion after all. Speaking of which.

"How's your head?" Just because he was her adversary didn't mean she couldn't be polite. Besides, she was going to win, and the poor guy was going to walk away with a knot on his head for a consolation prize.

"Better."

"You should probably see a doctor when you get home."

He tweaked a brow, his eyes homing in on hers.

She hadn't meant to be so presumptuous, but she'd given this a lot of thought since Wednesday. She was the local girl, the one who cared about the town. And her plan was a winner for the community. Maybe Mrs. Simmons was a bit eccentric, but she wasn't foolish.

"What?" she asked when he continued to eye her.

"Little sure of yourself, aren't you?"

PJ took a sip of coffee. "Nothing wrong with a positive attitude. You seem a little tired; you should order something. They make a great Americano. My sister Madison is a big fan of their coffee beans, though she had to cut back, and my other sister, Jade, swears they make the best mocha frappe on the planet, though I wouldn't know because I don't like milk." He was staring at her funny. "What?"

"You talk a lot."

Of all the— "Well, someone has to."

"Why's that?"

"Why's what?"

"Why does someone have to talk?"

Her lips parted. Was he being serious or just goading her? She couldn't tell. "Some people happen to like it. Some say my energy is contagious, and my way with words is a gift. It's called conversation. You should try it."

"I would if I could get a word in edgewise."

PJ clamped her mouth shut, narrowing her eyes. Where was a potted plant when she needed one? She went back to her Americano, determined not to say one more word until Mrs. Simmons appeared.

From the corner of her eye she saw Cole open a newspaper, spreading it in front of him. Thank God he'd be going soon. They couldn't go three minutes without bickering.

A few minutes later Mrs. Simmons entered. She went first to the counter to order a drink, then she approached, cupping her pink smoothie.

Cole pulled out the chair for her. *Nice touch.*

Mrs. Simmons patted his hand. "Thank you, dearie. Hello, PJ. I'm sorry to keep you both waiting. Snowball got locked in the moving truck, and it took forever to find her. Poor thing was traumatized. I think she'd do anything to avoid that airplane crate, but I can't have her in that dark truck all by her lonesome all the way to Colorado, can I?"

"Of course not." PJ eyed Mrs. Simmons's bejeweled hand, still curled around Cole's. Not good.

Unless it was sympathy. That's what it was. Sympathy.

Mrs. Simmons offered Cole a drink, and he politely declined. She set her other hand over PJ's. Could she be turning them both down? Maybe she had decided to sell the house after all and open a new hospital wing instead. A fresh wave of anxiety made PJ's heart pound.

"I'm sorry it's taken so long to reach a decision. After Wednesday, I knew I had a lot of thinking to do, and these days that takes a lot of time."

PJ traded smiles with her. She didn't look at Cole. He wasn't even here. Wasn't in this race. *Please, God.*

"Well, I know you're both anxious to hear my verdict, but the truth is . . . I just can't decide."

PJ frowned. Then tried to smile because she didn't want to

offend Mrs. Simmons. Her eyes darted to Cole. His expression was as unreadable as ever.

"I—what does that mean exactly?" PJ asked.

"I need more time. I need to see your plans in action."

"But," PJ said, "that's not possible."

Mrs. Simmons's eyes sparkled like diamonds. "That's what I thought at first! But then I thought, why, the house is so big. Plenty big enough for Cole's kids and PJ's restaurant." She squeezed both their hands. "So for one year you'll share it. You, my dear, will open your fine dining establishment." Her eyes swung to Cole's. "And you will have your transition housing!"

Cole ran his knuckles over his jaw, still quiet.

"I've got it all figured out." Mrs. Simmons fanned her aged fingers out. "Those kiddos of yours need a place to stay while they finish high school. PJ, you're opening a restaurant, and you need a staff. Voila! Built-in employees."

She looked between the two of them like she'd just discovered the key to world peace. Apparently seeing their lack of excitement, she continued, "Don't you see? Your kiddos can live in the house and staff the restaurant to earn their keep, develop a strong work ethic, maybe even pick up new skills that'll make them employable. See?"

PJ saw all right. She saw teenagers who couldn't fry up a grilled cheese sandwich trying their hand at coq au vin. Saw kids who didn't know the difference between rice and risotto cooking in her kitchen, handling her fresh produce.

"But . . . but . . ."

"You have one year to show me what you can do. I'll check in with you from time to time, and on June 1 of next year you'll do another presentation for the board. This time you'll have real-life statistics, and I'll be able to see which opportunity is truly the best fit for my family home.

"In the meantime, the community will benefit from the restaurant—we don't have anything grand for miles—and your children will get a temporary home through their senior year." Mrs. Simmons pressed her palms together. "It's just perfect, isn't it? I know there's a detail or two to work out, but I'm certain we can handle it."

"That's a very . . . creative approach, ma'am," Cole said, finally finding his voice.

"The community will love it—a hearty competition being played out right in front of them. Plus a lovely restaurant and a noble cause to boot." She sat back, looking so proud.

"I'm sure they will." He prodded PJ with his look.

"Um . . ." PJ cleared her throat. "Mrs. Simmons, this may be more complicated than you've figured. I mean, how can high school kids be expected to cook fine cuisine? And where are we going to live in the meantime?"

"Why, you'll teach the kids, dear! You're a McKinley. I'm sure you're up to the task. And there's plenty of room for the both of you. PJ, you'll take the first floor, and Cole will take the second. It won't take much at all to add a little kitchen up there. I've thought it all through. I'm having the agreements drawn up as we speak, and they'll be ready to sign next week."

She squeezed both their hands. "Now, I really hate to run, but Snowball is traumatized from her difficult morning, and I really must get back to her."

She gave one last slurp of her smoothie, her wrinkled red lips pursed around the straw. "I'll call you next week, and we'll meet to sign the papers. I'm so excited! I can't wait to see how it all turns out. Have a lovely afternoon, dearies."

PJ watched her leave, watched the door fall shut behind her. A squeak escaped her throat. More customers entered and exited. She couldn't tear her eyes from the door.

Cole broke the silence. "What just happened? We can't share the house, and my kids aren't serving in some froufrou restaurant for rich people. They've had enough people looking down their nose at them."

PJ glared at him. "Now you find your voice? Where was it two minutes ago when Mrs. Simmons was sitting right in front of you?"

"You didn't tell me she was nuts."

"She's not nuts. She's . . . eccentric."

"Well, we have to talk her out of this."

PJ closed her eyes, past experiences with Mrs. Simmons flitting through her mind. The community garage sale, the theater ticket incident, the annual auction.

"What?" he asked.

"You don't know how stubborn she is. She's not changing her mind."

"We have to talk to her. Make her understand it won't work. We can't pour all this money and energy into a house we might lose."

"You're right, it won't work. So why don't you just do the honorable thing and back out?"

"Since when is quitting honorable? And if you're so fond of the idea, why don't *you* back out?"

Had she thought his green eyes mesmerizing? She bit her tongue, literally, and looked away. They had to fix this. It couldn't work. Could it?

He leaned into his elbows. "Listen, I need this more than you—"

"How do you figure?" She was out on her own with hardly a penny in the bank and working in a freaking candy store.

"These kids need this."

She pictured the images from his poster board and felt a stab of guilt. "And my business venture is self-serving, is that what you're saying?"

He clenched his jaw and looked out the picture window.

"My enterprise will help this community. And it's *my* community. *My* home. *I* belong here."

He looked at her. Something flickered in his eyes before they shuttered.

She remembered his foster kid childhood and felt another prick of guilt. He probably hadn't felt as if he'd ever belonged anywhere. An ache swelled in her gut. "Listen, I'm sorry, I—"

"This isn't feasible. We can't get along for five minutes, much less live under the same roof for a year."

She shrugged. "We don't necessarily have to live there."

"Speak for yourself, Sunshine."

PJ crossed her arms, the ache inside fading fast. He had her all pegged. "You don't know me."

"We need to talk to her, and we need to do it together." He gave her a pointed look.

"What? You don't trust me?"

"Why would I? You're a stranger."

"I nursed you back to health!"

"You gave me a concussion."

She glared at him. She wasn't getting anywhere with him. Just like she wouldn't get anywhere with Mrs. Simmons. The woman would talk in circles until their minds were spinning like blender blades and their signatures were scrawled across the dotted lines.

"Fine. We'll talk to her. But don't get your hopes up."

Chapter Seven

PJ SHUT HER CAR DOOR AND PULLED HER SWEATER TIGHT against the evening chill. Gravel crunched under her Sperry's, and a cricket chirped nearby. She walked around the side of her parents' farmhouse, breathing in the smell of freshly cut grass. In the distance newly planted cornfields stretched over rolling hills all the way to the setting sun.

Home.

After the day she'd had, she needed this. The conversation with Mrs. Simmons had gone just as she'd suspected. She and Cole, slightly dizzy from the older woman's monologue, had left the house with signed copies of the contract.

Okay then. She would make this work. She'd find a way to turn a profit and convince Mrs. Simmons that her restaurant deserved a place in the community.

As she neared the backyard the sounds of laughter, chatter, and family were almost enough to draw a smile. The smell of grilling chicken grew stronger until her stomach rumbled in anticipation.

She rounded the corner, entering the backyard with its shade trees and cozy patio. The twinkle lights were already on, though the sun hadn't set. A game of two-on-two stopped at her arrival.

"PJ's here!" Mom called, coming in for a hug. Everyone descended at once. Her dad. Ryan. Jade and Madison with their husbands.

She scanned the group for her six-month-old nieces. Only then did she see the banner and balloons.

"Wait," PJ said. "What's going on?"

Mom pulled back from the hug. "I ran into Mrs. Simmons at the café. She refused to tell me the decision outright, but I could tell . . . What's wrong?"

"Where do I start?"

"What happened?" Madison asked. "I thought you had this all sewn up."

PJ looked from sibling to sibling. Smart Madison with her successful veterinary practice. Jade, newly married to the mayor, with her musical talent and her very own adorable twins. Dependable Ryan, who seemed to succeed at everything he did. Marriage notwithstanding.

"Well, it's sort of good news," PJ said.

Jade shifted a fussy baby to Daniel, who walked toward the house for a bottle or something. "Then why the long face?"

"Let's go sit down." Mom tugged her to the cloth-covered picnic table, already set with tableware, a Ball jar of freshly cut pink peonies in the center. Her siblings sat opposite her, while her dad, Beckett, and Grandpa returned to the grill nearby.

It was time to look at the bright side. This was happening, like it or not, and the alternative wasn't acceptable. Besides, she couldn't stand to see I-told-you-so looks on her siblings' faces.

"Bottom line is, I'll be opening the restaurant, just not the bed-and-breakfast—at least for now. So it's good. I get to run my own restaurant right out of culinary school. How many people get that opportunity?"

"But what are you going to do with all those rooms?" Ryan asked.

"Have babies?" Jade's rings clinked together as she laced her fingers.

"Not funny," Mom said. "Let's get her married first."

Jade gave a wry grin. "Gee thanks, Mom."

Mom rubbed her shoulder. "Now, honey, I didn't mean anything by that. You know we couldn't love the twins more."

"Seriously." Madison tossed her long brown hair over her shoulders just in time for Beckett to come up behind and rub them. "Why not the B & B? I thought it was a sound idea, if a bit much to take on."

A bit much for PJ, she meant. "I could've handled it just fine. But Mrs. Simmons felt Cole Evans's plan had merit also." She sighed and let them in on the rest of the plan. "She couldn't make up her mind, so she wants to see our plans in action. We have one year to make a go of it, and then she'll make her final decision."

"Wait," Dad said, a chicken breast hanging from the massive tongs in his mitted hand. "You have to wait a year?"

"That's ridiculous," Mom said.

"Yes." PJ's leg bounced under the table. "It's like a trial run. We'll each have our separate enterprises."

"Separate!" Jade said. "You'll be under the same roof. What do you even know about this guy?"

"I don't like this, PJ." Dad lowered the chicken to the grill and closed the lid.

"You need to think this through, honey." Mom stilled PJ's

leg with a hand. "Getting a restaurant up and going will be expensive."

"You know, most businesses don't even make a profit the first few years," Madison said.

"Do you think I haven't thought this through? I won't have to pay rent, so my overhead will be low. If, God forbid, I lose, I can store all the equipment and open my restaurant later. As for operating expenses, I can work part time if I need to." And staff would come really cheap, but she wasn't about to go there. Besides, she didn't see that working anyway.

"But you'll have the construction loan," Beckett said, taking a two-second break from Madison's massage.

"I'm aware of that. I'll keep the build-out to a minimum."

"What if he's dangerous?" After what Jade had been through in Chicago, it was a legitimate question. A date rape had left her pregnant and alone. It was only after coming home that she'd managed to find stability again—and Daniel had played a big part in that.

"His background check was clear," Ryan offered.

PJ shot him a look of gratitude.

"Isn't it kind of a weird coincidence that he showed up on her doorstep, rented the same house?" Mom said.

"Apparently the house got caught in the middle of the Tacketts' divorce," PJ said. "Deb rented it to me, and Herb rented it to Cole."

"I still don't like it," Mom said.

"I can ask the sheriff to run a more thorough investigation if that'd make you feel better, Mama Jo." Daniel wasn't one to throw his mayoral weight around, so it was hard to be offended by the offer.

"Thanks, Daniel."

"He may have already done that for Mrs. Simmons," Ryan said.

The sheriff was Mrs. Simmons's nephew, after all. It made sense she'd want to check his background before letting him move in.

"Cole has a good heart," PJ said. "He wants to help foster kids, and his business plan is viable. He even has his funding in place already." Why was she taking up for him? "I'm not saying it won't present some challenges, but I can make anything work for a year."

"You seem awfully solemn for a girl about to move in with Mr. Tall, Dark, and Handsome," Madison said.

"Oooh, you never said he was good-looking," Jade said.

Daniel gave Jade's shoulder a squeeze. "Hey now."

Jade kissed his knuckles. "Just don't sign anything until you get the background check—I don't care what he looks like."

"And have an attorney look over the documents," Ryan said.

Too late. On both counts.

Dad crossed his arms. "I still don't like this. I'm going to have a talk with Mrs. Simmons."

PJ stopped short of rolling her eyes. "No, Dad. I'm an adult. I can handle this."

Mom patted her back. "That's right. She's an adult. I'm sure everything will be just fine. And we'll pitch in, won't we, kids?"

"Sure."

"Of course."

PJ didn't miss the skeptical looks on their faces. She clenched her teeth. She was going to win this house if it killed her.

It was late by the time PJ left her parents' house, worn out from the questions. Why was she always defending herself? No one questioned Madison when she wanted to become a vet. No one said a peep when Jade wanted to start teaching guitar or when Ryan wanted to be a volunteer firefighter. Hello, he was risking his life.

Okay, it wasn't that they hadn't said anything to the others. Her family always had plenty to say. But it was obvious they didn't trust PJ to make big decisions. They just didn't think she was capable of making it on her own.

She inhaled, then exhaled hard. It had been a long day at the fudge shop, then the awkward meeting with Mrs. Simmons and Cole, and the family meal . . . all of which made her want to sink into her comfy bed with her familiar quilt and feather pillows.

Or better yet, hit the kitchen and whip up something delicious—a raspberry cheesecake . . . crème brulee . . . a nice chocolate ganache cake? Mmm, that sounded good. She'd been noodling over a new recipe. But she needed a quality bittersweet chocolate and heavy cream.

PJ swung left when she reached Main Street. The market on the other side of town was her best bet, but it closed at eleven. Despite her need to hurry, she went slowly through town. Sheriff Simmons liked to sit back in the Acorn Street alley and catch people going thirty-four in a thirty.

The sidewalk had been rolled up hours ago, the only movement coming from the Rialto theater lights running in their never-ending rectangle and the whipping of the flags in front of the courthouse.

She accelerated as she exited town and rounded the curve by

the marina. The lights twinkled off the Ohio River. Overhead a nearly full moon brightened the sky.

On the other side of the road, the park was quiet and empty save for a truck at the back of the lot. She squinted and eased her foot off the gas. Was that Cole's truck? It had sat in her driveway for two days, an old-model blue Ford.

She couldn't tell the truck's color in the dark, but it had to be his. No one in town drove one like it, and it was unlikely to be a tourist this time of night.

What was he doing here? Taking a midnight stroll? She saw a movement in the front seat and pressed the gas pedal again. Why was he sitting in his truck this time of night instead of settling in his hotel room?

Unless . . .

The night he'd shown up he'd said—once he regained consciousness—that he had no place to go. And she'd made it clear he wasn't welcome in her shed. She followed the road, looking in her rearview mirror, guilt wedging into the tight spaces of her heart.

Chapter Eight

PJ STEPPED OUT OF HER CAR AND LOOKED UP AT THE WISHING House. It was all hers. Well, not *all* hers. Just the first floor, and only for a year. But it was about to become her very own fine dining establishment. She bounced on her heels. She could do this.

She walked up the steps to the lawn and stopped, envisioning the sign she was going to order. It would go right beside the walkway, in front of the beautiful flower garden. She'd been planning to name it Wishing House Bed & Breakfast and call the restaurant The Grille. But since the B & B was on hold, she'd decided to name her restaurant Wishing House Grille. Classy but not pretentious. She'd add the B & B to the sign after she earned the house.

The sweet fragrance of lilacs drifted over on a breeze, mingling with the scent of freshly mown grass. A mourning dove called from the branches overhead, its call soft and lamenting.

A door slammed behind her, and PJ turned. Cole strode up the steps. She remembered seeing his truck at the park and knew he must be even more eager than she to take possession of the house today.

He wore a black T-shirt and worn jeans. His short hair was mussed, and a few days' stubble covered his jaw. Neither diminished his looks one bit.

"Morning," he said.

She returned the greeting, dragging her eyes back to the yard. "I was just envisioning where the sign should go. Right here, I think. These flower beds are beautiful, but they're going to take a lot of work." She scanned the yard. "A lot of grass to mow too. Maybe some good chores for your kids, right?"

The corners of his mouth tightened. "My kids aren't going to become the help around here, if that's what you're thinking."

PJ crossed her arms. "You're the one who was going on about teaching them responsibility and work ethic."

"That doesn't mean they're going to be your free labor. And while we're on the topic, they're not going to be your personal minions in your kitchen either."

"Like I really want a bunch of untrained teenagers messing around in my kitchen."

They stared each other down.

Holy moly. It was only the first day. The first two minutes. PJ drew in a lilac-scented breath and let it out slow and easy. "I think we should keep things separate as much as possible. Separate jobs, separate entrances, separate floors."

"Fine."

Finally they agreed on something. She'd have to find a way to ease into this relationship. It had started badly, but that could be rectified. She was a pro at making friends. She just needed to try harder.

"The architect will be here at nine thirty. She did work on my sister's veterinary practice. She's good and, equally impor- tant, not too expensive."

"I don't need an architect."

PJ frowned. "What do you mean? Won't you have to tear

down walls and move things? Add a bathroom or two and a kitchen?"

"I'll do it myself."

"But what if you tear into a load-bearing wall? Or bust a water line?"

"I know what I'm doing," he said as he walked away.

Maybe he wouldn't be making many changes. The less work for her when she made that space into her B & B.

He was just going to have to keep his distance, Cole figured. Wouldn't be easy working in the same house, but if they kept to their own floors it would be fine.

The upstairs looked even better than it had online. Four bedrooms, most big enough for two; two full baths; a small attic. He could take the attic room for himself, turn one bedroom into a living room and another into the kitchen. Heaven knew Sunshine wouldn't be sharing hers. That left two bedrooms—enough for four kids. The thought put a bounce in his step. He only had funding for three, but maybe if he budgeted carefully . . . After all, he'd figured on paying the full utility bill, and now he only had to pay half. Plus Lizzy wouldn't come until April.

He ran his hands along the uneven plaster walls as he walked down the narrow hall. They needed a coat of paint. The wood floors creaked under his feet, a familiar sound that reminded him of home, his real one. The one he'd had before the accident.

He checked out the bathrooms. The plumbing was ancient but in decent shape. The bedrooms needed additional electrical outlets, and the whole upstairs was in dire need of decent lighting. The fancy draperies would have to go eventually, but that could wait.

He was making good progress on his hardware store list when Lizzy called. She didn't have many friends, but with all the attention she got from the boys, she was a train wreck waiting to happen. Cole was going to do everything in his power to make sure she wasn't taken advantage of.

He asked after their foster parents, and they chatted until she had to get off the phone. He told her he loved her before he hung up. Although Becky and Greg told her that often, he knew she needed to hear it a lot. Her father had abandoned her at birth, and her mother was a drug addict who saw her only sporadically. He pocketed his phone and flipped the hall light switch, but nothing happened.

The stairs creaked behind him. PJ was standing in the middle of the wide staircase, her hand curled around the mahogany banister.

"Sorry. Didn't mean to eavesdrop."

He shrugged, trying the light switch again. "How'd it go with the architect?"

"Good. I'm really excited to see what she comes up with." PJ trotted up the rest of the steps, her ponytail swinging like a pendulum. "How's it going up here?"

"Everything's pretty sound." The fewer details she knew, the less she could fuss over.

"Except the hall light?" Her eyes flickered upward, then back to him, and her smile drew his eyes for a long second.

"Yeah." He walked into the nearest room and tried to open the window. He'd need to air the place out when he painted.

After a little tugging, the window went up. The old wood sash, weighted with a balance, was nearly painted shut.

"The downstairs windows are new." She'd followed him into the room, bringing her sweet flower smell with her. "Too bad she didn't replace these. They look ancient."

"As long as they open, they'll do for now." He brushed past her and entered the next room, repeating the process. This window put up more of a fight.

"Our heating bill is going to be atrocious." She came up next to him and ran a fingernail along the chipping white paint.

They were nice hands. Long, slender fingers tapering down to short but well-kept nails. Her skin looked softer than anything he'd touched in a long time.

"I don't think she spent much time up here," PJ said. "Her bedroom was downstairs."

"There's a bedroom downstairs?" Maybe he could fit a couple more kids in. He'd have to get more funding, but—

"Down, boy. That's *my* bedroom."

"I thought you already had a house."

"A rental, remember? And only through July. Once renovations are complete, I'm moving in."

He ran his knuckles over his face. He'd just assumed it would be him and the kids.

"Don't worry, it's big enough for both of us—and a handful of teenagers." She followed him to the next room. "Hopefully your girlfriend's understanding."

He frowned, then realized she must've overheard his parting words to Lizzy and made assumptions. He wasn't going to correct her. Better she thought him taken.

For that matter, she probably had a boyfriend of her own.

Cole hoped the guy wouldn't go ballistic at the setup. It wasn't like they'd be here alone. By the time her renovations were complete, there'd be a houseful of kids.

"So when are you moving in?" she asked.

"Today." After a week in the car he could hardly wait to sprawl out on the floor.

"Which room you taking?"

Didn't she have something better to do than follow him around? "This one for now. The attic after I clean it out."

"Oooh, nice. I always wanted an attic room. I never had a room to myself until I rented my house." She peeked into the closet.

Since she was otherwise occupied, he checked her out. Her long brown hair was pulled into a sloppy ponytail. Her neck was exposed, and the slope of it made him want to press a kiss where it met with her shoulders.

What the heck was he thinking?

His eyes fell on her square shoulders and traveled past her trim waist, down her long legs.

"Omigosh." She looked over her shoulder.

He jerked his eyes back to the window.

"My jeans alone wouldn't fit in here."

He was sure his kids wouldn't have that problem.

"So where you from? I don't think you ever said."

"North of here. Fort Wayne."

"Big city compared to Chapel Springs."

"Yep."

She followed him into the next room. The window wouldn't budge.

"How'd you hear about the contest?"

"Ran across it online."

"Yeah, I couldn't believe she was giving this place away. But, hey, when you've got more money than Bill Gates . . . Need some help?"

"I got it." He used his legs, his arms straining.

"So you have any siblings?"

The whole truth was too painful and would only lead to more questions. Especially with Sunshine. "No."

"I can't imagine. I have a brother—you met him—and two sisters. I had another brother, Michael, but he died when he was seventeen."

So they had something in common. He glanced over his shoulder as a flicker of sadness passed over her face. He almost mentioned Noelle. Almost. But then PJ's smile was back in place. He went back to the window.

"It was hard for all of us, but it was extra hard on Madison. She was his twin, and it took a long time for her to really live again. Michael loved to sail. Bought a boat when he was sixteen instead of a car. He dreamed of being the youngest winner of our annual regatta, but he never got to try—you have to be eighteen."

"Sorry to hear that."

PJ shrugged. "Yeah. Well, two years ago Madison got it in her head that she needed to win it for him. She ended up taking sailing lessons from Beckett—he's her husband now, but there was no love lost between them back then! Anyway, she and Beckett ended up winning the regatta and falling in love all at the same time. It was pretty special. She's the vet. You have any pets?"

He moved his hands to the top of the sash and tried again. "Uh, no."

"Me neither. I had a fish at college, but he didn't make it. Always wanted a dog, though. We had animals around the farm, strays that Madison brought home and stuff, but not a family pet. My brother's allergic to cats, and Mom always said she had enough responsibility. I guess with five kids, she was right. Plus Daniel."

"Who's Daniel?" And why did he want to know?

"Here, let me help." She wedged in between Cole and the wall, grasping the sash at the bottom. They gave it a few tugs, then Cole pulled out his pocketknife and started cutting through the dried-on paint.

PJ leaned against the wall, too close. The smell of her perfume or hair or whatever it was teased his nose.

"Daniel's my brother-in-law. He's also the mayor, but before that he was kind of an honorary brother. Always hanging around, basically part of the family. His parents live in DC. His dad's a senator, so he grew up here with his grandma. How about you? Any family to speak of?"

"Not really."

"That must be hard. How in the world did you get all that funding without connections?"

"Mostly from church."

"Oh, we have a great church here. A couple of them actually. You might be able to get more funding if you need it."

She was trying to help him? What was her deal?

He pocketed his knife and grabbed the window sash.

PJ turned and helped. "How old are you, anyway?"

"Twenty-six."

"I'm twenty-two."

The window went up this time. A breeze drifted in, flirting with the loose hairs around her face.

"So what's PJ stand for?"

"Penelope Jane—after my grandmothers. It only gets used when I'm in trouble, and even then it's just my mom."

"It doesn't suit you."

"I know, right? Hey." She checked her watch. "It's been five minutes, and we haven't argued once."

He gave a wry grin. "World record."

"Maybe we should quit while we're ahead."

"Best not to jinx it."

"Right." She smiled wide.

She really did have nice lips. And why was he looking at her mouth again?

Chapter Nine

PJ RAN THE ROLLER THROUGH THE PAN AND APPLIED THE paint to the plaster. The white walls showed through the fresh burgundy paint. "It's definitely going to take two coats."

Ryan was masking off the picture window in the room that would soon be the main dining room of her restaurant. "At least."

She'd gotten the plans back this week. They only had to move one wall to broaden the kitchen. The restaurant would consist of two rooms, the former living room and sitting room. The wide porch would provide patio seating. She couldn't wait to see it all completed.

The front door opened, and Cole entered with bags from the hardware store. He'd been gone most of the evening.

"How's it going?" he said.

PJ lowered her roller. "Hi."

Cole's eyes darted between PJ and Ryan, then he started for the stairs.

"Wait," PJ said. "You remember my brother, Ryan?"

Cole's gaze swung to Ryan, and recognition passed over his features. He shifted some bags. "Vaguely. Thanks for the medical help, man."

Ryan stood, jerking his chin upward. "Least I can do when my sister's handing out concussions."

50

PJ elbowed him in the gut and got a satisfying grunt in return. "It was self-defense."

Cole gave a huff of laughter and started up the steps with his load.

"Need some help?" Ryan called.

"I got it. Thanks."

Cole disappeared, and seconds later his footsteps creaked overhead. A radio came on, a driving beat with a wailing electric guitar filtering down the stairs. Sometimes she felt a little bad for him. On his own with all that work to do upstairs, while she had her whole family helping out.

"So what's his deal?" Ryan asked.

"What do you mean?"

"He's kind of quiet. Have you learned anything else about him? What about that report Daniel was getting?"

PJ shrugged as she pushed her roller back and forth in the pan. "It didn't turn up anything. He doesn't talk much about himself, but he's fine. He's not dangerous or anything."

"You don't know that. You're not exactly the best judge of character."

Ouch. Ryan had no idea he'd just stuck an arrow into a soft, vulnerable spot. None of her family knew about Keaton.

"Give me some credit. I'm not twelve anymore."

"Just be careful. Maybe you shouldn't be here without one of us."

PJ rolled her eyes. "I don't need a babysitter. You wouldn't be having this conversation with Madison or Jade."

"It's only because I care."

She didn't want to think about this anymore. It just stressed her out.

"So I heard you went on a date last weekend. Who was she?"

Ryan ripped off a strip of tape with his teeth. "The new receptionist at school. You don't know her."

Ryan taught and coached football at Chapel Springs High School in addition to volunteering for the fire department.

"Where'd you go? Did you have fun?"

"It was fine, I guess."

PJ looked over her shoulder at him. "You ask her out again?"

"Not yet."

"It's a Friday night and you're helping your sister paint—not that I don't appreciate it. You should ask her out again. Are you going to?"

"You're the nosiest sister on the planet."

PJ blinked innocently. "It's only because I care."

Ryan shot her a look over his shoulder, his lips pressed together.

She knew she wouldn't get any more out of him. Likely he'd go on a few dates with the woman and then things would fizzle out. It seemed to be his pattern these days. She wondered if he'd ever find someone he'd love as much as Abby. PJ had loved her too. The rest of the family had never really warmed up to her, but they'd been heartbroken about the divorce.

She wanted to ask Ryan about her, but it wasn't a welcome topic, even after all this time.

PJ started on the next wall, smoothing out drips of paint as she went.

"The paint's really darkening the room," Ryan said.

"It'll be romantic. I want a dimmer switch on the overhead chandelier and candlelight on the tables. It'll be perfect."

"What are you doing for tables and chairs?"

"I'm getting some things from Grandma's Attic." Their mom's store was a treasure trove of used furniture. "It'll be mismatched-eclectic. Not my ideal, but it'll do for now."

"Got your menu all planned out?"

"Almost. Part of my final project at school was to create a restaurant menu. I already have most of the main dishes and a couple desserts—which reminds me, there's cheesecake in the fridge. Take it with you. I need feedback."

"Happy to help. If you need someone to test your entrees, feel free to bring me dinner anytime."

"Bachelorhood getting to you?"

"Frozen food gets old quick."

"I could teach you to cook, you know. I was thinking about having cooking lessons on slow nights to supplement the restaurant income."

"Great idea. It'll help during the winter season. I can't see you being open every night."

He was right. She'd have to make her money during spring, summer, and fall when the tourists came. Winter was going to be dead. And the restaurant wouldn't open until late summer at the earliest. How was she going to turn a profit this year?

And she had to if she was going to convince Mrs. Simmons to give her the house. Either that, or Cole was going to have to flub up big-time.

Her dad had cosigned on her loan this week. So much money. The commercial kitchen was the kicker. She'd need silverware and dinnerware. She'd splurged on her pots and pans—beautiful copper Bourgeat cookware. She couldn't wait for their arrival.

What if it didn't work out? What if she lost the house? What if a year from now she found herself still working at Fiona's Fudge Shoppe, thousands of dollars in debt?

Her lungs tightened at the thought. She focused on breathing in, expanding them. Breathing out. Her heart raced, and her breathing quickened. She set her roller in the pan and walked across the drop-cloth-covered floor.

What was wrong with her? It felt so strange, so awful, like someone else was looking out her eyes. Fear bubbled up, vague and undefined, but strong, seeping into the deepest reaches.

Everything was going to be fine. She wasn't going to fail. She wasn't.

But right now it was hard to believe she was going to live through the moment. *Get it together, PJ.*

"What's wrong?"

PJ shook her head, still trying to get her breathing under control. "My heart's racing." She started pacing. Somehow it comforted her.

Ryan applied a strip of tape, finishing the baseboard. "I'm sure you're fine." He stood and checked his watch.

She *was* fine. *You're fine, PJ. Stop stressing. You're doing this to yourself.*

"I have that meeting at the firehouse."

PJ nodded. Blew out a breath, wishing he'd go so she could panic in private.

"Sure you're all right?" Ryan asked as he opened the door.

She nodded and tried for a smile. That was all she could do. And then he was gone.

She paced through the room, focusing on her breathing, which couldn't seem to keep pace with her heart. *Please, God.*

Minutes passed, but they felt like hours. She stopped by

the window overlooking the backyard. Peaceful trees. Peaceful gardens. Peaceful shade. She drew in breath after breath, blowing it out through her mouth.

What was wrong with her? This wasn't normal. Right?

"PJ?"

She closed her eyes, not daring to look over her shoulder. Why couldn't everyone just leave her alone for two seconds?

She worked to steady her breath. "Yeah?"

"You wouldn't happen to have a—"

In. Out. *Come on, PJ. Relax.*

"You okay?"

Go away. Just go away. She nodded.

Muted footsteps fell behind her.

"Have a what?" she made herself ask.

She felt his presence closing in. Smelled the musky scent of him, now familiar. She tucked her trembling hands into her pockets and focused on an old tire swing that hung from a thick branch of a towering oak tree.

"You're not okay." He was beside her now. "What's wrong?"

She shook her head. Blew out a breath, focused on the tire swing, swaying gently in the breeze.

He took her wrist, pulling her hand from her pocket, and set two fingers at her pulse.

Her heart did a funny flop. The swing disappeared. Her awareness dwindled down to those two fingers.

"I'm fine—I—I've just worked myself up, I guess. I do that sometimes. Think something's wrong when it's really not."

His gaze was on her, green eyes that saw everything. Piercing.

She looked away. She didn't want him to see her like this, vulnerable.

He released her hand. "It's high. A hundred and twenty beats per minute."

"I'm feeling better now." It was true. Just the fact that she was thinking about his eyes, his touch, proved it. She rubbed her wrist. Slowed her breathing.

She still felt his eyes on her. She pushed the window sash higher. The June breeze kissed her face. "You were—what was it you wanted?"

"Channel locks. You don't have a pair, do you?"

She blew out a breath. Definitely feeling better. "I don't even know what that is."

"Ah. Never mind then." He backed toward the stairs. "Sure you're all right?"

"Yeah." Her heart was settling into a normal rhythm, her thoughts clearer, the intense fear fading. "Hey," she called.

He turned at the foot of the steps, one hand resting on the mahogany turnout.

She was going to thank him for his concern, but the words stuck in her throat. "We could share tools. I mean, you know, to save money. You're welcome to my painting supplies when I'm done."

He gave her a long, penetrating gaze. "All right," he said finally.

After he disappeared up the stairs, she wondered if she'd have been better off just saying thanks.

Chapter Ten

His heart raced as he crawled through the wreckage. His mind screamed, but no sounds came out. The smell of fumes and burning rubber choked him. *Mom! Noelle! Dad!* his mind screamed.

It was too dark. His hands felt for life. Found the booster seat. An arm. "Noelle!" Finally his voice worked. He shook her. But she wouldn't move. Wouldn't answer.

He ran his hand down to her wrist. Two fingers, they'd taught him in school. Not the thumb. He couldn't feel anything. *Come on, come on.*

Her small hand was still warm, the chubby fingers curling lifelessly. He moved his fingers, searching. Finding nothing. No pulse. No beats. No life.

"Noelle!"

Cole's eyes flew open. The room was dark. The floor beneath him hard. His ragged breaths punctuated the silence.

He closed his eyes again, one part wishing for the oblivion of sleep, the other knowing it wasn't safe tonight. It had been years since he'd had the dream. He threw off the blanket. It was going to be a long night.

The dream lingered in his mind, the details haunting him. Details absent from tonight's nightmare—everything that had led up to that accident.

The familiar ache started in his gut, twisting into a hard knot, and he welcomed it.

The bell jingled, and PJ looked up to see Jade entering Fiona's Fudge Shoppe. "You're early. I thought we were meeting at the house."

"Daniel's taking the girls to his grandma's, so he dropped me on the way."

PJ was glad the Saturday crowd had dwindled. "I'll be right back." Fiona was in the back cooling fudge on the marble slab. She was sure her boss wouldn't mind her taking off a bit early.

A few minutes later she and her sister headed to the house, catching up on the way.

"I can't wait to see what you think," PJ said as she pulled up to the curb. "I got the first coat of paint on the dining rooms yesterday."

"Wow, I'd forgotten how huge it is," Jade said as they approached the porch.

"Won't it make a great B & B?" PJ had to keep her dream in sight. "I can't wait to have the whole thing."

"You have to win it first."

They pushed through the screen door. Pounding noises from upstairs echoed through the house.

"Your friend's working today?"

"He's not my friend. He's my competition." She thought

of Cole's kindness yesterday when she'd spaced out and felt a twinge of guilt.

"Who're you kidding? Everyone's your friend."

PJ flipped the switch for the grand chandelier, but nothing happened. "He must have the electric off. It's going to be a little dark."

She showed Jade around the main level, detailing her plans.

"So this is the wall that's coming down. The commercial ovens will go here. I've got my eye on some equipment from a restaurant that's going out of business in Columbus—cross your fingers. The wood floor's got to go. Ceramic tile. Dad's going to lay it."

"Hmmm."

Pounding sounded from directly above them, almost deafening.

"What's he doing up there?" Jade asked.

"Who knows." She led Jade down the short hall. "And this will be my room once everything's done."

"Kind of small."

"Well, sure, but I won't be in here much. And once I win, I can move wherever I want."

"Upstairs with the guests?"

"Or the attic. It's huge and has this gable that overlooks the backyard. It would make a great master suite."

"Sounds nice."

The pounding stopped.

"Want to see the upstairs?"

"Maybe we shouldn't intrude."

"You don't want to meet him? It'll only take a minute."

As they entered the foyer, the floor creaked at the top of the staircase. "PJ . . . you seen my new hammer? The one with the long handle?" He sounded annoyed.

She'd used it last night to hammer the paint lid on tight. "Oh, sorry." She ran into the dining room and retrieved it, then climbed the steps, motioning Jade to follow.

At the top of the steps Cole reached for the hammer, frowning.

"Sorry," she said again.

He moved aside as they reached the second floor. The light from a bedroom window hit the side of his face. Dust coated his dark hair, sweat glistened on his forehead, and a mask hung around his neck. His eyes looked tired.

"Jade, this is Cole, my, well, the guy I told you about. Cole, Jade, my sister."

They shook hands.

"Nice to meet you."

"Same here."

"Jade's the one married to the mayor. Daniel? My honorary-brother-turned-brother-in-law? She teaches guitar and has adorable daughters named Ava and Mia. They're twins." She didn't know why she added that. Or why she kept talking. "Cole's from Fort Wayne. He's opening the transition house for foster care kids. Obviously." *Shut it, PJ.*

"Right," Jade said.

"So . . ." PJ pocketed her hands. "How long's the electric going to be off? I need to put another coat on, and those rooms are pretty dark."

"I told you I was tearing down the wall today."

"I know, but . . . I didn't realize . . ."

Cole drilled her with those green eyes until she shifted, the floor creaking under her feet.

His jaw clenched. "Fine. I'll turn it back on." He brushed past her.

"Thank you," she called down the stairs.

"Hot, but kind of grouchy," Jade whispered when he was out of earshot.

"Must be having a bad day," she said, then wondered why she was making excuses for him.

"Where's your sister?" Cole asked.

PJ turned on the ladder, her eyes temporarily blinded by the aluminum lamp she'd borrowed from her parents.

"One of her girls came down with a fever. I didn't get squat done today." She regretted turning down her mother's offer of help this afternoon. But Mom had her own business to run, and ever since her heart attack last year, they'd all been careful of her workload.

When her vision returned, she saw Cole standing in the doorway, hands on his hips. The sleeves had been ripped from his shirt, and her eyes fell to his sculpted arms. Speaking of ripped.

"I ran into a few snags myself."

She pulled her eyes to his face. He was looking the dark walls over with a scowl. She wondered if he was calculating the time it would take to repaint after he owned the house. Well, she'd save him the effort by winning.

She rested the roller on the ladder and gathered her hair off the back of her neck. "Did you turn down the air or something? It's sweltering in here."

"I turned it off."

"What?" She stepped down the ladder and headed toward

the thermostat behind him, stepping carefully over the drop cloths. "No wonder I'm dying."

"You have the windows open," he said as she brushed past.

"Look at this. It's eighty degrees in here." She turned it on, and blessed cool air filtered in.

"If you're going to turn it on, at least shut the windows."

"I'm not finished yet."

"Look, Sunshine, maybe you can afford to blow money out the window, but I can't."

"I'm not going to breathe paint fumes. Why are you so grumpy today?"

"I'm not—" He ran his knuckles over his jaw. Blew out a breath. Bits of plaster still clung to his hair.

They stared each other down. For heaven's sake, she just wanted to cool the place down. She reached into her pocket and pulled out the ten-dollar bill she'd stuffed there after lunch and tossed it at him.

He caught it against his chest.

"That should cover it." She passed him, shooting him a final look just as her foot caught on the drop cloth.

She pitched forward. Her other foot shot out, snagging on the material.

Cole's arm caught her around the stomach. She grabbed on as he snatched her back. Her body hit his with a dull thud, stealing a breath.

She stilled, fully aware of the length of his body pressed against hers. Of his solid arm around her middle. Of her fingers, curled around his thick forearms. She breathed in his musky scent, felt his warmth at her back. His breath stirred the hairs near her temple. Her heart pounded at the near fall.

Yeah, that was it—the near fall.

She turned. Made eye contact with his lips, inches away. "Thanks."

"You're welcome."

She watched his lips form the words, then wondered if he could feel her heart thumping rapidly against his chest. It was all the motivation she needed.

She uncurled her fingers, easing away.

He released her, taking a step back, then another. He gestured toward the stairs. "I'm going to go . . ."

"Yeah. I'm about done here too."

He turned up the staircase and was gone.

As she waited for her heart to settle, her eyes fell to the floor. The bill lay forgotten between the folds of material.

Chapter Eleven

PJ WAS HOPING TO FIND THE CONTRACTOR STILL AT THE house, but his truck wasn't out front. Neither was Cole's. She walked through the front room and into the kitchen area. Brad had made good progress today. The wall was finally down, the room gutted. She surveyed the open spot, her eyes seeing what wasn't there: stainless commercial stoves, lines of prep tables, her new Bourgeat copper cookware hanging from a pot rack in the center of it all.

Thick copper, stainless steel lining, cast iron handles—the pots were so gorgeous she couldn't resist peeking at them every day. She'd taken home a fry pan last week and put it to the test with savory crepes made with a creamy chicken, ham, and mushroom filling. She couldn't wait to cook with them in her new kitchen.

Just a quick peek. PJ walked across the subfloor and moved aside the plastic sheeting covering her soon-to-be bedroom.

Her eyes fell on the empty space where the boxes had been. They traveled around the room and back to the empty space. Her heart thrashed against her ribs. Where were they?

She'd left them right here. Maybe someone had moved them. She bustled past the plastic and through the kitchen, scanning the area. She looked in the dining rooms, in the closets. She took the stairs quickly and looked in all the rooms upstairs, even though there was no reason they'd be up there.

She raked her fingers through her hair, squeezing at the roots. It made no sense. They couldn't have just disappeared. Her eyes fell on the attic steps. She hadn't been up there since he'd moved in. She didn't want to think it of Cole, but the cookware was worth a lot of money—almost five thousand dollars.

You spent five thousand dollars on pots and pans! Pots and pans that are gone!

She trotted up the attic steps and tapped on the narrow door, just in case. After a moment of silence she swung it open. One twin mattress hugged the bare floor across from her. A crate, turned upside down, held a book, a shadeless lamp, and a tube of ChapStick. Other than a duffel bag and some stacks of clothing, the room was empty.

Where could they be? The only person who'd been in the house other than Cole was the contractor. But Brad had come highly recommended by her pastor and had given her a reference list a mile long. She hadn't actually called any of the names; she was too eager to get started, but still.

Wait. While she was at work, her dad had come by to unplug the sink drain in the bathroom. Maybe he'd moved the boxes. She pulled her phone from her purse, then remembered he had a committee meeting tonight.

She went back downstairs, deep in thought, her mind working hard on the puzzle. The front door opened as she reached the foyer.

Cole blew in, a hardware bag rattling in his hands. "Hey."

"Hi." She looked him over, biting the inside of her mouth,

wondering if he was capable of stealing from her. He didn't seem the type, but—

"What?" he asked.

She realized he was right beside her, trying to go upstairs, and she was blocking his way.

"Have you—have you seen some big white boxes? They were in the room off the kitchen."

"Nope. Never go in there." He paused to look at her. "Why? What's wrong?"

His calm green eyes settled on her, probing, as if sensing her panic despite her nonchalance. Her thoughts went back several days to when he'd caught her fall. When he'd reacted so quickly, pulling her safely against him.

She was being paranoid. Cole wouldn't steal from her. He was starting a home for kids, for heaven's sake. Her dad had probably just moved them.

"Nothing. I just—misplaced something." Dad had moved them. That had to be it.

But the next day the cookware still hadn't turned up. Her father didn't even remember seeing them. She'd confronted the contractor, but he claimed not to know anything about any white boxes, and he seemed sincere, had even helped her look around the house. Maybe someone had come in off the streets while Cole was upstairs working.

She had no choice but to notify Sheriff Simmons, who wasn't very encouraging about recovering the cookware. Though the house was insured, PJ was supposed to take out a policy for the contents. She hadn't gotten around to it yet. Now she was short five thousand dollars and she still needed cookware. She was going to have to borrow money from her parents, a thought that sucked the life out of her.

~

Cole shone his flashlight under the sink. The leak had warped the cabinet base, and he was afraid water would go through to the floor when the sink was used regularly.

A drip beaded on the old pipe where a fitting bulged. He went for his toolbox in the other room. Downstairs was quiet. PJ hadn't been around all day, which was strange. She was usually there on Wednesdays. The house seemed empty without her self-talk and loud country music.

His lips twitched as he thought of her karaoke. Despite her bad harmonies, the girl sang with the gusto of a rock star. Something miraculous must happen between her mouth and ears, because if she heard herself the way he did, she'd never sing another note.

He grabbed the pliers and crawled into the space under the sink, the smile falling away as he worked the pliers. The rusty fitting wouldn't budge. After another minute he took a break, frustration setting in.

That emotion hovered pretty close to the surface these days. Between the pressure of getting this house ready, his worry over Lizzy, and his attraction—yes, he was going to call it what it was—to his opponent, he was a little on edge.

He couldn't help staring at her sometimes. She was so different. Quirky. And yeah, she was beautiful. Those big brown eyes, that wide smile. When they weren't bickering she was fun, even if her mouth did run constantly. It sure was a pretty little mouth, though.

Cole clenched his jaw and went at the fitting again. What was he doing? He had no business thinking of her that way. But ever since he'd caught her in his arms, he'd hardly been able to think of anything else. It had been so long since he'd held a woman. And she'd been so soft, her slender curves pressed against him. Smelled so good. It wasn't perfume, he'd surmised from that too-short embrace. It was her hair that smelled all sweet and womanly. He'd wanted to bury his nose in there and never come up for air.

That's enough, Evans. Last thing she needs is someone like you screwing up her life.

"Cole?"

He jumped, his forehead banging against the trap. He bit back a few choice words. "*What?*"

PJ's bare feet stopped at the doorway. Hidden in the cabinet, he let his eyes travel up her long legs to the cutoffs, which was as far as he could see.

"I'm starting to think grumpy is your default."

"What do you want?"

"Just wanted to tell you to keep the house locked up, even when you're here."

He gave the pliers another futile twist. "Why's that?"

"Someone stole my cookware."

He lowered his arm and eased out of the cabinet, sitting up. "What?"

"Those boxes I mentioned yesterday—they're gone. Along with the very expensive cookware inside."

"Are you sure?"

"They didn't walk away."

He didn't miss the flicker of suspicion in her eyes. It wasn't the first time he'd seen that look. Seemed once you were in foster care everyone assumed you were a bad person.

She crossed her arms. "I filed a report with Sheriff Simmons, but he wasn't too encouraging. He might want to ask you a few questions at some point, since, you know, you live here."

"Sheriff Simmons . . . Is he—"

"Yeah, Mrs. Simmons's nephew. Great-nephew, I think. He was there the night you showed up at my house, but you probably don't remember."

Great. He was suspected of theft by a family member of the woman deciding his fate. "I'm happy to answer his questions, but I never even saw the boxes." He thought of the contractor who'd been working in the house. "I doubt someone just walked in off the street and took your stuff."

She arched a brow. "Got any better ideas?"

He clenched his teeth. She was thinking it, but she wasn't going to say it. "What about that contractor you hired?"

"I already checked him out."

"Did you tell the sheriff about him?"

"Of course."

"Is anything else missing?"

She shrugged. "Just my cookware. I don't suppose you're missing anything?"

"Not that I've noticed. If someone broke in, they'd take more than that, wouldn't they? We have tools lying around."

"You'd think." She continued looking at him.

He wished she weren't standing over him, looking down her pert little nose at him with a seemingly innocent expression. He should just say it, get it out in the open.

"Just—keep the doors locked, okay?" She turned and left.

He shoved back under the sink and a few minutes later finally worked the fitting loose. But the ugly feeling swelling inside him didn't go away.

Chapter Twelve

PJ DASHED UP THE WISHING HOUSE PORCH, DUCKING IN out of the rain. It had poured all day, and the fudge shop had been dead. She entered the house, shaking the water from her hair. The stale smell of paint fumes lingered in the air, mixing with the smell of sawdust and rain.

She entered the kitchen, admiring the first coat of paint she'd applied the night before. It was only glossy white, but it brightened the place. One more coat. The ceramic tile was being laid tomorrow, an expensive but necessary expenditure. The warped wood floor wouldn't do, and it would be too hard to replace the flooring later after the appliances and steel shelving were installed.

"Yoohoo!" a voice called from the foyer. "PJ?"

"In the kitchen."

Madison appeared in the doorway, a T-shirt hanging on her like a burlap bag. "Got my painting gear on."

"I hope you're wearing shorts under there."

Her sister gave her a look. "It's one of Beckett's old shirts. Mom'll be here after supper. And just so you know, she's planning to confront you about church. Like a good sister, I'm giving you advance notice."

"Great." It was true she'd missed a few Sundays. Okay, more

than a few. But she was on a tight schedule here. Surely God understood.

"She also heard you're going to be open for brunch on Sundays, once the restaurant opens. She's worried about you."

"It's true I'll be working Sundays for a while, but once my staff settles in, they'll be able to handle it without me." She'd get back to church once all the craziness passed.

Madison wandered into the dining room, and PJ followed, wanting to check the touch-up she'd done late last night.

"Hey, this is looking great. It'll be romantic with some soft candlelight."

"I think so too."

Madison stopped abruptly. "Uh-oh."

PJ looked over her shoulder, noticing the water that covered an entire corner of the room. She followed the source to the window. The curtains she'd rehung the day before slapped against the wall. Rain still pelted in.

"What in the world?" PJ hustled to the window and put the sash down. Water, an inch deep, seeped into her tennis shoes. She splashed back to the center of the room where it was dry. She'd closed that window last night. She knew she had. She'd been a little paranoid about having them open since Cole had complained about the air conditioning.

"You have any towels?"

"In the kitchen."

"You should go downstairs and see if it's leaking through."

Madison soaked up the water while PJ checked the basement.

"Any leaks?" Madison asked when she returned.

"No, thank goodness."

PJ grabbed a dry towel and helped with the last of the mess, water soaking through her jeans. "I thought for sure I shut this window last night." She'd done it after putting the lid on the paint can and wrapping the wet brush with Saran Wrap. Hadn't she? Yes, she was practically positive.

"At least there's no permanent damage."

That still didn't explain the window. Had Cole opened it? But she couldn't imagine why he'd need to. It had been hot and muggy, and she already knew he wasn't a fan of open windows.

Unless . . . No, he wouldn't do that. Wouldn't purposely flood her dining room.

Would he?

The suspicions she'd stuffed down over the past week rose to the surface again. Anyone could've taken the cookware. It was worth a lot. But who else would want to flood her dining room?

It had started raining right after she'd left last night. Could Cole have come down and opened the window? He wanted the house badly. As badly as PJ. But would he stoop to sabotage?

As a foster kid he'd probably scrapped for everything he had. Was he scrapping for the house too? At her expense?

She sat back on her haunches and opened her mouth to let Madison in on her suspicions.

"Unless you have a ghost, you need to be more careful, PJ. This could've been a lot worse, and you really don't have the money to waste—or the time."

She wanted to defend herself. Tell Madison it hadn't been her fault, that she suspected it was Cole's. But she'd been defending him since day one. Her family already thought she lacked good judgment—she'd been chided about the expensive cookware. She wasn't setting herself up for a round of I-told-you-so's.

Besides, it was possible it wasn't Cole, right? He'd been distant since she'd asked him to keep the house locked up. An image of him under the bathroom sink formed, his long legs extending out into the hall, his T-shirt riding up, exposing a couple inches of his muscled stomach. She'd almost forgotten what she'd come for until he'd snapped at her.

Stop that, PJ.

If she thought about it, he'd actually been distant since the tripping incident. Since he'd caught her against him. She'd found herself reliving those long seconds too often. The way he'd felt against her. The way his breath had stirred her hair.

The man is likely sabotaging you, and you're getting swoony over him?

What was wrong with her? Was she just missing Keaton?

After piling the wet towels by the front door, the sisters started painting in the kitchen. Madison caught PJ up on her husband's family. Beckett's dad was still sober and doing well. Layla's home-staging business had taken off. She and Seth had just returned from a long weekend in Gatlinburg and were trying to get pregnant. PJ already knew half of this. She ran into Seth almost every time she went to his hardware store.

As Madison chattered, PJ found her mind wandering to Cole and the suspicious incidents.

"Where's the edger?" Madison asked.

"The old one has burgundy paint on it. I think I have a new one. I'll get it."

She rooted through the plastic bags in the foyer. She hadn't wanted to think badly of Cole. She always gave people the benefit of the doubt. It was her nature to be optimistic. But even she couldn't ignore the evidence staring her in the face.

The more she thought about it, the angrier she got. They

were going to be sharing this house for a year. At this rate he could squash her dream in weeks. She had to nip it in the bud, however unpleasant it might be.

The door swung open, hitting her in the hip, pushing her forward. She caught her balance and turned to glare at Cole.

"Sorry." He shifted his grocery bags and pocketed his keys. "You didn't lock the door."

"My sister just got here." She reached around him and turned the deadbolt, conscious of the way he didn't budge. Of the way his nearness made the hairs on her arms rise. The way his muscles bulged under the weight of the grocery bags. Good heavens, his arms were the size of her thighs.

Why? Why did he have to be the one to make every cell purr like a kitten?

"Hi. I'm Madison."

PJ stepped back to safety while Madison and Cole traded greetings.

"Better get the groceries in," he said when they were finished. "It's hotter than blazes out there."

"Nice and cool in here though," PJ blurted.

"Yep."

"All the windows are closed, though, so don't worry." PJ shot him a knowing look.

His brow furrowed. "Okay . . . Good."

He started to pass her.

She stepped in his way. "Have you seen my edger? It was in one of these bags."

He stopped beside her, close. His musky scent filled her nostrils, and the warmth from his body washed over her.

"No, I haven't."

She nudged her chin up. He was so freaking tall. "Are you sure? I've been all through them."

He fixed her with a look that she felt clear down to her marrow. His arm brushed hers as he shifted a bag, but she made herself stay still.

A muscle in his jaw ticked. "You're welcome to mine. They're in the first bedroom on the right."

She crossed her arms, backing off. "That's okay. Don't worry about it."

"Suit yourself, Sunshine," he said quietly, the low tone humming through her ears.

He trudged up the stairs, his footfalls fading away. Only then did PJ let out the breath she held. She felt Madison's eyes on her as she headed back to the kitchen. If Cole had more groceries to bring in, she wasn't hanging around to see him again.

She picked up the roller and filled it, then realized it was already full. The roller made slurping sounds as she spread the paint on the wall.

"So *that's* what's going on," Madison said.

PJ smoothed out a paint drip from pressing too hard. "What?"

"There's enough chemistry between you two to keep a high school lab busy for a year."

"Chemis—" PJ stopped rolling and looked at Madison. "If by chemistry you mean mutual dislike, you'd be right."

"Whatever you say."

"He has a girlfriend."

"Who is she?"

"I have no idea. I hear him on the phone sometimes."

"So you haven't actually seen her?"

PJ huffed. "No."

Madison smirked. "You're prickly tonight." She sounded more amused than put out as she dipped her brush in the can. "He puts you on edge."

No, the theft of her cookware put her on edge. The attempt to flood her dining room put her on edge. "I've got a lot on my mind."

"He calls you Sunshine. That's so cute."

"Trust me, it's not a compliment."

"He's awfully good-looking."

PJ glared at Madison. "Can we talk about something else?"

Madison's lips twitched, her eyes widening, innocent. "Of course."

It was after nine when Madison and their mom left. The kitchen walls were finished, the brush and rollers washed and drying in the bathroom sink. PJ was tired and hungry, and she had to get up early for work.

The drone of a saw carried into the house. She followed the sound to the kitchen window and stared across the backyard to the light shining through the shed windows. Cole had been out there since shortly after he'd gotten home.

She thought about her cookware, the window . . . It hadn't been far from her mind all night. Her mom had even commented on how quiet she was. Madison had covertly quirked a brow at PJ, as if she had the inside scoop.

The truth was, whatever chemistry she and Cole had or didn't have was irrelevant. The man was out to steal her dream, and she wasn't letting him get away with it. Her heart beat faster.

There was nothing sunshiny about the thoughts she was having. And there was no use putting off a confrontation. She'd just go home and toss and turn.

She slipped out the patio door and into the muggy night. The first fireflies of the season flashed over the flower garden, and the smell of rain hung heavily in the air. The loud whine of the saw grew sharper as she neared. She hoped he didn't plan to work much later or they'd have angry neighbors.

The old wooden door swung heavily on its hinge as she entered, and the smell of sawdust assaulted her. Big enough for a car, the room held only some old boxes and a makeshift saw table Cole had set up. He hunched over it, his back to her, guiding a piece of plywood under the blade.

Sawdust littered the cracked cement floor. He wore a ratty T-shirt, a pair of paint-speckled jeans, and work boots that had seen better days. When he finished the cut, he slid the board to the floor and began measuring another.

PJ watched him work, reminding herself to remember what he'd done. To remember the beautiful cookware she'd spent her very limited cash on. Money she'd have to pay back with interest. Maybe the open window hadn't caused any lasting damage, but it could've. What if she hadn't come over tonight? What if he did something worse next time?

"Something on your mind?"

She jumped, not realizing he was aware of her presence. She lengthened her spine and raised her chin, though he couldn't see her; he was still hunched over the table.

"Where's my cookware?"

He took his time measuring. Marking. "Finally got up the nerve to ask, huh?"

"That's not an answer."

He looked over his shoulder, drilling her with those green eyes. "I didn't take your cookware."

"I don't suppose you had anything to do with the window, either."

"What window?"

"The window you opened last night. While it was raining. The window that let in a ton of water and practically flooded my dining room. Lucky for you, there was no permanent damage."

He straightened, turning. His nostrils flared. "I don't know anything about an open window. And I didn't take your pots and pans."

He was good, she'd give him that. Firm tone, direct eye contact. She almost believed him. But the evidence was even more convincing. She supposed it was possible she'd forgotten to shut the window, but someone had taken her cookware, and no one had better opportunity or more motive than Cole.

"You don't believe me."

"Should I?"

"I'm not a thief." Something shifted in his eyes, and he raised a brow. "And why would I try to flood a house that's going to be mine?"

Cocky, arrogant jerk. She narrowed her eyes. "We'll see about that."

"I will win this house. But I'll do it fair and square."

"Don't be so sure. The Grille will make a profit. Crossroads will be a financial drain."

"Well, maybe it's not all about money for me, PJ."

She thought of those faces on his presentation board and her face heated. It wasn't all about money for her either. It was about proving herself. To her family. To the community. To herself. But he didn't need to know that.

"Maybe not, but Mrs. Simmons will certainly take that into account. And if any more *incidents* happen, you can be sure I'll be passing along my suspicions to her."

A shadow flickered over his jaw as he clenched it. "You do that."

"I will." PJ turned on her heel and left the shed, her heart beating up into her throat.

Chapter Thirteen

PJ JUMPED FROM RYAN'S TRUCK AND WENT AROUND TO THE
back where all her belongings were piled in the bed. It would've
gone faster with more people, but her sisters and their husbands
were conveniently busy today.

"I really appreciate your help," she said.

"Don't forget you promised me pot roast. And mashed
potatoes—homemade."

"The beef's in the Crock-Pot as we speak. I even seared it
and used my secret rub."

He lowered the tailgate and pulled a box forward. "It better
be good. You have a ton of junk."

"Of course it will be. And it's not junk. It's kitchen equipment."

"How many blenders does one person need?"

PJ grabbed a box and started inside. The last three weeks
had sped by in a flurry of renovations, work, and hiring. July was
almost over, and PJ had set a grand opening date of August first.
Her nerves were getting the best of her. She'd had two more
anxiety episodes this week. They'd left her shaky and scared.
She hoped she didn't have another today in front of Ryan.

At least there had been no more suspicious incidents. She and
Cole had settled into a sort of stalemate. They spoke only when
necessary and tolerated each other's noise and presence. She had

a feeling it was about to get harder now that they'd be living under the same roof.

An hour later, her belongings were settled into the house and the bed put together. She helped Ryan push it against the wall.

"So where's your partner today?" he asked.

"He's not my partner. And I don't know or care where he is."

He smirked as he set her nightstand in place.

"What?"

"Nothing. It's just, that's not what Madison said."

PJ pursed her lips. "Madison is a lovesick newlywed. She's seeing things that aren't there."

"I trust her instincts. Which is more than I can say for you."

He was joking, but the barb stung. It was true she seemed to have a radar for losers. Never more so than with her last relationship.

The doorbell rang as PJ set her lamp on the nightstand. "That's Layla."

"Saved by the bell," Ryan said.

She smacked the back of his head as she passed him, then scooted past before he could retaliate.

Layla was their brother-in-law Beckett's sister. A home stager, she'd offered to help PJ arrange the tables and find inexpensive wall hangings and centerpieces.

PJ hugged her at the door. The woman had always been beautiful, but since she'd married Seth Murphy in a whirlwind wedding a year and a half ago, she downright glowed.

"You get prettier every time I see you," PJ said. "I could almost hate you."

"You're one to talk. Hey, this place is great."

"It should be. I've been working my butt off."

"Seth said you practically live at the hardware store these days."

PJ made a face. "I have the bills to prove it."

Ryan entered the foyer. "Hey, Layla."

"Hey, Ryan. I heard you're the work mule today."

"Basically."

"Don't feel too sorry for him. He's getting paid in food."

"And I'm going to eat like a pig, so make plenty." He turned to PJ. "If we're done here, I'm going to take off."

"Don't you want to stay and help pick out centerpieces?" PJ asked.

He scowled. "What time's dinner?"

"Five thirty. Don't be late."

"I'm the one who's late," Layla said. "Sorry. I just got assigned the Avery house and had to stop there first."

Ryan turned on the threshold, eyes alert. "The Avery house? It's for sale?"

Ryan's ex-wife had loved the house. It was just down the street from the Wishing House—a charming brick Craftsman with a wide front porch and a lawn shaded with ancient oaks. PJ knew they had dreamed of buying it one day, raising kids there.

"It's going up next week, and my boss wants it finished as soon as possible."

All of the playfulness had drained from Ryan's face, and sadness flickered in his eyes.

"Why do you ask?" Layla said.

"I didn't know they were moving," PJ said, shifting the attention from her brother.

"Just to a smaller home. They wanted a bedroom on the main floor."

"Makes sense. Speaking of bedrooms on the main floor, maybe you can take a peek at mine. I don't think I like the way we arranged it." She tucked her arm in Layla's and started for the bedroom. "See you in a few hours, bro."

"See you."

She tried to focus on what Layla was saying, but her thoughts returned to Ryan and the wound that had just been reopened.

Chapter Fourteen

COLE SET THE CAN OF PAINT AND A FEW ODDS AND ENDS ON the counter and greeted Seth Murphy, owner of Murphy's Hardware.

"Back already?" Seth asked.

"It's always something. What are you doing here this late?"

"My manager's wife had a baby a couple days ago, and my high school worker's on vacation."

Seth rang him up, and Cole forked over the cash. The renovations were costing more money than he'd anticipated. More time too. On top of that, he'd had to get a permit and a license, fill out government forms, and work with the local foster care network. Lots of red tape.

Seth handed him the receipt. "How's the house coming?"

"I should be ready for kids in a few weeks." He had a stack of applications for kids about to age out of the system. How would he even decide who to turn away?

"You just missed PJ. I guess her grand opening is this weekend. Layla's been staging the restaurant."

Cole had seen Seth's wife around the place the past few days. "It's looking good." He'd poked around when PJ wasn't there. Heaven knew she wasn't going to offer him a grand tour.

"You need any help with that range hookup, just give me a call. I've put in a few."

"Wouldn't that be consorting with the enemy?"

Seth shrugged. "Just keeping the customers happy."

"I'll keep that in mind. Thanks."

A minute later Cole pulled out of the hardware lot. Darkness was starting to fall, and katydids buzzed in the hills around him. He drove toward the house, the road winding alongside the river.

As he neared town he saw PJ's car at the mom-and-pop gas station. The gas hose ran to her car, and she was sitting inside. He took a second look as he passed. Her head rested on the steering wheel. He guessed he wasn't the only one worn out.

He entered town and braked for the light in front of the Rialto Theater, though there was no traffic. The town had pretty much cleared out for the evening. He couldn't get the image of PJ hunched over the steering wheel out of his mind. She was always hopping with energy.

Was she really just resting? Or was she upset over something? He remembered finding her in the house weeks ago, pale and shaken, her heart racing. He hadn't noticed any more episodes, but it wasn't like they'd been hanging out together. She'd moved in a few days earlier, but even so, they kept to their own floors.

Ever since she'd accused him of stealing her cookware, he'd stayed out of her way. The accusation still stung, though he didn't know why. They weren't friends, though he must've begun to think in those terms; otherwise, why would he care what she thought?

The light turned green, and he accelerated. His eyes drifted to the rearview mirror and settled on PJ's car, still parked in front of the pump. The streetlamps flickered on, pushing back the impending darkness.

If he didn't check on her, he'd just worry. He swung his truck around at Cappy's Pizzeria and headed back toward the station. He'd just drive by and make sure she looked okay. Hopefully it was dark enough she wouldn't notice him skulking past.

But when he slowed, the gas line was still connected to her car, and she was still slumped over the steering wheel. Frowning, he braked, pulling into the lot.

The sweep of his headlights over the vehicle did nothing to alert her. He stopped beside her car and shoved his truck into park before getting out and rapping on the passenger window.

She raised her head, and he released a breath he didn't realize he'd been holding. "You okay?"

She nodded, looking away. But she didn't look all right. Her eyes seemed distant, and she looked pale under the harsh station lights. He tried the door and found it unlocked.

He planted his palm on the car's roof, leaning down. "You sure? You're breathing kind of fast."

"Go away, Cole." Her chest rose and fell quickly. Her forehead was shiny with perspiration, though that could be because her car was hot as Hades.

He went around the car and replaced the gas pump, capping her tank, then got in on the passenger side. He turned the key over and cranked up the air.

"What are you doing?"

He took her wrist from her lap. She tried to pull it away, but he held tight and took her pulse.

"I'm fine." She closed her eyes while he counted.

"It's 130," he said a moment later. "You feel dizzy?"

"No." She drew in a shaky breath. "I'll be fine in a minute. Just go away. Please."

"Have you seen a doctor?"

Her hand felt cool and clammy. It trembled in his until she pulled it away. She lowered her head, hiding behind the curtain of her hair. She still hadn't answered him.

"Have you seen a doctor?"

"I'm fine, Cole. I just—just work myself up sometimes."

"I'll take that as a no." He got out and parked his truck, then opened the driver's door. "Scoot over."

"Why?"

"I'm taking you to the ER."

"I said I'm—"

"If you say you're fine one more time, I'm going to pick you up myself. Move over."

"I don't have time for this. Not to mention the money. I have a lot to do; I open in three days."

"And what are you going to do when this happens in the middle of dinner rush?"

Her hands trembled as she lowered them. She pressed her lips together, and her chin wobbled. "Fine." She unfastened her belt and maneuvered to the other seat.

He slid into the car, buckled her belt and then his own, and pulled from the gas station. Riverview General was just a few miles outside of town. PJ was quiet until they pulled into the lot.

"They're not going to find anything. I'm always working myself up over nothing. Just ask my family."

"How about we ask the doctor instead. Want me to call someone?"

"No."

Someone came to the curb and helped her inside while Cole parked the car.

Three hours later, PJ gathered her things and left the triage room. She was still shaky but now just from missing supper. The deductible was going to hurt her wallet, but at least she had answers.

Walking down the sterile hall, she rooted through her purse for her keys, then remembered Cole had driven her car here. She'd have to call him or call her family—neither option was appealing.

She felt for her phone, then remembered she'd left it charging in her car. Great. Entering the lobby, she was headed toward the counter when a movement from the lobby drew her attention.

Cole was walking her way. "All done?"

"I didn't expect you to wait."

"Feeling better?"

"Yeah."

He ushered her out the door, leading her to the car. She started for the driver's side.

"I'll drive," he said.

"It's my car."

"You just left the ER." He held up the keys. "And I have the keys."

She scowled at him as he led her to the passenger side and opened the door.

"Anyone ever tell you you're bossy?"

"You're the youngest of five; you should be used to it."

Unfortunately, she was too used to it. She tried to be angry with him, but it was hard when he'd just wasted three hours in an ER lobby for her.

"So what'd you find out?" he asked as he pulled onto the street.

She hesitated at sharing private information. They weren't exactly best buds. But he had brought her here and waited on her. "Apparently my thyroid is high. I guess that can cause panic attacks."

"I wondered if that's what they were. My mom used to have them."

He'd never referred to his family before, and she wasn't going to let the opportunity pass. "What happened to her?"

The Main Street lamps washed over his face as they rode through downtown. His mouth tightened, and a haunted look settled over his features. She was suddenly sorry she'd asked.

"Car accident."

"I'm sorry."

"It was a long time ago."

She wanted to know more. What about his dad? Where had his grandparents been? Why did he end up in foster care, and how old was he when it happened? But she didn't exactly deserve answers to her personal questions. She'd accused him of sabotage, had barely spoken to him in the past five weeks.

"So did they give you meds or something?" he asked.

"I have to make an appointment with an endocrinologist." And she was opening in three days. Three days. She still had to purchase food, pick up her menus, finish training the staff, and proof the ad for Friday's paper. "I don't have time for this."

"You don't have time to ignore it."

"I know. It's just bad timing." They passed the gas station. "Hey, your truck."

"I'll get it tomorrow."

When they reached the house, she followed him up the path. A cricket chirped nearby, going silent as they passed. The porch was dark, and the door creaked as Cole opened it. The big old house was quiet. The smells of paint and polish lingered in the air. He flipped on the light while she locked up behind them.

"Night," he said, heading toward the stairs.

"Good night." PJ watched him go, his loose gait now familiar and somehow reassuring. "Hey," she called quietly.

He turned halfway up, his hand resting on the mahogany rail.

"Thanks for taking me tonight."

He studied her a minute, his eyes dark and unfathomable in the shadows. There was so much she didn't know about him. Despite her initial plan to draw him out, he was more of an enigma now than when he'd moved in.

"No problem."

He turned and continued climbing, leaving PJ to wonder what secrets those eyes held and if she would ever get to the bottom of them.

Cole turned over in bed, staring at the darkened ceiling. PJ's question had stirred memories better forgotten. And no matter how much he tried to push them back down, they surfaced relentlessly.

Some people lost their memory of the moments leading up to an accident. He only wished his mind had been so generous.

No, he remembered every detail. Every word. Every expression that had ghosted over his mom's face. And he remembered everything leading up to that awful night.

It had been a bad week all the way around. On Monday his baseball game had been rained out halfway through the third inning. He'd been pitching so well, and they'd been in the lead 4–0 against their biggest rival. His mom was on a business trip and his dad was working, so he'd had to walk home in the pouring rain. At twelve he was old enough now.

When he rounded the bend he was glad to see his dad's car in the drive. Cole could tell him how well he'd pitched. His dad liked it when he played well, even if he always did see some way Cole could've done better. Cole told himself that was why he'd improved so much. Why he'd made the All-Star team three years running. Why he'd been drafted up early this season.

The lights were off when he entered the house. The TV light flickered, but a scan of the living room told him his dad wasn't watching the ESPN highlights on the screen. He heard a woman's laughter down the hallway.

His mom was home early. He hadn't seen her car, but she parked in the garage. Noelle must still be at daycare because if she were home, she'd be wrapped around his rain-soaked leg, begging for a pony ride.

He followed the voices into the hallway. He hadn't seen his mom in three days and was surprised she hadn't gone straight to his game. She was always in the stands cheering for him.

The bedroom door was cracked open, and he was glad because if it were shut, he'd have to go away. He knew what his parents were doing when they locked the door. Jared Parker had filled him in two years ago. He hadn't wanted to believe it, but his other friends had confirmed it. Now every time his parents shut the door, he wished Jared Parker had kept his big fat mouth shut.

He heard his dad's laughter now, his voice rumbling low. He was in a good mood. Cole smiled as he approached the door. It had been awhile since he'd seen Dad smile, much less laugh. It was a good time to tell him about the game.

Cole pushed the door, and it fell silently open. His eyes settled on the bed, where two figures were tangled beneath the sheets. He stopped in his tracks as his mom's laughter drifted to him, and he thought belatedly that he should close his eyes. Quick.

But then he saw the black hair spread across the pillow. Saw the long, tapered fingers running up his dad's bare back. The bright red nails curling into Dad's short hair.

He spun and hurried down the hall, careful not to make a sound. His skin felt hot and tight, and his stomach felt like it did on Halloween when he plowed through his bucket of candy.

He went out the front door, into the drizzle, and around back where no one would see him. He scrambled behind the air-conditioning unit and slid down the wall until he was tucked into a ball. Tugging his ball cap lower, he closed his eyes and went someplace else. To the ball diamond where he was on the mound, where his mom was in the stands watching him pitch, and his dad was at work, exactly where he was supposed to be.

Chapter Fifteen

"WHY AREN'T YOU PLAYING?" JADE SETTLED NEXT TO PJ AT the picnic table and began picking at the leftover brownies.

"I'm saving my energy for tomorrow." PJ pulled Ava closer, breathing in her sweet baby scent.

On the court nearby the game of two-on-two grew louder as Madison protested Ryan's block.

Joanne McKinley stopped by the table, arms out for baby Ava. "You've had her long enough. Come here, sugars."

"Say hi to Grammy." PJ handed off the baby.

The eight-month-old gave a gummy smile and kicked excitedly. "Ga, ga, ga!"

"Where's Mia?" PJ asked Jade as their mom made off with her Ava.

"Daniel's changing her diaper. She had apple juice today . . ."

"That's a bad thing?"

"Let's just say he might be awhile. So, I saw in the paper that Brad Wilshire was arrested yesterday. Isn't he the guy who did your renovations?"

"He was arrested? What for?"

"He was doing some work for Bernadette Perkins, and she caught him stealing her antique jewelry. You're lucky he didn't rob you blind. Not that you had much to take."

The cookware. Brad had stolen her cookware. She was sure it was long gone. It had been a month and a half. "I guess you're right."

"So, no more Fiona's Fudge Shoppe, huh?"

"Yesterday was my last day. At least I hope it was. If things get slow over the winter, I'll have to take a part-time job."

"Are you ready for the grand opening? Mom said everything looks great."

"Layla did an amazing job. I loaded up on fresh produce from the farmers market. The walk-in's full of quality meat, and the staff is trained and scheduled. I just hope people show up."

"Well, you know the family's coming. And that ad in today's paper should attract a lot of customers. It was awesome."

"It should've been—talk about expensive. Did you see the Grand Opening banner?"

"You can't miss it. The community will support you. I'm sure it'll be great . . ." There was something in her tone. Something about the way Jade's green eyes darted away, toward the court, then down to her fingers as she laced them, her rings clinking together.

"But . . ."

"There's no *but*." Jade brushed the brownie crumbs from the checkered tablecloth. The bench squawked as she shifted.

PJ might not be a mind reader, but she knew when her sister was hiding something. "Out with it."

"Are you sure?"

"Does it have something to do with my opening?"

"Yes."

"Then spill."

Jade's shoulders sank as she exhaled. "It's not a bad thing. I just didn't want to make you nervous . . . You sure you want to know?"

PJ shot her a look.

"Daniel had an interview with the paper today. He found out they're sending Maeve Daughtry to your grand opening."

Dread congealed in PJ's stomach like refrigerated chicken stock. "The restaurant reviewer?"

"So that's great, right? She'll be majorly impressed, write an awesome review, and people will come by the droves."

"Or she'll get bad service, overcooked steak, write a terrible review, and people will go to the Burger Barn."

Jade elbowed PJ. "What has happened to our little Tigger?"

"She's been cooped up in a dusty old mansion with her adversary."

Jade tipped her head back, her eyes lighting knowingly. "Ahhhh . . ."

"Don't *ah* me. It's not like that."

"That's not what Madison said."

PJ glared across the court at her oldest sister as she dodged Dad and put up a shot. "Seriously? Why don't you two focus your romantic energies on Ryan? Cole's got a girlfriend. He's the last man I'd ever consider." She'd learned her lesson about taken men.

"He's awfully cute."

Not the word PJ would've used. Hot, maybe. Appealing, definitely. Infuriating, sometimes. But he was kind, too, she thought, as she remembered the way he'd checked on her at the gas station and taken her to the hospital.

And now she knew he definitely hadn't taken her cookware. Or flooded her dining room. She must've forgotten to close the window. It wouldn't be the first absentminded thing she'd ever done. She shook the thoughts from her head. She didn't want to remember the way she'd accused him so boldly.

Daniel appeared, straddling the bench across from them, Mia balanced on his thick arm.

The baby held her arms out to Jade. "Ma, ma, ma, ma, ma!"

Jade reached across the table, taking her daughter. She kissed the girl's chubby cheek.

Daniel scowled playfully at Jade. "You owe me for that one."

"I'm not the one who fed her apple juice," she said smugly.

Daniel swung his leg over the bench, facing them. "I heard you ended up at the ER this week. Feeling better?"

"They gave me Ativan for the panic attacks, but it makes me feel zoned out. I can't afford that right now."

"It's a thyroid issue though?"

"Yeah, but they can't really make the thyroid produce less hormone without killing the gland. We're hoping it sorts itself out. Until then, I just have to deal. So Jade told me about Maeve Daughtry. Any tips on impressing her?"

"I hear she's a sucker for great presentation and hates a long wait."

"All right then. So fast and beautiful. If I can add scrumptious to that, it'll be a home run."

"It'll be all that and more," Jade said. "If there's anything you can do, it's cook."

"Ga, ga, ga!"

"See, Mia agrees."

PJ only hoped Maeve Daughtry felt the same.

Chapter Sixteen

PJ DRIZZLED THE GARLIC BUTTER OVER THE RIB EYE, SPRINKLED chopped parsley over it, and set it in the window. "Order's up! Callie, how's the risotto coming?"

"Perfect, Chef. Where's Ronda? The tenderloins are dying."

Ronda appeared at the window and grabbed the plates. "Sorry, I'm in the weeds. I need a baked potato on the fly." And she was off.

"How long on the fettuccine?" PJ asked Nate.

"Two minutes, Chef."

PJ turned to the next order. Filet, brisket, and tilapia. She worked on automatic, in her element. They were a good three hours into the opening, and she was running high on adrenaline. Everything was going like clockwork. Well, almost everything. She'd overcooked a sirloin, Nate had gotten a minor cut using one of her new Wüsthof knives, and a server had spilled a tray of coffee—thankfully not on anyone.

But they'd had a full house all evening and nothing but compliments so far. Her family had come and gone, peeking into the kitchen only long enough to rave about the food and service.

She brushed the hair from her damp forehead with the back of her gloved hand. She'd informed her staff about Maeve Daughtry before the doors had opened. The reviewer had been seated fifteen minutes ago. She'd ordered the filet that was in the oven now.

"Coming through," Callie said, whizzing past with a hot skillet.

A second later the kitchen went dark and quiet. The hum of the refrigeration unit, gone. The buzz of the heat lamps, silent. The grind of the blender, still.

"Chef?" Callie said.

A power outage? *Oh please, not now.*

"It's not storming," Nate said. "The lights are still on in the dining room." The only light filtering in came from the next room.

"Thank God." PJ removed her gloves. "Okay, it must be a fuse or something. You just flip a switch, and it comes back on, right?" She did not have time for this.

"Don't ask me," Nate said. "I live in an apartment."

"I think there's a box, right?" Callie said. "Like in the basement or something?"

Heart pounding, PJ ran to the basement steps, only to find the lights down there were off too. She wasted precious time looking for a flashlight, all the while thinking of Maeve's thick steak cooling in the oven.

She shone the light around the dank basement. "Come on, where are you?" If only her dad were still here. She would call him if she couldn't figure it out quickly.

There in the corner. A big gray box. The door squeaked as she opened it. She frowned at the rows of black switches. Which one?

At a loss, she called her mom's cell but there was no answer. The home phone went over to voicemail.

No.

She pocketed her phone, realizing her breath was coming too quickly. Panic rolled in like fog over the river. *No. Not now. Please, not now.* She tried to push it back.

Her heart raced, and her lungs worked to keep up. A sweat broke out on the back of her neck, despite the coolness of the basement. She bent over, planting her hands on her apron-covered knees. Why hadn't she taken her meds?

Focus, PJ. You can do this. Breathe.

She drew in a breath, fighting back the overwhelming sense of panic. It would pass. She'd be fine. She focused on her breathing, tried to turn her attention to the switches, but she couldn't even think past the panic.

Cole looked up from the board he was measuring as another set of car lights swooped across the shed. Things were hopping at PJ's grand opening. The newly paved parking lot off the alley was full. He suspected cars lined the curb out front as well.

He felt conflicted about her success. She'd been so nervous—hadn't been able to sit still for two days straight, never mind that everything looked like perfection inside. She was especially nervous about her family coming. That he understood. He'd never been more nervous as a pitcher than when his dad had been in the stands.

PJ had also been nervous about that reviewer from the paper. Cole had tried to stay out of her way tonight, working in the shed, but his eyes kept coming back to the kitchen window. He wondered how it was going. If her staff were doing their jobs. If her customers were being kind. Strangely, he felt protective of her. Surely people would understand any little glitches. It was to be expected on opening night.

But he'd worked as a contractor long enough to know some customers were high on expectations and low on mercy.

Dropping the board onto the stack, he glanced at the window again. The square of light was gone. He frowned. Why would the kitchen light be off?

He skirted the worktable and headed toward the house, brushing the dirt from his hands. When he entered the kitchen, the aromas of grilled steak and garlic teased his nose. Something sizzled low nearby.

"PJ?"

"Cole." Callie approached in the darkness, sounding frantic. "The electricity's out. PJ went to the basement to take a look. Do you know anything about it?"

"It's only out in the kitchen," someone else called.

"I'll go see." This was a disaster. Worse, he thought as he hurried down the basement stairs, she probably thought he'd done something to sabotage her big night.

He found PJ in front of the circuit box, hunched over her knees, a flashlight at her feet. "You okay?"

"Not really—stupid panic attack." She was breathing too fast. "Can you fix it?"

"It's probably just overloaded." He picked up the flashlight and scanned the rows of switches. There. He flipped the switch off, then back on, relieved when it stayed in position.

"That should do it." He looked at PJ, still hunched over. "Can I get you anything? Some water?"

She inhaled through her nose, blew out the breath, shaking her head. "Can you—check upstairs?"

"Do you need your meds?"

"Please, just—the kitchen . . . steaks . . ."

"All right." He rushed upstairs. The lights were on. Everyone in the kitchen was scurrying around. A middle-aged guy was chopping away like a madman.

Callie was stirring something on the stovetop. "Thank God! The orders are pouring in."

Cole checked the oven and found steaks inside. "What should this be set on?"

"Broil. But I don't know how much longer she had on them. Especially since the oven was off." Fortunately he'd helped his foster father grill a ton of steaks.

He checked the orders. Another minute on the filet, two or three on the sirloins.

"Where's PJ?" Nate asked.

"She'll be another minute. What else can I do?"

"Wash your hands."

When he was finished Callie tossed him an apron. "Here. Check the fettuccini. It was almost done when the electricity went off. Should be al dente—that means—"

"I know what it means." First he removed the filet from the oven and set it on a white plate. After checking the order he added a scoop of risotto and a few spears of asparagus.

"Hold on." Nate drizzled garlic butter over the meat and added a pinch of something green over the top. He tucked a sprig of something into the risotto. By the time he was finished, the plate looked like a piece of art. He set the plate in the window.

Cole found the fettuccini done and pulled it off the heat, then drained it.

Callie appeared with a plate. "Right here."

He poured the noodles onto the plate, and she followed with a fragrant white sauce and slice of garlic toast. A pinch of Parmesan. More sprigs.

Cole was checking the steaks when PJ rushed into the kitchen. "Sorry, guys." She peeked into the oven. "Where's the filet?" Panic edged her voice.

"Relax." Cole removed the two sirloins and plated them. "It's already been served."

PJ pressed her fingertips to her temples. Her eyes were frantic. "That was Maeve Daughtry's steak. The reviewer from the paper."

Callie patted her shoulder as she passed. "It's okay. Cole handled the steak—it was perfect. The risotto was spot-on. Nate did his thing with the presentation. It's all good, I promise."

PJ looked between them, settling last on Cole. "Yeah?"

"Yeah," he said.

She blew out a breath, the anxiety falling from her face. "All right then. We have a ton of orders, so let's get back to it."

~

"Thanks, guys," PJ said as the last of her staff went out the back door. "Good job."

"See you in the morning."

The door shut and PJ went to lock it. Morning. There was so much to do before they opened for brunch. She couldn't think about any of that now, though. She only wanted to bask in the success of the evening.

The electricity had held out the rest of the night, but she'd called an electrician friend of her dad who was coming tomorrow morning to have a look. She'd sneaked an Ativan at her first opportunity. Zoned out she could live with. Panic attacks she could not.

She glanced around the kitchen, making sure all was in order. Her cookware was bright and shiny and hanging overhead. They weren't the Bourgeat, but they'd worked just fine.

She should be tired, as late as it was, but the excitement of the night lingered, making her jittery with energy. Or maybe that was the coffee she'd drunk while counting receipts. Another reason for excitement. She'd raked it in tonight. Of course every night wouldn't be so profitable, but it gave her hope.

The fading aromas of steak and garlic mingled with the pungent smell of sanitizer. Everything was back to sparkly new, the ceramic floor clean and still wet in spots. She flipped out the lights. She couldn't even think about going to sleep right now, never mind that she'd have to be up at the break of dawn.

Besides, there was one more thing she had to do.

She scaled the stairs to the second floor and walked down the hallway. Things were coming along up here. Almost finished. The walls painted, the bathroom put back together. The last two rooms had become a small kitchen and dining room that opened to a living room. It was a small but cozy space where the kids could gather for TV and meals, though there were no furnishings yet.

At the top of the attic stairs a sliver of light shone beneath the door. PJ headed up, her heart in her throat for some silly reason. It was only the caffeine making her heart race, making her hands tremble.

She rapped lightly on the door.

"Come in."

She turned the knob and opened the door. Cole was sitting on a rug, his back to the wall.

"Hi," she said.

"Hey."

He wore only jeans. She thought maybe there was paperwork or something spread around him, but she couldn't seem to tear her eyes from his bare chest. The perfection was marred by a scar that ran from his shoulder to his heart.

"Congrats on your opening. It seemed like a huge success."

She forced her gaze away, quickly scanning the room. He'd acquired a real bed and a couple pieces of furniture since her last jaunt up the attic stairs.

"Except for the little matter of losing electricity and having a full-blown panic attack in the middle of rush."

"Both of which you overcame."

"Thanks to you. I didn't have a clue which switch to flip on the doohickey, and obviously I wasn't in any shape to handle it."

"You would've figured it out."

"Plus you rescued Maeve's filet. You don't know what that means to me."

The corner of his mouth turned up. "You haven't read her review yet."

"You're not very good at this."

"What?"

"You're welcome—it's the appropriate thing to say when someone offers their gratitude." She smiled to soften the words.

The way the lamplight washed over the planes of his face was pure artwork. She was pretty sure it was doing the same thing to his chest, but she didn't risk a peek.

He rubbed his jaw. "I was half afraid you'd think I'd caused it."

"What?"

"The overload."

She winced. It hadn't even occurred to her. But after the way she'd jumped all over him about the cookware, she couldn't blame him.

"I know you didn't. And I know you didn't take the cookware. I'm sorry I jumped to conclusions before. It wasn't fair."

He studied her face until she felt her cheeks heating, then seemed satisfied with whatever he saw. He nodded once.

"So . . . whatcha working on?" she asked.

He looked at the papers spread around him, sighing. "Applications."

"For . . . ?"

"Kids."

"Kids? Oh. *Kids*." There must have been fifty applications there. Her mouth went slack. "All of them? Those are all kids wanting to come here?"

"Yep."

She saw the painful quandary in his troubled green eyes. In the hunched set of his shoulders. Most of these kids would be turned out on the street? The glow of her opening night dimmed.

"How are you going to choose?"

He shrugged. "That's what I'm trying to figure out."

"Want some help?" Where had that come from?

"Don't you have to be up early?"

"I'm jacked up on caffeine and adrenaline."

He stared at her long and hard again before lifting a shoulder. "In that case . . ." He gathered a stack of applications and held them out. "Haven't looked at these. Put the most promising ones in this pile."

"Promising meaning . . ."

"The ones most at risk. No family to turn to, learning disabilities, et cetera."

PJ took them as she settled on the rug across from him, folding her legs pretzel style. She ran her hand over the soft brown rug. "Love this."

"Garage sale. Still had the price tags."

"Nice."

She looked over the first application. Seventeen-year-old boy. Been in foster care for eight years. No living relatives.

No family. Ugh. PJ couldn't even imagine not having her family. She didn't need to read any more. She put it in the Promising pile and started on the next one. Girl. Mild learning disabilities. Mother was a drug addict. Father was in jail. Eight foster homes. Eight. Promising pile.

Boy. Father unknown. Mother deceased. Abused in first foster home. She thought of Cole's scar and wondered if abuse had put it there. How many knocks could one kid take? She put the file in the Promising pile.

She read through the next three, her heart tugging at each one as they went into the same pile.

"PJ."

She looked up.

"You can't put them all in that pile."

"But they all need help."

His face softened. His eyes filled with shadows. "I can only take four—and one spot is already spoken for."

A lump formed in her throat. She hated this. It wasn't fair. Why did she have a boatload of family, and these kids had no one? She thought of Cole and how strong he must be to come out of the system and find a way not only to support himself but to help others like him.

"I need to narrow it down to ten," he said. "If I try to interview all fifty-seven I'll be at it till Christmas."

Fifty-seven.

"As it is, they'll barely get to finish high school."

Because he could only guarantee they'd have a place until June 1. Frowning, PJ went back to the applications.

It was amazing how fast fatigue set in once the adrenaline and caffeine faded away. Once she was making decisions that would put parentless kids on the street.

After they'd been at it awhile, a yawn sneaked up on her. But she only had a handful left.

"What time do you have to be up?" he asked.

"Five."

He checked his watch. "That's in four hours. Go to bed. I'll finish up."

She stretched, her neck and shoulders aching from sitting hunched over so long. He was right. She was going to be exhausted tomorrow, and she had her first brunch to get through. Strawberry crepes, maple-flavored bacon, quiche lorraine tartlets, and so much more.

"All right." She handed him the few she hadn't read and headed for the door. "Good night."

"Night."

At the threshold she turned. He was already bent back over an application, a frown marring his forehead. He rubbed his chin with a knuckle.

When she stopped seeing him as her competitor, she could see what her sisters saw—a very appealing man. Not just on the surface but way down deep where it mattered most.

He looked up, the frown easing away. "What?"

"Nothing, it's just . . ." PJ bit her lip, considering her words for once. "I think what you're trying to do is really great, that's all." She eased away from the door, not waiting for a response. "Night."

"Good night."

PJ startled at the ringing sound. What? Where was she? She opened her eyes, orienting herself. The earliest rays of dawn crept through the curtains. More sleep.

Her cell phone. That was the ringing.

"Hello?" she croaked, her head falling back into the pillow.

"'There's a new little gem in town, and it sits on the corner of Main and Ruby—'"

"Mom?"

"'The restaurant lives and breathes in the beautiful historical Wishing House, formerly the home of longtime resident Evangeline Wishing Simmons.'"

PJ sprang up in bed. "The review!"

"'Wishing House Grille is a winner with its upscale cuisine and down-home charm. On opening night friendly staff were outshone only by the succulent dishes prepared by owner and chef Penelope Jane McKinley.'"

PJ whooped. "Succulent!"

Her mom laughed. "Shhh. I'm not finished." Her mom went on to read Maeve Daughtry's descriptions of the "outstanding presentation," the "tender filet of beef," and the "crisp spears of asparagus." By the time her mom finished, PJ wore a wide smile and was pacing the room with restless energy.

"Congratulations, honey. Looks like opening night was a huge success. Your dad says to tell you he told you so."

PJ laughed. A few minutes later she rang off, took thirty seconds for a well-deserved happy jig, then started the shower. She had a brunch to prepare and a restaurant to run.

Chapter Seventeen

COLE MADE HIS WAY TOWARD THE LIVING ROOM SLASH kitchen he'd converted from two bedrooms. He couldn't believe his kids were finally here. The last few weeks had been chaos, filled with final touches on the house and paperwork. Knowing he'd soon be tied to the house, he'd gone to Fort Wayne to visit Lizzy last weekend. She seemed down and quiet. He hoped the girls at school weren't harassing her again. April couldn't come soon enough.

PJ's restaurant seemed to be a raging success, and he was feeling the pressure. Not only to make Crossroads look successful but to help these kids who were trusting him to guide them into their futures.

He entered the living room and found them waiting for him. Zac and Shaundra sat at opposite ends of the brown couch. Josh stood behind the tweed recliner as if not sure he'd be here long enough to make himself at home. Last time Cole had peeked into Josh's room, the boy hadn't unpacked. He'd been moved around more than the others. Eight foster homes in three years.

Cole perched on the recliner. "Everyone get settled in okay?"

Zac nodded his chin upward.

"Is it okay if I took the dresser?" Shaundra asked.

"That's fine. You won't have a roommate until April. Josh?"

The boy pushed his wire-framed glasses up, a skeptical look on his face. "Who's paying for all this? I mean, it's gotta cost a bunch of money, right?"

"Don't worry about that. There are donors who fund Crossroads, but as I explained in the interviews, you'll be expected to work part time while you're still in school. Everyone will be contributing. Think of it as teamwork."

Cole went over the house rules, which included expectations like curfew, behavior, and chores. He'd come up with a points system that rewarded personal responsibility, saving money, and good behavior while discouraging misconduct and indolence.

He explained that he was arranging for people from the community to come in the first Monday of each month to coach them on things like balancing a budget, insurance, and home maintenance.

He reiterated that they'd have to find a job and another living situation by June 1 and assured them he'd help in any way he could. Afterward he showed them around the kitchen and pantry, going over the chore chart. When he dismissed them, Josh slipped quietly from the room.

Zac grabbed Cole's hand and gave it a hearty pump. "Thanks, man. This is pretty cool. I'm not going to blow it."

"I know you won't. I'm still working on setting up that internship with the local garage, but I think it's going to pan out."

"Sweet." After chatting a few minutes, he said good night and headed to his room.

Shaundra had hung back by the oak table he'd found at a garage sale. She played with one of the many braids hanging past her rounded shoulders.

"Got any questions for me?" he asked.

Shaundra's eyes always gave her away, and she tended to voice her thoughts directly. He'd admired that at her interview.

"My best friend said this was too good to be true."

He tilted his head. "What do you think?"

She took a good long look at him, her big brown eyes seeming older than her years. "I hope she's wrong."

"You've had some tough breaks, Shaundra. It's going to take time to build trust, but I hope in time you'll feel at home here."

"Me too." She headed toward the door, but a few steps out she turned. "I didn't know where I was gonna go."

He nodded. He knew the feeling.

"So . . . thanks."

Something welled up inside of him. The kind of feeling that made all the hard work, all the begging for money, all the red tape he'd cut through, worth it.

"Thank me by becoming a self-sufficient young adult."

She rolled her eyes good-naturedly. "You're worse than my caseworker—always riding my tail."

"Count on it." He was smiling as she left. He knew Shaundra's caseworker, and he was definitely up for the challenge.

PJ reached for another slice of pizza and set it on her plate. Cappy's Pizzeria was a far cry from The Grille, with its dark paneling, red vinyl booths, and questionable salad bar. Still, the blaring TVs, active pool tables, and lively atmosphere invited friends to come hang out. Since it was her night off and cooking wasn't on her agenda, it fit the bill. She deserved a break from the hectic pace she'd been keeping.

Across from her, Ryan signaled the server for another Coke. She'd invited their siblings, but Jade and Daniel were eating with his parents, and Madison and Beckett were having supper at Layla and Seth's place.

"So what are they like?" Ryan asked.

"The kids?" PJ shrugged. "Loud. But in all fairness, anything overhead would probably be loud. The girl seems nice. She reminds me of a cherub, kind of all round and soft with these cheeks that you want to pinch—not that I would. And the guys seem pretty cool. One's kind of quiet, and you get the feeling he doesn't miss much. The other one's really outgoing."

She bit into her pizza, unconsciously appreciating the tangy sauce with its blend of garlic, oregano, and basil with just a hint of cayenne pepper.

She remembered the applications she'd sorted through with Cole. Sometimes she wished she could forget them. The details of Shaundra's had stuck with her for some reason. The girl had been molested by four family members before she'd ended up in foster care at age fourteen. She had a learning disability and struggled in math, and she had no idea what she wanted to do with her life.

"What's with the face?"

PJ lifted a shoulder. "Those kids . . . I helped Cole sort through the applications, and—"

"You helped the competition?"

PJ gave him a look. "It was the least I could do after he saved my rear end on opening night. Anyway . . . it's just really sad what these kids have been through, you know? Josh, the quiet one, arrived yesterday with a garbage bag full of stuff. That's it. All he had."

"Wow."

"And I just—" PJ shook her head. "It's hard to fathom, that's all. The other two probably didn't have much more. Their apps were heartbreaking, all of them. I don't know how he narrowed it down."

She bit into her pizza, but the flavor had lost its appeal. She washed it down with a sip of root beer.

"Have you heard from Mrs. Simmons?"

"She calls regularly to see how things are going. Called to congratulate me on the great opening. I'm sure she's getting updates from Cole too."

"What's going to happen if you win?"

"What do you mean?"

"To the kids."

"What do you think will happen?" She hadn't meant to snap, but who liked the thought of putting disadvantaged kids out on the street?

"I just meant, will Cole move Crossroads somewhere else?"

"Oh, sorry. No, the overhead would kill him. He doesn't have the funds for that."

They'll be almost nineteen by then, out of high school. Independent.

"Tough break," Ryan said.

"If I win, Wishing House will employ locals and serve as much-needed housing for the community."

Ryan put both palms out. "Hey, I'm on your side. You're my sister, remember?"

But what about all the other kids?

PJ was relieved when the conversation turned to Ryan's job. But even as she drove home along the winding curves against the river, she couldn't shake his question from her mind.

Chapter Eighteen

"I can't believe you talked me into this," Ryan said.

PJ walked him out the door of her restaurant and onto the back porch. She'd had six students in her first cooking class, including Ryan—she'd worked her charm on him at Cappy's on Sunday.

"You'll thank me later when you're whipping up meals for women and they're begging for more."

"I don't have the qualifications to be here."

She jabbed him in the stomach with her finger. "It's Cooking 101. The only prerequisite is that you like to eat, and you definitely qualify. Besides, you prepaid, and if you quit I'll think I'm a lousy teacher."

A low growl escaped his throat.

She patted his cheek. "Go home and get to bed. You're overtired and cranky."

After he left she sank onto the porch swing. Darkness was falling fast. She'd probably be eaten alive by mosquitoes, but the fresh air felt so good. The flower garden around the porch shared its fragrances, a sweet blend of begonias and phlox. There was just enough light to see that the bed was already overgrown. She'd been too busy since The Grille opened to handle her end of the landscaping.

And how are you going to stay afloat if you have a B & B to run next year too? As busy as she was now, she couldn't imagine being responsible for those rooms and the guests. *You won't be able to handle it, PJ. You'll be in over your head.*

The back door creaked open, and Cole came out.

"Smells good in there."

"Basic spaghetti sauce. My first cooking class."

"How'd it go?"

"Nobody burned down the kitchen, and they're coming back next week—even Ryan."

"You suckered your brother in?"

"Hey, he needs to learn his way around the kitchen."

"Your idea or his?"

She notched her chin up. "It was mutual—after a little convincing."

Cole sank onto the chair across from her, stretching out his long legs to the edge of the porch. He scanned the backyard, no doubt watching the night's first fireflies. The porch light gave his skin a golden glow, and he wore a couple days' stubble on his jaw. A shadow settled into the subtle dip over his upper lip. His lower lip was pleasantly full, soft looking, like it was made for a delicious kiss.

He turned and caught her staring.

PJ looked away, cleared her throat. Darn guy was too handsome for his own good. She'd overheard a couple of the single ladies in tonight's class whispering about him. They'd probably signed up hoping to get a glimpse of him, but he was pretty busy with the kids these days.

"How goes it upstairs?" she asked.

"Not bad. Zac got a paid internship at the garage this week, and Shaundra got on at Sassy Nails."

"That was *my* first job."

"You'll have to share your trade secrets with her. I think it's a good fit though. She sure seems to like all that stuff."

PJ frowned at her fingers. "My nails haven't looked good since I worked there."

They were short and blunt and hadn't sported a fresh coat of polish since, let's see . . . her last date with Keaton. Shame swelled at the memory of the night she'd discovered his secret. She shoved the thought away. She refused to become mired in bad memories.

She pushed the swing instead, the rhythmic squeak of the chains punctuating the silence.

"So I was wondering about the cooking lessons," Cole said. "The kids need some basic kitchen skills—actually, I do too. In the future I'd like to be able to teach them myself."

"You want to take my class?"

"I'd like all of us to, but the funds aren't really there. I was hoping we could work out a trade or something?"

"What kind of trade?"

"I don't know. I must have something you want."

PJ's mind went straight to her thoughts of his lips. She forbade her eyes from dipping south a few inches, but she couldn't stop the heat working its way up her neck and into her cheeks. Thank God it was almost dark.

"Can't think of a thing." Even she couldn't miss the flirtatious note in her voice.

He took a few seconds to study her face. "I've been told I'm pretty useful to have around."

"By whom?"

"People."

"Women?"

His eyes twinkled under the porch lights. "Haven't had any complaints."

She'd imagine not. She bit the inside of her lip. It was impossible to tear her gaze away from his mesmerizing eyes. She hadn't seen this relaxed, playful side of him, and she liked it. Liked it a lot.

"I need a new closet," PJ offered.

"What's wrong with the old one?"

"It's an old maid's room. The closet was built for three uniforms and a pair of orthopedic shoes."

"I'm pretty sure they didn't have orthopedic shoes at the turn of the century."

"I want a walk-in with shoe shelves and wire baskets. Are you up to the task?"

"Bring it."

"And cubbies for purses!"

"You're getting awfully excited about this closet."

She shrugged. "I'm a girl."

His eyes skimmed her figure so quickly she wondered if she'd imagined it. He cleared his throat. "So, where's this closet going to go?"

"You know where it is now, to the left of the door? I thought we could just bring it out a few feet."

"We?"

"Well, I'll be supervising."

"Perfect."

"I'll buy the materials."

"No, that's on me. You're teaching four beginners to cook—believe me, you'll earn it."

"When would be a good time for the lessons? Sunday anytime after brunch ends would work, or Monday before my six o'clock class."

"The kids work after school, but Sunday would be good. Our weekly meeting is at three, so four or five?"

"Let's make it five, then we can eat the spoils for supper."

"Deal."

A radio blared on upstairs, shattering the peaceful night.

PJ winced. "Wow, that's some loud, uh, music?"

"Zac's partial to screamo. He does play a mean electric guitar though." He stood. "I'll tell him to turn it down before our neighbors kick us out."

They said good night, and PJ watched him go, admiring the broad set of his shoulders and the lean cut of his waist. Another cooking class scheduled, and she was going to have her dream closet. All in all a good day.

A song pulled PJ from her sleep. She freed her arms from the covers and grabbed her phone as the familiar ringtone woke her fully.

Keaton.

Her breath quickened and her heart raced. She released the phone and it clunked onto the nightstand.

The song seemed to go on forever, and as much as she wanted to deny it, her fingers itched to answer. She clasped them tightly until her blunt nails cut into her palms.

Only when the tune stopped did she lie back against her

pillows. Why was he calling? She hadn't heard from him since she'd left Indy. Since the week after he'd broken her heart.

The memories rushed in like a thick fog. She'd met Keaton at a fund-raiser for Meals on Wheels. They'd been in line at the cash bar and had struck up a conversation about the line that never seemed to move. He was so handsome and charming in his fitted black suit with his striking blue eyes. He had sandy blond hair that toppled over his forehead, giving him a boyish appearance. But that was the only thing boyish about Keaton.

He was a sales rep for a printing company, and he came into Indy weekly on business. PJ was drawn to his commanding presence and dry sense of humor. They left the fund-raiser later and met at a coffee shop, staying until the lights were being turned off.

Afterward she didn't hear from him for almost two weeks and had moped around her dorm until Kayla had been ready to beat her with a spatula. Then on a cold Tuesday evening, with snow drifting down into soft blankets, he came back into her life.

They began spending every free moment together when he came to town. He was smart and ambitious. He listened when she talked and believed in her dreams and goals.

They'd been dating three months when he took her to St. Elmo's. It was the most romantic night of her life. She'd always wanted to go to the restaurant, but it was out of her budget. The food was everything she'd been told. And the company . . . It was there, over a candlelit table, Keaton's blue eyes intent on hers, that she realized she was falling in love.

She'd always scoffed at her lovesick friends, at her sisters, with their moony eyes and furtive smiles, but later that evening as Keaton walked her to her dorm, his body shielding her from the cold, PJ knew what it was all about.

When he touched her, her heart sighed. When he kissed her, she melted. They stopped by the deserted entrance, and he boxed her in against the brick wall. His eyes caught her and held her captive, and her body begged for a kiss. He didn't disappoint. Her knees were as limp as overcooked noodles by the time he drew away.

"Thank you for tonight," she whispered. "I had the best time. I wish you didn't have to go home."

"I wish I didn't either."

"I miss you when you're gone." His phone calls were sporadic, and their schedules made it hard to connect. It seemed she was always leaving voicemails. But when he was here . . .

He ran his finger down her cheek, and she felt it to her toes. "I miss you too. I'll be back next Tuesday. Where would you like to go?"

She pulled a pout. "I have a class on Tuesday night, remember?"

A group of girls busted out the door, talking loudly.

He pulled away, but leaned back in for another kiss. "I'll call you. We'll set something up for Wednesday."

"Okay. Night."

As he turned, she pulled out her phone and punched in his number. When it rang in his pocket a few steps away, he checked the screen and turned, smiling.

"I miss you already," she said into the phone.

He stalked toward her, his eyes like magnets. "You're hard to leave, PJ." When he was close enough, he lowered the phone and gave her a kiss to remember. She inhaled his spicy cologne and cuddled into the warmth of his body. For the first time she wished she had her own apartment. He didn't draw away until she was trembling.

As she opened her eyes, they caught on the phone in his hand. "Where's your iPhone?"

He glanced at the cheap-looking phone. "My, uh—this one's for personal use. My iPhone's for work."

"Oh." That was strange. She'd seen him texting a friend more than once. At least that's what he'd said.

After they parted, PJ was in a funk. The phone bothered her. What if he had another girlfriend in Illinois? Kayla pulled it out of her when she was still tossing and turning an hour later.

"That is kind of odd," her roommate said after PJ explained. "And I'll be honest, there are other weird things too. You said you always get his voicemail when you call—"

"He's just busy."

"And he calls at odd times."

"He works late."

"Did he ever accept your friendship request on Facebook?"

"No, but he said he hasn't been on there in ages. I'm sure it's nothing. He's a really good guy. We had the most romantic time tonight, Kayla. I think I might be—"

She looked at her friend and was sure she had that same moony expression Jade had worn the night Daniel proposed. "I've never felt this way."

Kayla studied her from across the darkened room. "Just be careful, okay? I don't want you to get hurt."

As much as PJ wanted to wallow in the giddiness of new love, she couldn't shake the suspicions from her mind over the next week. She hadn't always chosen the best boyfriends in the past. Was Keaton a poor choice too?

His visit the following week did nothing to allay her concerns. In the middle of the Circle Centre Mall Wednesday night he excused himself to take a phone call—on his iPhone. She couldn't hear his words as he greeted the caller, but his tone of voice was gentle, like when he spoke to PJ.

When she asked casually who it was, he said it was his boss. The suspicions didn't go away as her attentiveness picked up on other details over the next couple weeks. The way he turned his phone away from her when he texted sometimes. The way he always stepped away to make a phone call at nine o'clock.

Several times he asked her if everything was okay, and she brushed him off, afraid an unfounded accusation would ruin things between them. But when he visited her in early spring, she made a bold plan. She was going to follow him back to Illinois. It was only three hours. She'd be exhausted for classes in the morning, but she had to do it for her own peace of mind. For her heart, which shuddered in her chest at the possibilities.

She borrowed Kayla's car, tucked her hair inside a baseball cap, and followed the silver Verano at a distance even though it was night.

Two hours later a traffic snarl caused her to get closer to him than she liked. She ducked behind a semi, her heart pounding hard. If he caught her following, what could she say? If he wasn't hiding anything, he'd never forgive her.

What was she thinking, following him all the way home? A few minutes later the jam cleared, and she followed at a comfortable distance. Maybe she should turn around. She was being stupid.

But then he took the south ramp onto 57. Mount Vernon was north of 64. Her nerves clattered. She turned off the radio and turned the heat down, suddenly too warm.

Awhile later he took the Benton exit. PJ followed him

through a small town and into an older subdivision with nice, large homes. She lengthened her distance.

Please, God, let there be some reasonable explanation.

His brake lights flashed, and he pulled into a drive. PJ tugged her cap lower and passed by, turning around at the cul-de-sac.

Her hands trembled on the steering wheel. Why had he lied about where he lived? Less than a minute later, she eased up the street and parked in front of the house next door in the shadows along the curb. She ducked down in the seat, watching as Keaton exited the detached garage and walked up the porch steps.

When he reached the top, the door flew open. A little pajama-clad boy barreled into him. Keaton swooped him up into his arms.

PJ's breath caught in her throat, choking her. Then a woman appeared in the doorway, her willowy frame silhouetted by the light behind her. Light glinted off her short blond hair.

PJ couldn't tear her eyes away as Keaton drew her close and bent for a slow kiss. As one mass, they disappeared into the house, shutting the door, leaving PJ out in the cold, broken and alone.

Keaton had been lying about everything. The realization carved out a hollow shape in her middle. Worse than that, she'd been dating a married man! Had been kissing a married man. She was in love with a married man. She was the Other Woman. The empty place filled with shame until it swelled, spreading to every space inside her.

Now a ding pulled her from the nightmare as a voicemail hit her phone. She waded through the shame, reached for it, and deleted the message, dropping the phone as if it were poison. Because really, that's exactly what Keaton was.

Chapter Nineteen

MONDAYS WERE QUIET WITH THE RESTAURANT CLOSED AND the kids in school. The perfect day to finish PJ's closet.

Cole grabbed the wire shelf and began attaching the top one into the clip. The extended closet was tight for two people with the shelving in stacks. The sweet flowery scent of PJ teased his nose. He'd put in a brighter light, but now the heat it gave off was too much.

"A little lower," PJ said. "I can't reach."

"Here?"

PJ edged around him and rose on tiptoe, reaching up. "Should be fine. The purse cubbies are going over here, right? With the wire cubbies under them?"

"Uh-huh." He popped the first end into the slot and proceeded to the other side. "Excuse me."

"Sorry." PJ eased into the corner. "Need help?"

"No." The shelf popped into place. He jiggled it to make sure it was secure before moving on to the next.

"Not there."

"Why?"

"I want to hang dresses on that side."

He eyed her up and down. "You own dresses?"

She narrowed her eyes in a mock glare. "Just move it down."

"Just saying, I don't remember moving any dresses out of here." Never mind the red skirt she'd worn to her presentation. He happened to know those long legs deserved to be on display.

"What do you call this?"

He glanced over his shoulder and frowned at the pink ball of froth in her arms. "A cotton candy explosion?"

"It's a bridesmaid dress. It was a lovely wedding—and the happy couple are still together."

He squatted down. "I find it hard to believe that anything that started with that could end happily."

"Marriage cynic." Her eyes teased. "I had you pegged from day one."

He couldn't help thinking of his parents. "Marriage is fine for some people."

"Not you?"

Anxiety swirled through him at the thought. He craved that kind of intimacy. Nights got lonely, even with a houseful of kids. Sometimes he just wanted someone to pull close, to hold against him and know she was his alone. Someone like PJ.

You don't deserve it, Evans. Not after what you did.

"I'll take that as a yes," PJ said.

He couldn't even remember the question.

"Well, when I get married someday," she said, "I'm not going to pick some ugly confection in a hideous color."

"So you admit the dress is ugly."

"It's . . . aesthetically challenged."

He looked for the next shelf. "Why do brides do that anyway? Are they trying to make sure their friends don't outshine them by putting them in the silliest thing they can find?"

"Doraphine would never do such a thing."

"Doraphine? Well, that explains it all." He squinted at the dress. "Are those feathers?"

She set it aside. "So I won't wear it again—ever. I still plan to buy dresses someday, and I'll need a place to hang them."

"Fine, fine. This suit you?" He held the shelf against the wall.

"Perfect. No, wait, up a little. Down, down. Right there."

"When you said 'supervise,' I didn't think you meant it so literally."

She shoved his shoulder, hardly enough to budge him. He liked this side of her. She was playful and fun when she wasn't working so hard to prove herself.

"This is my first real closet. I shared with Jade growing up, then with my roommate at college. And now I finally have a whole big closet all to myself—with purse cubbies!" She gave a happy little clap.

His lips twitched as he stood, moving to the next shelf, high enough to accommodate stacked rows of shirts and pants. His mood had been in danger of a major dip, but somehow she made him forget all that.

He worked the wire into the clip, but this one didn't go easily, and the longer shelf was making it awkward.

"All right, Sunshine, settle down and help me with this clip."

She moved in closer. "Where? Here?" She reached around and began pushing with him. "No leverage. Let me in."

He moved aside, letting her in front of him, his arms on both sides of her. Big mistake. Her sweet scent wafted up his nose and seemed to curl around every cell in his body.

Arms extended, she pressed against the shelving unit, her back coming up against his body. He held the shelf in place, swallowed hard. *The shelf, Evans. Focus on the shelf.*

But she was so close. She felt so good against him, and if he lowered his arms, his palm would fit right into the curve of her waist, her back into the cradle of his chest. He could slide his hands around to the planes of her stomach, draw her flush against him, and bury his nose into the side of her neck. That spot he was always wanting to kiss.

His arms trembled as he pushed the shelf, leaning into her.

Pop. The wire snapped into the clip.

"Got it." PJ turned to him, her lips turning up.

She was inches away. His lips nearly grazed her temple. A strand of hair, resting against her cheek, fluttered under his breath.

Her smile fell away.

His eyes scrolled over her face, stopping at her big brown eyes. He couldn't remember the last time a woman had looked at him like that, like she was melting under his gaze. He didn't allow himself in these situations.

He should pull back. Step away. Now. But then he made the mistake of inhaling her sweet scent, and his body was having none of that.

Instead he tucked the strand behind her ear. Then he couldn't seem to stop his fingers from following a path down her long hair. It was so soft. Like silk.

She shivered. "What—what are you doing?"

He swallowed hard. Denial. Denial was always good, especially when it let him keep touching her. "Installing shelves."

If installing shelves felt this nice, he'd do it every day. Heck, every hour.

"We probably shouldn't be . . . you know."

Was it his imagination or had she just leaned a fraction

closer? His fingers took another heavenly trip down the silk of her hair. Last time. Then he'd step away. But his hand continued its trail down her back, settling at the curve of her waist. And he was right. It fit there like the hollow had been made with him in mind.

With him in mind? What was he thinking? PJ hadn't been made with him in mind. No woman had. He'd had a family once and what had he done? Who was he to think he deserved a woman like PJ? Any woman at all?

His hand fell to his side. He stepped back, clearing the thickness from his throat. "I need to—go."

PJ blinked, a look coming into her eyes he didn't want to see.

He left the closet, strode from the room, and escaped out the back door. He was in sore need of some fresh air.

PJ's breath left her suddenly, leaving her as limp and wilted as week-old lettuce. She could still feel Cole's touch. Still feel his fingers sliding down her hair, sending every follicle into a frenzy. Still feel his strong hand settle into the curve of her waist like he was staking his claim. She'd never liked the thought of that, but then, she'd never known Cole.

This wasn't good. She wasn't looking for a relationship. Someday, yes. But she didn't trust herself to make good choices, to see beneath the good looks and rippling muscles. Not after Keaton. She seemed to be missing the good sense gene when it came to men, because by all appearances Cole was taken too. She'd heard him on the phone, using the tender tone reserved for a woman. He had a girlfriend tucked away somewhere who might have no idea he was holed up in a house with another woman. Installing her shelves, tucking her hair behind her ears, making her shiver.

There was no way she was going there again. Bad enough she had to dodge Keaton's calls and texts. She didn't need to add Cole to the equation.

Besides, he was her rival. In nine months one of them would be leaving, and she fully intended it to be him. There was no chance of a future here, girlfriend or no. And the way he took off like oil across a hot skillet, he was in complete agreement.

Chapter Twenty

SEPTEMBER FADED INTO OCTOBER, BRINGING BRIGHT autumn foliage and chilly days. They switched the air conditioning to heat at night. Fewer people chose to dine on the wide veranda, and PJ became anxious about the long winter months ahead.

She and Cole had made it through the cooking classes, but he'd been pretty scarce since the closet incident. She was glad. She was. If she was a tiny bit hurt it was only because she was a people person. She got lonely for adult company.

November arrived with cold, gusty winds, and the tourists were suddenly gone. How would her restaurant survive the off-season? Her first cooking classes were over and round two hadn't drawn the crowd she'd hoped. At her worst moments, when she tallied up her profits for the week, a terrible dread filled her.

She was going to lose the contest. Lose the house, her restaurant, all the money she'd put into it. Sometimes it was enough to bring on a panic attack. She'd work through it, then give herself a pep talk and go through her routines and somehow put the negative thoughts behind her.

Meanwhile, things upstairs seemed to be going swimmingly. Cole's kids had jobs, and she'd heard nothing but good things from Dan at the garage and Wanda, the manager at Sassy Nails. Yeah, she'd splurged on a manicure. Probably not the best idea she'd ever had.

She was glad it was going well for them, but living with a bunch of teens had its frustrations. One day in September she'd come home to find half the flower garden mowed down. She took a deep breath and told herself at least the weeds were gone too.

The next week a huge oil stain blotched her beautiful new concrete parking pad where Zac had changed his oil. Rather than confront Cole—because that would require a conversation—she grabbed the dishwashing liquid and a scrub brush and went to work. It came out. Mostly.

Josh continually used her front door, Shaundra did her dance squad routines above the dining room during restaurant hours, and someone liked to pilfer food from her fridge.

Through it all, PJ gritted her teeth and reminded herself they'd be out in six months. She didn't even let herself worry about where they'd go. After all, they had jobs, and they'd be graduated by then.

Adding to her stress, Keaton continued texting her. Sometimes she read them before she deleted—it was impossible not to, when they were only one or two lines.

MY MARRIAGE IS OVER. ARE YOU THERE, PJ? PLEASE CALL ME.

The texts made it impossible to put him behind her. They were a constant reminder of her poor judgment, covering her with a blanket of shame. Was he really divorcing? Had *she* caused the divorce?

Worse yet, she sometimes remembered their tender moments together, their laughter, the space she'd given him in her heart. At her loneliest moments, she was tempted to text him back. If his marriage was really over, what was the harm? Then she'd feel horrible for being tempted. What kind of person did that make her?

Keaton, the kids, the restaurant, Cole. It was all simmering on the back burner, ready to boil over as she headed into the holidays.

On the Monday before Thanksgiving, she went Christmas shopping with her mom. The season's first snowflakes drifted down as they made their way back to her mom's Enclave, arms laden with bags.

Mom lowered her chin into her scarf. "It's freezing!"

"I hope the snow sticks," PJ said as they piled the bags into the back.

Her mom smiled. "You would."

"It's so pretty . . ." PJ spun around, arms out. "And it's our first snowfall. How can you not like it?"

"Someone's in a good mood."

"Spending money always puts me in a good mood. Especially when it's someone else's." Plus, she'd managed another Monday away from the house, avoiding a quiet day at home with Cole.

Her mom chuckled as she started the car, and the strains of "White Christmas" filtered through the radio.

"You want to grab dinner somewhere?" PJ asked. "You can bring something home for Dad."

"I should probably get home and do some laundry." Mom backed from the parking spot. "I was hoping you'd make it to church yesterday. We miss you. Everyone asks about you."

PJ knew her concern was really about her spiritual walk, not her vacant spot in the pew. "I was going to let Callie handle brunch, but her little girl got sick."

"Maybe next week. I know the restaurant is important, but if you don't set priorities, life has a way of setting them for you."

"I know. I'll try and make it."

A text dinged in. PJ felt the vibration in her pocket. She thought immediately of Keaton and ignored it.

Mom pulled onto Oak Street. "I think that's yours."

On the other hand, it could be any number of people. She was being paranoid. She pulled her phone from her pocket and checked the screen. Her mood took a dive to the floorboard.

"'I miss you'?"

"Mom!" PJ shut off the phone.

"Sorry, didn't mean to look over your shoulder. It's none of my business."

PJ hated that he'd texted her. And why now, of all times? It was almost as if he were sitting in the car with them. If her mom knew what she'd done, she'd be so ashamed.

PJ was glad they weren't going out to eat now. She wanted to go home and put her phone down the garbage disposal. The commercial one. Maybe it was time to change her number.

"I know it's none of my business, but that text . . ."

PJ looked out the passenger window so her mom couldn't read her face.

"Honey, if things are heating up between you and Cole, I think you should be careful."

"Me and Cole?"

"He seems like a nice man, don't get me wrong. But he's had a rough time of it—and I know it sounds callous, but honey, you don't go through all that and not come out with a lot of baggage."

"Mom, there's nothing going on between me and Cole." She brushed away the memory of him in her closet.

"Oh? That's not who the message was from?"

She'd done it now. Last thing she needed was more prying questions. "Everything's under control. You don't have to worry about me."

Her mom's blue eyes burned into PJ, until she was sure her mom saw everything, right down to the butterfly tattoo she didn't know about.

"He's an awfully attractive man."

"You too?"

"And I'm sure you feel bad for him—you're softhearted, and I've always loved that about you. But relationships are challenging enough without that kind of baggage. From what I understand, he was in foster care for a long time. I don't know what put him there, but it can't be anything good—and that's without all the experiences he may have endured once he was there."

"I know, Mom. You don't have to worry."

"So there's nothing going on between you two?"

"*Mom.*" She thought of Madison's husband and his baggage— an alcoholic father and a mother who abandoned him. Had her mom butted in as their relationship progressed? She doubted it.

Mom put her palm up. "Sorry. None of my business, I know. Just promise you'll be careful."

"I promise." PJ was nothing these days if not careful.

A few minutes later, Mom pulled up to the curb behind PJ's car. The exterior lighting, set on a timer, was on, and Wishing House glowed under a velvet sky.

"Good heavens, what happened?"

PJ followed her mom's eyes to the back of her red Monte Carlo where the Enclave's headlights shone. Onto the heavily dented bumper.

"What in the world?" PJ got out and marched to her car.

It was no little fender bender. Someone had bashed in the whole back side.

"That's pretty bad." Mom bent to examine the damage. "Surely it wasn't a hit-and-run. Not here in Chapel Springs."

It wasn't. PJ knew exactly who'd done it. Josh always parked his Oldsmobile beater right behind her. She'd wanted to complain to Cole because it was an eyesore but she hadn't.

But she was going to now. "I have to go."

"You should probably call the police," Mom called. "And your insurance company."

"Oh, I will."

"And take pictures! What about your bag?"

"I'll get it Thursday."

Cole fanned through the mail, picking out the one piece addressed to him and setting the rest back on the table. He climbed the steps to the second floor, then to the attic.

The house was quiet, the kids still working their after-school jobs and PJ having left early in the afternoon.

He closed the door to his room and ripped open the blue envelope. Lizzy was sweet to remember. He smiled at the funny caption on the card and set it on his nightstand beside the empty soup bowl and Coke can.

He flopped into bed and flipped on the TV. It was still an hour until Monday Night Football, but there was plenty of pre-game commentary. He'd looked forward to the game all week. How lucky was he that the Colts played on his birthday?

He arranged his pillows and settled against the headboard. He'd thought about buying a cheap sofa for his room, but it seemed like a waste of money. He liked to be out in the community living room as much as possible when the kids were home.

The heat kicked on, and he jacked up the volume. He loved the cooler weather, though the heating bill was wrecking his budget. On top of that, one of his sponsors had lost his job and had to renege on his pledge of support. Cole was going to have to find extra funds and soon.

He'd already taken a job installing windows for a home improvement company. But there had been unexpected expenses, like an insurance policy to cover their belongings. He also hadn't accounted accurately for the amount of food three teenagers consumed in a week.

There was a sharp rap on the door. He turned the volume down. "Come in."

PJ appeared. Her cheeks were flushed, her eyes sparking, and specks of snow dotted her dark hair.

"You need to come outside."

"What's wrong?"

"What's wrong? What's *wrong*? There's a huge dent in the back of my car. It's not even small enough to qualify as a dent— more of a complete smashing of the back side of my car!"

He leaned forward, snapping off the TV. "I'm sure there's—"

"You know it was Josh. He always parks right behind me, and his car's gone."

"Now wait a minute. Maybe it was—"

"A hit-and-run? Is that what you were going to say? Really?"

It was, but he wasn't saying it now, not with the way she was shooting daggers at him. "Josh was running late for work. I'm sure if he did it, he'll tell us. He has insurance. It'll be taken care of."

"And what about the flowers? Will those be taken care of? And the food from my fridge—"

"Wait, what?"

"—and the dancing over my dining room, and the tromping through my restaurant during open hours, and the oil on my concrete? Will all that be taken care of too?" She crossed her arms over her chest, which rose and fell quickly.

"Somebody's been holding back."

"Well, it's not like you've been hanging around the first floor. If you had been, maybe you would've noticed that you still haven't put the hooks up in my closet."

He clenched his jaw. "Anything else?"

She pulled in a breath and released it, her shoulders sinking. The fight left her face, her whole body. Her eyes found the rug. "No."

He'd had no idea she'd been so bothered by the kids. And she was right. He had been avoiding her. If he'd come around more, maybe he would've noticed. Maybe she would've felt free to tell him all this.

He exhaled hard, then stood and slipped on his shoes. "Let's go look at your car."

He followed her down the stairs and out the front door. Snow swirled around them, and he tucked his hands into his pockets. He could see the damage long before they reached the vehicle. It wasn't as bad as she'd made it sound, but it was a good-sized dent.

He ran his hand along the bumper. There were a couple white scuffs among the red. It was Josh all right. "I'll talk to Josh when he gets home. He was running late, and I'm sure he just didn't know what to do. He's a good kid."

She stepped back, huddling against the cold. She hadn't looked at him since her tirade. "And he has insurance for sure?"

"Yes. It'll be taken care of."

The deductible would probably cost the kid everything he'd earned, but he had to learn there were consequences for his actions.

"He gets home a little after nine. We'll come down, and you can get all his information."

By the time Cole was back in his room, the anticipation of the football game had long worn off, and he really wasn't looking forward to tonight's half-time show.

Chapter Twenty-One

THE RESTAURANT WAS BUSIER THAN SHE EXPECTED FOR THE
Saturday after Thanksgiving. Everyone must've been as tired of
leftovers as PJ was.

The back of the house bustled happily along as the evening
wore on. She couldn't say the same for the front. One of the servers, who was habitually late, had been a no-show. She had to find
a replacement.

She sautéed mushrooms and onions in a skillet, keeping an
eye on the sirloin and rib eye in the oven.

"Two Roquefort salads on the fly for VIPs!" one of the servers called.

Callie went to work on the salads while Nate arranged bru-
schetta on a plate.

PJ's car was in the shop for repairs. Josh had gone straight to
Cole when he'd gotten home from work. He'd apologized to PJ,
his face so contrite she felt bad about his deductible.

Cole had also talked to the kids about her list of complaints.
So far there'd been no more oil stains, no more dancing on the
ceiling, and no more missing food. She and Cole seemed to
have arrived at a tentative truce, though they both remained
guarded.

She wiped her forehead with the back of her gloved hand.

She wished she had a separate heating system for the kitchen. The one window hardly made a dent, and the fans only seemed to blow the hot air around.

"One sirloin, kill it," a server called.

PJ prepared the sirloin. "Callie, how long on the rice?"

"Two minutes, Chef."

She removed the rib eye from the oven and arranged it on a plate before sliding the mushrooms and onions on top. She handed it off to Callie.

"Chef?" Barbie, one of her servers, poked her head into the kitchen. "Someone wants to pay you his compliments."

Nothing made her happier than a satisfied customer. PJ pulled off her gloves and turned with a smile. It froze on her face when Keaton slid past Barbie.

Her smile fell. Her heart rate tripled, and her breath left her lungs. What was he doing here? In her restaurant? In her kitchen? In her safe little world?

"Hello, PJ."

She couldn't look away from his smiling blue eyes. Not even when she realized Callie had gone still beside her. A dozen memories flittered through her brain.

Her throat constricted. "Keaton," she managed.

His hair was shorter, barely curling at the nape of his collared shirt, that flop of bangs she used to love just touching his brow. His shoulders weren't as broad as she remembered, and his frame seemed smaller.

"The meal was delicious," he said. "Best food I've had in months."

"Thank you."

"The restaurant is amazing, PJ. Congratulations."

"Thank you."

She had to get him out of there before he sucked her back in with those mesmerizing eyes. With that boyish flop of hair and that way he had of making her feel like she was the only woman in the room.

She forced a smile. "It was good seeing you. Thanks for dropping by."

She turned back to the stove and worked on automatic, immensely aware of his continued presence. Of Callie, her movements uncharacteristically slow. Of Nate's curious glances.

"Can we talk?"

"I'm sorry . . . I'm pretty busy tonight." And tomorrow and the next day. If he'd just leave, she could forget he was ever here. She'd change her number and forget all about his gentle touches and tender kisses.

And the lies, PJ. Don't forget the lies. The wife. The kid. The marriage.

"Please, PJ."

He wasn't one to beg. If she refused, would he say everything he wanted right here in her kitchen? In front of her staff? She couldn't take that chance.

Swallowing hard, she removed her apron. "Callie, you got this?"

"Yes, Chef."

She left the kitchen, Keaton on her heels, and went out the back door and onto the porch. The cold air slapped her in the face, sent goose bumps skating up her arms under her stiff whites. She turned, wishing she could hide, wishing she hadn't installed the bright hundred-watt bulbs.

A shadow settled into the crease at the corners of his lips

as he smiled—those crescent-shaped almost-dimples she used to love.

She stopped a safe distance away and curled her arms over her stomach. "You shouldn't be here, Keaton."

He lifted his hands, palms up. "You don't answer my texts or calls."

"So you just show up in my kitchen during restaurant hours?"

"I miss you."

There it was. That way he had of catching her off guard.

"You don't miss me. You just miss the gullible girl who made you feel young again."

He took a step closer. "That's not true."

Distance. She needed plenty of distance. PJ stepped back.

"My marriage is over. I'm sorry about what happened. It was wrong, and I have to live with that. But I want you back, PJ, more than anything. What do I have to do? Just say it. I'll do anything."

Her heart clenched hard. She remembered the way she'd felt in his arms. Safe and loved. He'd never said the words, not with his lips, but he'd said it over and over with his touch, with the look in his eyes. He was saying it now, and it was tempting, oh so tempting, to take just a few steps forward and find herself back in his embrace.

No, PJ. They're only lies. That's what he does.

But what if it was true? What if his marriage really was over?

Then it's all your fault. She turned around, breaking the hold of his gaze. It was all she could think to do. Her heart and mind waged a vicious tug-of-war.

Her breaths quickened, panic rising from someplace deep inside, and she realized she'd forgotten to take her meds this afternoon. Of all times.

She closed her eyes and focused on her breathing. She tried to fight it back but it crept closer, choking her with its cold fingers.

"Can we open a window or something?" Zac said.

"No joke. It's like eighty degrees in here." Josh fanned himself with the sports section.

Having the living room above the restaurant's kitchen? Not such a great idea.

Cole walked to the dinette area and slid the sash up, letting the cold November air glide over his skin. The boys had decided to stay in for a *Drake and Josh* marathon. Shaundra was out with a school friend.

A voice carried up from the back porch, unfamiliar, male.

"Why didn't you answer my texts?"

"You have to ask?" It was PJ's voice.

He should move away from the window, but something held him. Something in her voice. It wasn't like her to leave the kitchen during dinner rush.

"I told you my marriage is over now. For real. Come for a drive with me. We need to talk."

"Go away, Keaton. Please." She sounded breathless. Upset.

Cole straightened. Zac and Josh laughed, making him miss what was said next.

"I can't do this right now." Panic laced her voice.

"I'm not going anywhere until we talk, PJ."

Cole didn't like the sharp tone of the man's voice. He headed for the door. PJ probably wouldn't thank him for interfering. It was none of his business, but he didn't like the way she sounded.

And the guy, an old boyfriend—and married at that—couldn't seem to take the hint.

He raced down the back stairs that he and the kids used and came to a halt at the side yard a few feet from the porch. The man and PJ were facing away from him.

"Go away, Keaton." PJ's shoulders rose and fell quickly. Her arms were wrapped around her middle. She looked small in her chef's uniform.

"No. We're talking now." The guy advanced on her.

"Hey!" Cole said. "Back off."

The guy whirled around, frowning, as Cole leaped up on the porch.

"Who are you?"

"You heard what she said. It's time to go."

The stranger turned back to PJ. "Who is this guy?"

PJ shook her head, obviously struggling to control her panic, but the moron didn't seem to notice.

"Is he the reason you won't return my texts or answer my calls? Seriously?"

"Please leave, Keaton," PJ gasped between breaths.

"All right, pal." Cole grabbed his collar and jerked him toward the porch steps.

The guy shook him off, straightening his shirt.

Cole placed himself in front of PJ, feet spread, fists ready.

"We're not done, PJ," the guy said, giving PJ, then Cole, a long look. A few seconds later he went down the porch steps and around the corner of the house.

Cole followed, making sure he left, then returned to the porch where PJ was pacing, blowing out breaths.

"Where are your meds?"

"In my purse. My room."

He returned a minute later, and PJ downed the pill with a glass of water. She had color in her cheeks again, and her breathing had evened out.

"Better?"

She nodded. "Is he gone?"

"Yeah."

Cole wanted to ask who he was. It didn't seem possible she had been seeing a married man. Not PJ. His gut tightened at the thought, and it had little to do with the marriage. He didn't like imagining PJ with any man at all.

"I have to get back to the kitchen." She walked away, stopping at the door. She turned and met his eyes for the first time since he'd shown up.

He saw relief and gratitude in her eyes. The look made him feel heady, as if he could slay all her dragons with the wave of his hand. He didn't even want to dwell on the reasons why that made him feel so good.

"Thank you," she said.

"Will he come back?"

Half a dozen emotions flickered over her face. "I don't know."

If he did, she wasn't going to be alone with him, not if Cole had anything to say about it.

"I hope not. He doesn't live around here. He'll have to go home eventually."

"Might be best to stick close to home for a couple days. Tell your hostess he's not welcome. You need help, come get me."

"Okay," she whispered. And then she was gone.

Cole said good night to the boys and retired to his room, adrenaline still buzzing through his veins. He was glad he'd been home, had overheard enough to know PJ needed help. He didn't know if the guy would've hurt her, but he wasn't about to find out.

He settled on his bed and flipped on the TV. Maybe PJ would've been just fine, but it had felt good to come to her rescue. To protect her. His thoughts flashed back to the time he'd fallen short, and he wondered if he'd ever be able to make up for his failure.

Nothing had gone right for the past couple weeks, and it had all been his mom's fault. He'd gotten one bad grade on his midterm report, and she made him go to bed at nine all week. He'd missed the Cubs game, and all his friends had been talking about the great comeback.

He wondered what she'd do to Dad if she knew about the woman with black hair and red nails. Dad should be the one getting Mom's wrath, not him. It was so unfair. It was only social studies, and who cared about a stinking midterm grade?

He sat back, adjusting his seat belt. On the other side of the car, Noelle was playing with her My Little Pony. Her chattering was getting on his nerves.

His parents were making him go with them to visit Mom's friend, some old lady who lived in a tiny boring house with no yard and no kids. Her old box television didn't even have cable or satellite. Even worse, it was a long drive, and his mom listened to country music.

Cars whirred past. There were too many curves and hills, and it made his stomach roll.

Noelle pulled another pony from her bag, and her chatter grew louder.

Cole leaned back, his hand over his stomach. "Keep it down, Noelle."

She didn't seem to hear him.

His dad glanced at him in the rearview mirror.

He was getting a headache too. Probably from too much sleep. Or all this chatter. "Horses can't even talk, you know that, right?"

"Stop it, Cole," Mom said.

"Well, she won't shut up."

Mom turned and frowned. "*Cole.*"

He wasn't allowed to say that, but lately it seemed like he wasn't allowed to do anything at all. "Are we almost there?"

"You know very well we're not," Mom said. "And you need to be on your best behavior this evening. Mavis isn't well."

They rounded a bend and his stomach churned.

Noelle's voice grew increasingly nasal with her pony-talk.

"Gosh, Noelle, knock it off."

Dad gave him a look in the mirror.

"Why couldn't I just stay home?"

"We've already been through this," Mom said. "It's a family outing, and it does Mavis good to be around children."

More likely she didn't want him staying home where he could sneak and use the computer. That's probably why Dad was coming this time too, so he couldn't sneak off and see the black-haired lady. He'd heard Dad talking quietly on the phone one night this week when he'd gotten up to use the bathroom and his mom was asleep. Cole could tell it was someone Dad worked with by the things he'd said.

"You can go outside and see if the neighbor's cats are around," Mom offered. "I think she had her litter of kitties."

"I'm not four, Mom, and I don't care about a bunch of cats. Can I have my Game Boy?" His mom had hidden it in the glove compartment when she thought he wasn't looking.

"You know you're grounded from electronics."

"That's not fair! I didn't want to come on this trip anyway."

Mom turned in her seat. "Well, you're the child and you'll do as I say. I don't like your attitude one bit, Cole. Keep it up, and you'll find yourself grounded from baseball too."

"Why not? It's not like I have a life right now anyway!"

His mom pursed her lips. "I'll be calling Coach Nick in the morning and telling him you can't play tomorrow afternoon."

"I'm supposed to pitch! *Dad!*"

His father didn't even meet his eyes in the mirror.

"I'm sorry, Cole," Mom said, "but I'm not tolerating your behavior."

"*My* behavior! What about Dad's?" The words were out before his brain even processed them, but he wasn't sorry. Mom was being so mean! And Dad wasn't even sticking up for him even though he was supposed to start tomorrow for the first time ever.

Dad met his eyes in the mirror. Cole looked away.

Mom looked between them. "What do you mean, Dad's behavior?"

"I mean that woman he had in his room two weeks ago."

His mom's eyes shifted to her husband. "Matt?" Her voice cracked on the name.

His dad's fist tightened on the steering wheel.

At his dad's silence, Mom's eyes swung back to Cole. The first bit of guilt pricked at the panic he saw there.

"What are you talking about?" Her voice was low and even, but there was something scary bubbling underneath.

Cole slammed his lips shut. He'd done it now. Him and his big mouth. He felt the heat of his dad's look in the rearview mirror—didn't dare look. Even Noelle was frowning up at him, a pink pony clutched in her chubby fist.

"Matt, what woman? What's he talking about?"

He could feel Mom's eyes on him, but he didn't want to look at her again. His heart beat like he was pitching the last inning of a tied championship game. Heat flooded his neck and his face.

Dad turned to Mom. "I don't know what he's talking about. He's just mad, honey."

"It's Elaine, isn't it?" His mom's voice rose and wobbled.

"Come on, Dee, this is ridiculous." He reached toward her.

Mom flinched away. "What's going on, Matt?"

"Honey, come on, he's just mad. Isn't that right, Cole?"

"Leave him out of this and answer me! Is it—"

The car swerved suddenly. A shriek sounded, and it was the last thing Cole heard until he opened his eyes in the hospital.

His head throbbed. His throat was so dry, and he could barely pry his eyelids open. His arm was in a sling, and tubes were attached to his hand. There were beeping noises and the sound of shoes squeaking on the floor outside the door.

He fell back asleep, but when he woke up sometime later a nurse was leaning over him. She was nice even if she was using baby talk. But he was too scared to be annoyed.

He was too sleepy to say much, but when he woke again later and asked for his mom, the nurse got all weird. That only scared him worse, and later he found out why. His mom had died at the scene of the accident and so had his dad. They had revived

Noelle in the ambulance and she'd hung on for almost a day, but by the time Cole was alert, she was gone too.

He was supposed to protect her. His dad said so all the time. And he'd failed her. Failed them all.

Hours passed numbly. A lady came in and visited. When they let him leave the hospital three days later, she took him to a yellow house in a neighborhood he'd never seen. There was a mom and a dad and two little kids—a family. But they weren't his family. His family was gone. He would never see them again.

Cole couldn't remember anything about the accident until days later. Not the accident or the argument that had come before. But when it all came bleeding back, when his thoughtless words replayed in his head, he wanted to die too. His family was dead, and it was all his fault. He kept the shameful secret to himself. That and the truth that seeped in with it: Cole didn't deserve his family. He didn't deserve anyone at all.

Chapter Twenty-Two

BALANCING ON THE LADDER, PJ STRUNG A GARLAND ACROSS the dining room doorway. She'd borrowed a few things from Mom and Layla to get the place looking festive. Some fragrant pinecones and red tapers, and one could never go wrong with twinkle lights.

The weekend had passed without another word from Keaton. This morning she'd breathed a sigh of relief upon awakening, knowing he had to be far away at work.

She put the finishing touches on the garland and stepped down from the ladder, surveying her handiwork. Not bad.

"Miss McKinley?" Shaundra appeared at the bottom of the steps in snug jeans and a teal T-shirt that complemented her skin tone. "Can I ask you something?"

"Only if you call me PJ."

The girl smiled. "Okay. Well, see, we're studying the Middle East in school, and I got this project that's due tomorrow. I have to bake something called baklava?"

"I'm familiar."

"I have to go get the ingredients, but there's something called phyllo in it?" She scrunched up her nose.

"It's a really thin dough that you layer with the nut mixture.

You'll find it in a box in the frozen section near the pie shells and desserts."

"Oh, thanks. That doesn't sound too hard to find." She shifted. "I was also wondering . . ."

"What is it?"

Shaundra tugged on her braids. "Um—do you maybe have a cake pan I can borrow? I promise I'll bring it back."

"Of course. You want some help making it?"

"Oh, I couldn't. I'm sure you got stuff to do, and it's your day off."

"Actually, I love making baklava. And I have a super recipe, if you need one."

Her brown eyes lit up. "Really? You'd help me? 'Cause I've never really cooked anything except, you know, in the class we took with you, and that was real food."

"I'd be happy to."

"Thanks, Miss . . . I mean PJ. And I'd love to use your recipe too. I found mine online so I don't know if it's any good, and I could really use an A on this project."

"I'll get the recipe then. Let's meet in the kitchen around seven."

When the timer went off, PJ checked the oven window. The top of the baklava was golden brown.

Shaundra stirred the honey mixture over the burner. She was a natural in the kitchen, focused and following directions to a T.

"It looks great," PJ said. "How's the honey mixture coming?"

"It's got one minute left."

PJ handed her the oven mitt, and Shaundra pulled out the baklava. The fragrance of cinnamon and cooked pastry filled the kitchen. It looked golden and crispy and smelled like heaven. PJ's mouth watered.

"Mmmm, I want some now," Shaundra said.

"We should've made an extra one just for us."

"Okay, now what?"

"Read the recipe." PJ handed it over.

"It says to spoon the honey mixture over top, then let it sit."

PJ turned off the burner and oven. "Go for it."

The honey mixture oozed onto the pastry and nuts as Shaundra spooned it on. "It smells so good."

"It is good, trust me. It earned me an A plus in my pastry class, and my professor was no easy grader." She'd made the dough from scratch.

"That's good, because my last test took my history grade down to a C. My friends say grades don't matter after you apply to colleges, but I'm keeping them up just in case."

"Where'd you apply?"

"Ball State, Vincennes University, and Ivy Tech. I'm really hoping for Ball State, but I'll need some major scholarships, and it's a stretch with my GPA anyway."

"Well, maybe it'll happen. What are you going to study?"

"Not sure yet. I'll probably start with general courses until I know what I want to do." She set the spoon back in the pan and smiled at the results. "That turned out really good."

"It did. Nice work."

"It was fun too. A lot more fun than a test."

PJ laughed. "In culinary school, baking *is* the test."

As they cleaned up and washed dishes, Shaundra started

talking about Cole, raving about his kindness and generosity. "He's pretty good-looking, don't you think?"

"If you like that type."

Shaundra arched a brow. "The really fine type?"

PJ laughed. The girl was not the queen of subtlety. "I have two sisters, you know. I recognize matchmaking when I see it."

Shaundra shrugged. "You could do worse, all I'm saying."

When they were finished, PJ set the baklava off to the side. "You can swing by and pick it up on your way out the door tomorrow."

"I hope my class likes it. Shouldn't we put it in the fridge or cover it?"

"Baklava is best at room temperature, and covering it will make it soggy. Trust me, your class is going to flip over it." PJ reached into a drawer and pulled out some cupcake papers. "You can serve it in these."

The girl threw her arms around PJ. "Thanks, PJ!"

PJ was caught off guard for half a beat, but then she returned the embrace. "You did a great job, Shaundra."

"Thanks for all your help."

"You're welcome," PJ said to Shaundra's back as she dashed away.

Chapter Twenty-Three

PJ WAS WAITING FOR KEATON'S CALL. SHE KNEW SHE'D HAVE to answer or risk a repeat appearance. She'd expected it would come when she was in the middle of dinner rush—not that there was much of a rush these days—or when she was in the middle of cooking class.

But no, it was better than that. It came in the middle of a family lunch the next Sunday after church. She was reaching for the pot roast when "The Time of My Life" sounded from her pocket.

"Shame, shame." Jade fed Ava a bite of sweet potatoes. "No cell phones at the table."

PJ shut off the phone, meeting her mom's knowing eyes.

"So who gave you the time of your life?" Ryan asked.

PJ made a face at her brother and served herself a slice of pot roast.

"I'll bet it was Tom Brady II," Madison said.

Jade handed Ava's spoon to Daniel. "Nobody's taking that bet."

"I thought he had a girlfriend."

"You need me to have a talk with him, just let me know," Ryan said.

"I heard he had a talk with someone else." Madison's eyes sparkled.

PJ frowned at her sister.

"Bernadette Perkins said some man stopped by the restaurant to talk to you, and Cole chased him off."

"Is that true?" Dad asked.

"I don't know where she heard something like that." PJ stuffed her mouth with mashed potatoes.

"From Dottie Meyers, who heard it from Peggy Golan, who heard it directly from Callie Owens."

"Sounds like a reliable source to me," Ryan said.

PJ was going to be having a talk with Callie. What happened in the kitchen stayed in the kitchen, darn it.

"Just a bunch of gossip," Mom said.

"Mama Jo's right," Daniel said. "Remember the rumor that went around about Jade and me?"

"Well, I hope this one's true," Jade said. "'Cause we could use a little romance around here."

"Hey . . . ," Daniel said. "I'm romantic."

"Not *we*, we. PJ we." She grabbed Daniel's face, running her thumb over his jaw. "Sweetie, you are the definition of romance."

It was true. Long before Daniel had admitted his feelings for Jade, he'd sent her the most romantic secret admirer notes and poems.

"That's what I thought." Daniel pecked Jade on the lips, eyeing her like they weren't in the middle of feeding their two tots. Never mind surrounded by the rest of the McKinley clan.

"Come on . . . " Ryan grumbled. "No PDA at the table."

"I have to maintain my standing," Daniel said.

Mia banged the table with her chubby fists. "Da da da!"

"That's right, peanut. You tell 'em."

PJ returned Keaton's call the minute she was in her car, her breath fogging in the cold air. She turned up the heat as her headlights swept across the snow-dusted street.

The phone rang in her ear, and her heart skidded across her chest. Only part of her wanted him to answer—the part that needed to find closure. The part that still missed him. The other part prayed it would ring over to voicemail so she wouldn't be faced with temptation.

A few rings later voicemail clicked on, and his familiar voice sounded low and confident in her ear. She wouldn't leave a message. Even so, she listened to the end and then hung up, angry with herself for wanting to hear his voice. What was wrong with her?

She thought of last Saturday when Keaton had come. But strangely her mind fast-forwarded to the part where Cole had shown up. To the way he'd jumped onto the porch, telling Keaton to back off. To the way he'd placed himself between them as if Keaton was a physical threat.

He'd never given her reason to fear him, but it had felt good to be protected. Cole made her feel safe. Ironic, given that he'd scared her to death the day he'd come barging into her life.

When PJ got home, she went to her bedroom and finished a marketing book she'd borrowed from the library. Cooped up in her room, she longed for a living room of her own to spread out in. Soon, she thought, then felt a pang as she realized that to have one she'd have to displace Cole and the kids.

She used leftovers to make a smoked salmon and Gruyère grilled cheese sandwich for supper, then she looked over some advertising offers she'd received. She could hear the kids overhead. It sounded like they were playing Ping-Pong on the table Cole had bought. Their footsteps and voices were loud, but she couldn't bring herself to be upset when they sounded so happy.

She'd just changed into her pajamas and brushed her teeth when the familiar strains of the song played from her phone. She took a deep breath and answered, bracing herself for his voice.

"Stop calling my husband."

PJ froze. "What?"

"You heard me." The woman's voice shook. "We have a child—doesn't that mean anything to you?"

"I—"

"We're trying to work things out, and the last thing we need is you butting back into our marriage! Do you have any idea of the damage you've caused? The pain?"

"I'm so—"

"I don't want to hear it! You're nothing but a two-bit tramp. You think you're something special to him? You were nothing but a distraction, and you'd better stay away from him, you hear me? I know where you live. I will come down there and ruin you, don't think for a minute that I won't. I'll make you sorry you ever set eyes on him!"

The phone clicked in her ear. PJ dropped the phone on her bed. She felt the air rush out of her. It stuttered in her lungs before she sucked in another ragged breath.

He was a few days late on his portion of the bills, but finally one of his sponsors had come through. Cole ripped out the check and headed down the attic stairs. He passed the community living room where a rousing game of Ping-Pong was being waged between Josh and Zac.

He couldn't really afford the table, but when he'd seen it at the thrift shop, a little beaten up and priced to sell, he couldn't seem to help himself. Hearing their laughter now, he knew it had been worth every penny.

He took the second set of stairs and rounded the bend, heading back through the darkened kitchen and to PJ's door. It was cracked open, a sliver of light edging the side.

It fell open as he rapped on the door. "PJ?"

From the edge of the bed, she looked toward the door, then away from him. She swiped her hand across her face. "Yeah?"

He frowned, pushing the door open the rest of the way. "I brought the check for my half of the bills."

She cleared her throat. "Just set it on the bureau."

Either she had the world's worst cold or she was crying. Since she wouldn't look his way, he put his money on the latter.

"You okay?"

"Fine."

She didn't sound fine. His feet stuttered on the threshold. Should he go in? Stay away? He never knew what to do about tears.

Was she stressed out about the house? The restaurant? He couldn't help but notice that business had fallen off lately. And he hadn't helped matters by delaying his payment.

"Sorry I'm late with the payment."

She waved the apology away and shook her head. A sniffle sounded. Then another.

Overhead Josh must've scored game point, because his whoop practically shook the rafters. And the footsteps. It sounded like a herd of buffalo from here.

"Is it the kids? I'll go tell them to keep it down."

She shook her head. "They're fine." Her voice wobbled on the last word.

He'd thought they were complying with the rules. And PJ had made a big impression on Shaundra. It was always "PJ this" and "PJ that."

He took a hesitant step toward her. "If everyone's fine . . . what's with the tears?"

Whatever he'd said seemed to break something loose. She covered her face and a sob escaped. Even he knew he couldn't leave now. And strangely, he didn't want to.

"Hey . . ." He was at her side in seconds. He eased down onto the bed, and her pajama-clad thigh brushed against his. "What is it? Is it the restaurant? I know it's slow right now, but spring'll be here before we know it. The cooking classes are going well, right?"

She shook her head, her hands falling to her lap. "It's not the restaurant."

"What is it then?"

She dropped her head. Her lips quivered, and his fingers ached to still them. Tears cascaded down her flushed cheeks, one after another, dripping from her chin.

"Keaton," she said, sniffling.

He hadn't expected that. That's why it felt like a kick in the gut.

"We started dating last winter. He kind of just—swept me off my feet, you know?"

If he felt another kick in the gut, it was only because he felt her pain.

"I thought he was it. For the first time I was falling in

love . . ." She swiped a hand across her face. "But then things started happening—bad things."

If Keaton had laid a hand on her, Cole was going to throttle the man himself.

He hooked PJ's chin and turned her toward him. "What kind of things?"

"Little stuff. Like I couldn't reach him when he was away, and he wouldn't friend me on Facebook, and he called at odd times."

Cole tilted his head back as understanding dawned.

"I followed him one night, back to his house." Her face scrunched up. "There was a wife . . . a little boy . . . I'd fallen in love with a married man."

"Oh, honey . . ."

She closed her eyes. "I can't believe I'm telling you this. It's just that I can't talk to my family. They'd be so ashamed. And they should be. I didn't think I'd ever do something like that. I thought I was a better person than that."

"Whoa—wait. What exactly did you do?"

"I dated a married man!"

"A man you didn't know was married."

She nailed him with her wet brown eyes. "Somehow his wife found out, and I broke up a family! They're getting a divorce—at least that's what Keaton said. His wife said something else— plenty else. She called me just now."

"You didn't know, PJ. He lied to you. Did you keep seeing him after you found out he was married?"

"Of course not."

"Then you didn't do anything wrong. *He* was wrong. If his marriage is breaking up, that's on him."

She stared at him, those big brown eyes filling again. Her lip quivered and she covered her face, her body racked with sobs.

What was a guy to do? Cole put his arm around her shoulder, and that was all it took. She turned into him and burrowed in. He wrapped her up in his arms, letting go of a deep breath.

He felt her pain with every spasm of her body. And as she cried the old memory of the woman with black hair and red nails flashed into his mind. The woman who'd come between his parents and played a role in their deaths. He pushed the thought away. That woman had to have known Dad was married, didn't she? She was in his parents' bed, for crying out loud.

PJ sniffled, drawing him back to her.

He stroked her shoulder with his thumb. "Come on, now, it's going to be okay."

"It's not!" Her voice was muffled by her hands, by his chest. He could feel her tears soaking through his T-shirt. "I'm a horrible person."

He set her back until he could see her eyes, his hands framing her face. "Hey. You are not a horrible person."

"Yes, I am."

"You didn't know."

Her eyes began filling again. She blinked, and a tear chased a worn path. "But I know now . . . and I still want him sometimes." She said the words as if they were dug up from some deep, secret part of her heart.

He wished he could wipe away the shame he saw in her eyes. Her vulnerability pushed at all his walls. He drew her back to his chest.

She came willingly, sliding her arms around his waist, pressing her cheek against his chest.

Could she hear the way his heart thumped at the contact? The sweet flower smell of her rose to his nostrils, and he lowered his head, drawing her in.

Her shoulders shook as she sniffled, and guilt pricked him hard. What was he doing taking pleasure while she was hurting? *You're a real jerk, Evans.*

"I feel so guilty. I shouldn't be thinking these things. Shouldn't be missing him. What's wrong with me?"

"It's not a sin to be tempted. You're doing the right thing. That's what matters."

"I was doing so much better. I thought I was over him, but then he started texting and calling, saying he wanted me back. I ignored him but—"

"Change your number."

"But maybe he just needs closure or something. Maybe if I talk to him one last time, he'd understand it's—"

"You don't owe him anything, PJ. He knew what he was doing. He dragged you into this, manipulated you. You have to do what's best for you now."

She pulled away, wiping the last of the tears. She was finally settling down, her flushed cheeks dry now. "What if he just comes back?"

"Then he'll have to get through me."

Something washed over her face. Relief? Her eyes brightened. Her lips turned up at the corners. "Thanks."

She needed him. He thought that might be the best feeling ever. He'd even managed to calm her somehow. Him. A guy who was helpless in the face of tears.

"I'll change my number tomorrow. I don't know what I'll tell my family."

"Tell them you were getting unwanted calls."

She nodded. "Okay. Good idea."

Upstairs another wild game of Ping-Pong was under way. Feet shuffled overhead. Someone whooped.

He was suddenly conscious of PJ's thigh pressed against his, warm and firm. Of how close she was, just a breath away. He needed out of here before he started wanting.

Started *wanting*? *Really, Evans?*

The bed frame squeaked as he stood. "It's late. I'll go tell them it's time to shut it down for the night."

"Thanks, Cole," PJ said as he walked away.

"Anytime."

"Sorry about your shirt." She looked sheepish when he turned. She was the cutest thing in her pink pajamas, her bare feet dangling above the floor.

"It'll wash," he said. "Good night."

"Night."

He forced himself to turn, to shut the door and walk away. He should be used to that. He'd been trained for it all his life.

Chapter Twenty-Four

DECEMBER WAS PASSING IN A FLURRY OF HOLIDAY PREPARATIONS, cooking, and family. PJ was busy with the influx of early Christmas parties and tourists who came for the Silent Night Tour of Homes. As hectic as things were, she wondered what she'd do next year if she had a B & B on top of it all. The thought made her mind spin like beaters set to whip.

Keaton hadn't contacted her since his wife had called, though Cole stuck close to the house, making himself more visible during restaurant hours. After a few weeks, PJ began to relax. It seemed Keaton had given up. She could only hope he was working things out with his wife.

She hired Shaundra to help with kitchen prep for the Christmas season. The girl was quick and efficient once she got the hang of things. PJ found herself thinking she'd hire her full time come summer. Then she remembered that one of them wouldn't be there after June 1.

By Christmas Eve morning the kids had been off school for almost a week and were getting bored. It was evidenced by the blaring TV and short fuses. To make matters worse, a snowstorm two days before had left them cooped up together.

PJ got dressed, then flopped on her bed and began paging through the January issue of *Master Chef* for the third time. The restaurant had closed because of the storm and would be closed for the next two days because of the holiday. She was going to go stir-crazy.

She had to buy a recliner to squeeze in here. She could hardly wait until she had a living room of her own.

But then Cole would be gone.

He'd been coming around more lately because of Keaton. And if she were honest, she'd been seeking him out on occasion. It had nothing to do with his good looks or the way it had felt to be wrapped up in his arms. She just needed a good friend right now. Maybe he wasn't the wisest choice for that role, but he made her feel good. As though she could do this—even on weeks when she scraped the bottom of the barrel financially.

Overhead, the kids were waking and moving around. Awhile later, a Ping-Pong game started, and within minutes loud, angry voices carried through the ceiling. So much for a pleasant day off.

She had to get out of here. Breathe in some Christmas spirit, spread her wings. She tossed her magazine down and slipped on her boots. She was shrugging into her coat by the front door as Cole came down the stairs, wearing a scowl. The argument between Zac and Shaundra carried from the living room upstairs.

"Wanna get away?" she teased.

"Please. Save me. Where you going?"

"Out. Want to come?"

"Yes."

PJ tucked her chin into her scarf as she and Cole brushed snow from the windshield. The car gave a reluctant start, and PJ pulled from the curb.

Cole leaned against the headrest. "When does school start again?"

"You sound like a harried mother."

"I feel like a harried mother. It's not even Christmas yet. Where we going?"

PJ thought a moment. "Ice skating," she decided.

He rolled his head toward her. "Take me back."

She laughed. "Don't you like to skate?"

"I've never been. Hence my request."

"You're going to love it. Guys are naturals with their strong ankles. You'll be whizzing past me in minutes."

Twenty minutes later, PJ slipped her feet into the skates and started on the laces. The square was quiet this afternoon, only a few teenagers circling the frozen pond. The layer of snow had been brushed away, leaving a smooth, glassy surface.

Once PJ had laced up, she stood, replacing her gloves, and surveyed the landscape. Pine trees, their branches half covered in snow, towered nearby, and skeletal oak branches clicked together overhead. Multicolored lights twinkled dimly in the daylight, and the strains of "Santa Baby" floated from nearby speakers.

She took a deep breath of the crisp air. "It feels so good to be out. Doesn't this air feel great?"

"It's freezing."

"It's practically forty degrees."

Cole tied his skate. "If by 'practically' you mean minus ten degrees."

She grinned at him and gave him a hand up. "Come on, Half-empty, it's time to introduce you to ice skating."

They shuffled to the edge of the rink and took tentative steps onto the ice. Once both feet were planted, Cole pushed off, arms out and waving for balance. He pushed off again, mimicking PJ's motions. She'd spent a lot of winter nights circling this rink, usually with her siblings.

Cole was doing pretty well. He was still upright and moving forward, albeit a little shakily.

PJ turned gracefully and skated backward.

He scowled playfully at her.

"What? You're doing great. See, it's not so—"

His feet got tangled and he pitched forward, arms out.

PJ reached for him, and their skates shuffled. He was heavy on her arms. Her back worked hard to support his weight. Finally their feet shuffled to a stop, and a giggle worked its way into her throat.

His lips twitched.

One of her hands grasped his forearm, and the other was wrapped around his waist. His muscular thigh pressed against hers. Something fluttered in her belly.

"You have a great smile," he said.

She looked up and got caught in his green eyes, her smile falling away.

His breath fogged between them as his eyes fastened on hers. "Thanks."

Step away from the hottie, PJ.

She backed up, shaking off the moment.

"You should've let me fall," he said. "I could've hurt you."

"Not on my watch, big guy." She turned, pushing off. "Ready to race?" she called over her shoulder.

"Funny."

Cole watched PJ sail away as if she weren't moving on two narrow metal blades. How did people even do this? She did a fancy
twirl, her scarf flying around in a circle. It was good to see her
happy. She'd been so busy the past month, and he knew she'd
been worried her ex-boyfriend would interrupt her life again.
Cole had made it a point to stay close by during restaurant hours.
Just the thought of what he'd done to PJ made him want to lay
the guy out flat.

She made a U-turn and came up beside him just in time for
him to wobble like an elephant on stilts. He threw out his arms,
and PJ grabbed on.

"I thought you said I'd be a natural," he said once he had his
balance again.

PJ let loose of him. "You're doing great. The Olympics will
be back around before you know it. I think you have a shot at
speed skating."

He gave her a sour look, but really he was checking her out
and remembering what it felt like to have her arms around him
as he'd slipped. Dignity notwithstanding, it was enough to make
a man consider faking a fall.

"I'm going to take another turn around the rink," she said.
And then she was off, the ends of her scarf flying behind her,
before he could make good on his nefarious plan to get her back
in his arms.

An hour later they took a booth at Cappy's Pizzeria, having worked
up an appetite and not ready to return to the house. Colorful

Christmas bulbs dangled from the ceiling on shiny ribbons, and a silver Christmas tree huddled in the corner. The overhead pendants shed a soft light over Cole's handsome features. He had bits of snow in his hair, and her fingers twitched to brush them away.

"This is more like it," Cole said. "Stationary booths, warm environment, soft surfaces."

"Stop it. You did good."

"Then explain why my rear end's soaking wet."

PJ handed him a menu, lifting a brow. "Sounds like a personal problem to me."

A few minutes later the server took their order. Finally warm, PJ pulled off her coat and scarf, pushing them to the corner of the red vinyl booth. A nearby TV played a preview of tonight's bowl game, and a loud crack sounded from the poolroom as someone broke the balls.

"Sorry the kids have been kind of rowdy lately. They're stir-crazy, I guess. Plus the holidays can be hard when you don't have family."

She'd invited them to her family's house tomorrow, but Cole was spending the day at the house with the kids. It would give them a chance to bond. At least that's what he'd said. She wondered now if it was something more.

"What did you do before this year?" she asked.

"It varied. Sometimes I'd go to my foster parents' house, or someone from church would have me over. The holidays aren't that big a deal to me anymore."

PJ watched him sip his Coke and wondered if that were really true or just what he told himself.

"I've been out of foster care for nine years. I'm just used to it, I guess."

PJ did the math. "I thought you were twenty-six."

"Twenty-seven. Had a birthday."

"When?"

"Just before Thanksgiving, November 23."

About the time Josh had hit her car. She wondered if he'd even told the kids. She hadn't heard anything about a cake or a party.

"Why didn't you say something?"

He shrugged. "I guess birthdays aren't that big a deal either."

They were in her family. Even now that the kids were grown, the day still called for a party, cake, presents. She thought of Cole alone in his attic room while his birthday ticked away, and she felt the sting of guilt.

The server arrived, setting down an order of breadsticks. The aroma of garlic and yeast filled the air between them.

"I'm so hungry." Cole started on a breadstick.

PJ poured some cheese on her plate, her thoughts heavy. She'd known Cole over six months and still knew so little about him. She thought of what her mom said about his past. One thing about baggage, it was lighter when someone shared the load.

"I hope you don't mind my asking . . . You told me about your mom's accident, but what about the rest of your family?"

He swallowed and took a drink of Coke. "They all died in the same accident."

"All of them . . . ?"

"Mom, Dad, and my little sister, Noelle."

PJ's heart clamped tight. His whole family, gone in a moment. How would it feel to be the lone survivor?

"I'm so sorry. How old were you?"

"Twelve."

Her heart broke for the little boy who must've woken alone to the news that his family was gone.

"It was a long time ago."

"You didn't have grandparents? Aunts or uncles?"

He took another breadstick. "Mom's family disowned her when she married my dad, and he was an only child. His parents were older when they had him, and they died when I was little."

"So they just . . . carted you off to some foster home?"

The corner of his lip turned up. "They were good people. Looking back, I see they had their hands full with two young kids and a sulky preteen, but they always had time for me."

Sulky preteen? He'd lost everything and been shoved into another family.

"So they basically raised you?"

"I was only there for about a year. His work transferred him out of state."

"And just like that you had to go somewhere else?"

"Something like that. But I don't have any regrets. Greg and Becky were great, and that's where I met Lizzy."

Lizzy. The girl he'd been on the phone with. The one he'd told he loved.

She took a sip of her water. "Lizzy?"

"Another foster kid at the same house."

"She's your . . . girlfriend?"

"What? No, she's nine years younger than me. She's like a little sister."

"Oh." Why did the knot in her stomach suddenly release?

"She's the one I'm holding a spot for at the house. She turns eighteen in April." He cleared his throat. "So tell me about your childhood. What was it like growing up here? There are four McKinley kids?"

She set her breadstick down and folded her hands on the table. "Well, plus Michael, the twin who died. And Ryan's friend Daniel Dawson was practically a sibling, he was around so much. He was our honorary brother—so I get what you mean about Lizzy."

"Didn't he marry your sister?"

"Right, Jade, last December."

Cole arched a brow. "I guess he wasn't everyone's honorary brother."

"Guess not. They're really good together though."

"Your family is close."

"Yeah. It gets a little hectic, but in a good way, you know?"

"And you're the baby?"

"Ugh. Yes."

"Why ugh? I always thought my little sister had it easy. I doted on her, and my parents babied her. They were so much easier on her than they were on me."

"You sound like Ryan. But the baby has everyone stepping in to do everything for her. It has a way of making you feel incapable. And in case you miss the subtlety of the message, they're more than willing to verbalize it, always second-guessing your decisions or making backup plans for when you fail. I mean, I love them dearly, but they seriously don't think I can breathe without them."

He leaned forward, planting his hands inches from hers. "And sometimes you wonder if they're right."

PJ's lips parted. Then she pressed her lips together and lengthened her spine.

"It's not true," he said. "But sometimes you believe it anyway."

His gaze was direct, intense, like he could see down inside where no one else bothered to look. She wasn't sure she wanted him down there digging through all her stuff. But then, he already knew the worst of it.

"How'd you know?" she asked.

He lifted his pinkie and skimmed the side of her hand. "You're one of the most capable people I know."

"They didn't even think I'd make it through culinary school."

"But you did."

"Every weekend I'd come home, and there'd be this subtexting in their questions. Like they thought I'd lose interest and move on to something else or fail my classes and have to drop out. I think they're still stunned I actually graduated."

"Then they must really be surprised you're making a go of your restaurant."

She snorted. He hadn't seen her checkbook balance. Maybe December had been okay, but November had been the pits, and she wasn't expecting the next couple months to be any better.

"Don't discount yourself like that. You opened your own restaurant right out of culinary school. You know what kind of guts that takes?"

"Guts or stupidity? Because I'm thinking my family sees it as the latter."

"Then why were they always over there helping you with the renovation?"

"Oh, they're really helpful, don't get me wrong. And I feel like a complete jerk for complaining about my family when . . ."

"Don't. My problems don't negate yours. So they're not supportive of your restaurant?"

"It's not that exactly. It's just from the beginning it was, 'Don't get your hopes up, PJ.' 'This is an awful lot you're taking on, PJ.' 'There's an opening at Burger Barn, in case this doesn't work out, PJ.'"

His eyes darkened and his jaw flexed. "Burger Barn?"

"Okay, maybe it was the Candlelight Café, but still. They've been giving me backup options for months, like they see the failure coming." She looked down at the half-eaten breadstick on her plate, thinking of her bank balance and the weeks of winter left. "Maybe they're right."

"Hey. No matter what happens, you've worked your butt off to make that restaurant succeed. Win or lose, you should be proud of that."

Maybe so. But winning would prove she could do it. And she was coming to realize, it wasn't just her family she needed to prove it to.

Chapter Twenty-Five

CHRISTMAS AND NEW YEAR'S SLOWLY PASSED, AND THE kids returned to school. With the festivities over, the restaurant hit a lull.

PJ was returning from the butcher's with boxes of fresh steaks when she spotted Ryan sitting in front of the Avery house. Exhaust curled from the tailpipe of his truck, and the wipers came on intermittently, chasing away the flurries.

The house hunkered in the snow like a lazy groundhog, and a For Sale sign protruded crookedly from the frozen ground.

PJ pulled to the curb behind him, then got out and knocked on his passenger window with cold knuckles.

He startled, then unlocked the doors.

She jumped inside, shivering. "Okay, it's officially winter."

"You're only now noticing?"

"It's hard to remain in denial when it's three degrees and there's a foot of snow on the ground."

"Good point."

She breathed into her scarf, watching her brother from the corner of her eyes. He turned up the heat and settled back into his seat, one hand draped over the steering wheel.

He was a typical guy, not much of a talker, but she couldn't let this pass. "So . . . you're sitting in front of the Avery house."

"Yep."

Seconds ticked by. PJ surveyed the house. The walk had been cleared, but mounds of fresh snow covered the porch steps. The blinds had been pulled, giving the house a boarded-up feel. But she knew Ryan's being here didn't have anything to do with the house, not really.

"What are you doing, Ryan?"

He looked at the house, a wistful expression on his face as his eyes skated over the property. Finally he looked away, the stubborn McKinley look coming over his features.

"I'm going to buy it."

"What?"

"I'm buying the house."

Okay, maybe it was about the house. A really big house with at least four bedrooms, and a backyard meant for big family barbecues.

"But . . . why?"

He pulled his hand from the steering wheel, turned down the heat. He cleared his throat, a sure sign he was getting emotional. "I've always wanted it, you know that."

Actually Abby had always wanted it, but PJ wasn't about to say that. She wondered if he could afford it, then decided it was none of her business. She wasn't going to second-guess him the way everyone did her.

"Still . . . it's a lot of house for one person."

"Spring's just around the corner. If I wait, someone will put in an offer, and I'll lose it for good."

PJ wondered if they were still talking about the house. Someone had to talk him out of this. "Have you told Mom and Dad?"

"Nope. I'm putting in an offer tonight. It's reasonable. They'll accept."

She couldn't help but wonder how it would feel for him, living alone in Abby's dream home night after night. She shouldn't say anything. It was none of her business, and Ryan was one of the most sensible people she knew. Still, he was about to make a huge decision, and what if it was a monumental mistake? What if it only made him miss her more?

"Ryan . . . it won't bring her back . . . you know that, right?"

When he fixed his eyes on her, she knew she'd overstepped. She squirmed in her seat.

"You know, PJ, when you went after this restaurant thing, did I try to burst your bubble? No, I showed up and helped you paint, fixed your plumbing, and moved you in."

"I'm sorry. I'm only concerned about you."

"Well, don't be."

"I don't want you to make a mistake or look back and think I should've stopped you."

"Don't worry. If things turn sideways, I'll realize it's all my fault."

She wondered again if they were still talking about the house. For once she didn't know what to say or do. He was the older brother, the one with the answers. The one who always knew what to do.

He turned away. "Maybe you should go. The Realtor will be here any minute, and I want to handle this alone."

If that wasn't a dismissal, she didn't know what was. She reached for the handle. "All right. See you later." She got out and pushed the door shut, the wind tugging at her hair. He didn't even say good-bye.

Chapter Twenty-Six

COLE CLOSED HIS CHECKBOOK AND GATHERED THE STACK OF bills. Cutting it so close every month wasn't his idea of fun. His window installation work had dried up because of the cold weather, and he wondered if he could make it until spring when the home improvement business picked back up.

He'd had no luck finding another job or another donor. It seemed everyone was struggling to make ends meet. When Mrs. Simmons called to check on his progress, he focused on the positive things like Shaundra's decision to attend Vincennes University, Zac's improving grades, and Josh's softening toward the others. But at the end he'd have to give an accounting of the finances, and it wasn't going to be good.

He flipped on the TV and turned to ESPN, where they were previewing the upcoming Super Bowl between the Broncos and Packers.

The kids were in their rooms. The sound of Zac's guitar carried quietly through the walls, Cole's many lectures having finally paid off. After a hectic day of errands, he was glad to be home.

Home.

There was a word he hadn't used in a while. No place had deserved the title, not even Greg and Becky's. That he used the word now made anxiety flare up. This place wasn't his, not yet. Might never be. He knew better than most not to get too attached to people or places.

A car started up out back. PJ's cooking class must be over. She'd closed the restaurant on Tuesday nights in favor of the more lucrative classes. The smell of something sweet and chocolate wafted into his living room, making his mouth water.

He wondered if she'd come up tonight. She'd been doing that lately since their outing at Cappy's a few weeks ago. He understood her better now that she'd confided in him. It astounded him that she didn't see how capable she was. How amazing. Her smile lit a whole room. Her personality was like helium, lighter than air, making everything float.

He enjoyed their conversations, their banter. She played and teased and made him smile. But he was all too aware of his attraction. When she came up he was careful to sit in the recliner across from her. Careful to avoid touching her, to avoid getting close enough to catch a whiff of her sweet flowery smell. He was already infatuated, no need to tempt himself further.

They kept the conversation light. She seemed to have a lot of acquaintances but no close friends. He wondered about that. That she sought him out for friendship made him feel good—a feeling he needed to keep in check. Sometimes he caught her looking at him in a way that made him think she was feeling more too. He had to be careful. This couldn't go anywhere. She deserved so much better than him even if she didn't seem to know it.

"Knock-knock."

His spirits buoyed at the sound of her voice.

She swept into the room with a plate of heaven in her hand. "Chocolate lava cake, anyone?"

"For me?" Cole sat up, accepting the plate.

She sank onto the sofa beside him, close but not touching. "We had leftovers."

"Thanks. It smells great." He took a bite and let the flavors roll around on his tongue. "Mmm, still warm," he said around a mouthful.

"Where are the kids?"

"In bed, except for Zac."

"I hear him." She cocked her head. "'Sweet Child of Mine'?"

"For the thousandth time."

"That's a lot tamer than some of his other stuff. At least he's good."

"Speaking of good." He took another bite. "How do you do it?"

"Glad you like it. I created the recipe in school. It has coffee to bring out the chocolate flavor. I love making desserts. Unfortunately I love eating them too. If I keep it up, I'm going to bust out of my whites."

"Something tells me you have enough energy to work off more desserts than you'll ever eat."

He finished the dessert while she regaled him with cooking class stories. A group of ladies from the yacht club had signed up for the class. PJ was under the impression they were only trying to support her, but if they were learning to make desserts like this, they were the winners hands down.

On TV an interview with Coach John Fox rumbled quietly. They watched awhile, PJ rolling her eyes at Fox's claims of a confident win over the Packers.

Cole set his empty plate aside. He should take it over to the kitchen, put some distance between them, but the interview and PJ's commentary were engrossing. He'd get up when it was over.

"Oh, please," PJ said. "They don't stand a chance."

"You have something against the Broncos?"

"Have you seen Green Bay's offense?"

"They're good, but the Broncos are nothing to sneeze at. Heard of Peyton Manning?"

"I liked him better in blue."

"We all did." He grinned at her, loving the way she came alive so easily. "You really like football season, don't you?"

She shrugged. "Football season, basketball season, baseball season . . . it kind of runs in the family."

"Well, this has been an interesting season of my life, that's for sure."

"What do you mean?"

"This house, the kids, all of it."

"Me too, with the restaurant. It's like . . . my wishing season, you know? How appropriate that it's also the name of the house."

"I know what you mean."

They watched until the interview ended, then he took his plate to the kitchen sink and washed it. PJ came in as he was drying, leaning against the counter. The woman didn't sit still long.

"I sure miss Shaundra in the kitchen," she said. "I wish I could afford her year-round."

"There you go wishing again." He traded a smile with her. "Did she tell you she wants to be a chef?"

"No! That's great. She's been asking me a lot of questions—I guess that's why."

"She just told me yesterday."

"I'd be happy to sit down with her and go over some options.

A mini career counseling session. There are a few good schools that aren't too far away, and they have scholarship opportunities."

He loved when her brown eyes lit up. She was a bit of a roller coaster emotionally, but he didn't mind. She was full of life, and that was a good thing.

"I think she's settled on Vincennes, but I'm sure she'd love to talk to you about it. You've had a big impact on her."

"Well, she's had a big impact on me too."

Her phone buzzed as she collected her plate from him, and she checked the screen.

He wondered if she'd ever heard from Keaton. He hadn't shown up again that he knew of, and Cole had kept a pretty close eye out through December.

After returning a text, she slid her phone back into her pocket. "That was Jade. We're meeting for coffee in the morning."

"You ever change your number?"

"I did. The day after I, you know, fell apart in my room and blubbered all over your shirt."

"You didn't fall apart."

"I kind of did."

"Okay, you did."

They shared a smile. She had the prettiest one he'd ever seen. Wide and bright. He felt a pang as it fell away.

"He hasn't called or anything, so I'm hoping I've heard the last of him."

Cole tossed the towel on the counter and leaned against the sink ledge across from her. He wondered if she was still having withdrawal pains. She'd said she'd loved him, and clearly he'd broken her heart. The thought pinched him hard. He told himself it was because he didn't like seeing her hurt.

Yeah, that was it.

"It's gotten a lot easier," she said. "I wonder sometimes if it's really even him that I missed. Maybe I just missed being part of a relationship, you know? Feeling special."

He nudged her foot. "You are special. You're my little Sunshine, remember?"

Her eyes smiled before her lips. "Don't even pretend you meant that as a compliment."

"I don't know what you're talking about."

She laughed. "Sure you don't. You thought I was an annoying chatterbox."

"And you liked me so much more. You gave me a concussion."

"That was an accident!"

"You accidentally broke a pot over my head?"

She nudged his foot back. "You broke into my house."

"With a key."

Man, he loved the look on her face just now. Eyes shining, flirting almost. No, not almost. Feelings stirred inside like a million happy thoughts buzzing through his veins. He wanted to indulge the feeling. Just for a few minutes. It had been so long since he'd felt this good.

The twinkle left her eye, chased no doubt by the look on his face. He wished he'd kept up the banter instead of going quiet. Although the way she looked at him now wasn't half bad either, her warm brown eyes meeting his boldly, her lips slightly parted in the remnants of her smile.

"I should probably go," she said. "I have to be up early."

Well. He supposed that was that. "I think I'll turn in too." He flipped off the TV and lights and followed her toward the door.

Quiet rippled through the house once Cole shut off the TV. Zac's
guitar was silent, leaving PJ to her thoughts. The moment in his
kitchen had caught her unaware. All kinds of feelings welled up
inside as she crossed the room. Cole made her feel good. Safe.
Comfortable. Capable. She wondered if he knew. If he had any
idea how rare that was.

Gratitude for him swelled, and she turned on the threshold.
The stairwell light bathed the planes of his face in a golden glow.
He wore a day's scruff on his square jaw, and her fingers twitched
with the need to touch it.

"I don't think I ever thanked you for December—the way
you hung close to the house . . ." She remembered the way it had
felt, knowing he was nearby, during restaurant hours especially.
Feeling like he had her back. Her eyes stung. She blinked the
tears back, feeling foolish for getting emotional on him again.
He was going to think she was a basket case.

She swallowed against the lump in her throat. "I'm sorry.
You'll just never know what that meant to me, so thank you." She
reached out for a hug, wrapping her arms around his neck.

A fleeting second passed before he returned her embrace.
"You're welcome."

His breath stirred the hair at her nape, sending a shiver down
her spine, firing up the feel-good chemicals.

"My offer still stands." His voice rumbled into her hair. "I
know you haven't heard from him, but I'm just a call away."

"Thanks."

The heat of his palms burned through her thin sweater at her waist. She ached for them to come fully around her, pull her in close. Was she a fool for wishing?

"You make me feel safe," she said.

His chest expanded against hers, and the warmth of him seeped into her skin.

"You are safe."

She turned her face into his neck, inches from the bare skin above his collar. She drew him in. He smelled like heaven, all musky and male.

The moment stretched, going on too long—not long enough. He had to be aware of this, yet he hadn't pulled away either.

As if acknowledging her thought, endorsing it even, he turned his face into her hair. His breath feathered over her skin, and the moment slipped from hug to something more.

Her heart thumped so hard and fast he had to feel it, but she couldn't bring herself to care. She breathed him in again, brushing her nose along his neck.

She heard the quick hitch of his breath.

She shouldn't press her luck. She shouldn't. But then his thumbs moved at her waist, sweeping back and forth. The motion, so subtle yet so provocative, sent a wave of desire through her veins, thick and slow like honey.

She couldn't help herself. It was just his neck. Just one tiny kiss. A thank-you kiss. Her lips brushed the cradle between his neck and shoulder. His skin was warm and soft, faintly salty. Addictive.

His hands clenched at her waist. "PJ . . . ," he warned.

"What?" she asked, not because she wanted an answer but to hear that husky timbre of his voice again. When he didn't reply, she lifted her head from his shoulder.

A storm brewed in the warm, swirling waters of his sea-green eyes. They were intense, mesmerizing. She couldn't seem to look away. Her heart beat out an ancient tattoo that was a thousand generations old and yet somehow new and different.

Her gaze skated over his face, settling on his lips. She suddenly wanted them on her more than she could say. Needed to feel him. Taste him. Of their own volition her fingers found the scruff on his jaw. They tingled at the touch.

Her eyes found his again, locked in tight. She wanted to fall right in there and drown in the stormy depths.

He leaned closer until his breath brushed her lips. Her heart gave a hopeful sigh. And then he kissed her.

His lips were warm and soft and plush. He moved slowly, taking his time. Not lazy . . . savoring. She felt the distinct difference, relished it.

His arms slipped around her, pulling her close.

Finally.

She pressed against him as he deepened the kiss. Her heart sang a beautiful melody as her arms curled around his neck, her fingers threading into the softness of his hair while he worked magic on her lips. He tasted like chocolate, smelled like heaven, and felt like home.

How was it he'd been right here all this time, right upstairs? Why had it taken her so long to find herself in his arms?

He slowed the kiss. She sensed him pulling away emotionally an instant before he did so physically.

Their lips separated, and their breaths came heavily, inches apart.

He drew back until their eyes met. "I'm sorry."

The two simple words had the power to drop her stomach to her toes. The regretful look in his eyes didn't help. "You're not supposed to say that after you kiss a girl." Not when her lips still tingled with want.

His arms unwound from her, taking everything he'd given, leaving her empty and exposed. Wanting.

"This is a bad idea, PJ."

A sick feeling settled in her stomach. "Because . . ."

Something flickered in his eyes, and then it was gone. A shadow moved as his jaw clenched. "You don't want this. Only one of us will win the house. If it's you, I'll be leaving."

"And if you win?"

His eyes slid over her face. He tucked his hands in his pockets. "How would you feel about me then? After I stole your dream?"

Could she live with that? Be okay with him? He wasn't giving her the option of finding out. Her heart gave a squeeze at the thought. She couldn't stand the thought of their first kiss being their last.

"So . . . what?" she asked. "We can't be friends?"

Okay, so she didn't go around kissing her friends on the neck. Or the lips. She didn't have thoughts of pressing herself against them until she could feel their heart beating against hers.

"I think we'd better take a big step back."

Her heart fell the rest of the way down, through two floors, hitting the basement with a heavy thunk.

"A step back . . ."

His eyes, so stormy and full of want a moment ago, had shuttered, reminding her of their early days. Was that what he wanted to go back to? To stilted silence and formality punctuated by occasional quarrels?

"I think that'd be best," he said, taking an actual step back toward the attic.

Something about the motion stirred a firestorm inside. She'd never figured him for a quitter, but that's what he was doing. Quitting her, before he even gave her a chance. He didn't think she was so capable after all, did he?

She lifted her chin. "I guess there's nothing more to say then."

"PJ—"

"No, I got it," she said, turning before he saw her wet eyes. "Don't worry about it."

She forced her spine straight as she headed down the hall, down the stairs. Only when she reached her room did she hear the creaking above that indicated movement, and she shut the bedroom door behind her as easily as Cole had shut the door on her.

Cole stared at the darkened ceiling, the ache inside spreading until he hurt all over. Stupid! Why had he kissed her? He'd drawn lines, done so well at building a friendship while keeping his walls in place.

But then, he'd never felt her breath on his neck, felt her lips on his skin. He closed his eyes against the memory, and it was instantly replaced by the look in her eyes when he put the wall firmly between them again.

She'd told him he made her feel safe. What a joke. That alone should've had him pulling away. He was the last person to keep anyone safe. He'd failed at the job with the people he'd loved most. Best she learned that now before he proved it by hurting her worse.

Chapter Twenty-Seven

THE COACHLIGHT COFFEEHOUSE BUZZED WITH EARLY morning customers, and the rich smell of java hung heavily in the air. People dashed in, wrapped in thick coats, then left clutching steaming to-go cups. A few, like PJ and Jade, settled at small tables, chatting with their neighbors or reading the *Gazette*.

A gust of cold air slithered over PJ's shoulder as the door opened behind her. A sip of her Americano warmed her up.

She wondered what Cole was doing. She'd run into him on her way out the door when he was collecting the newspaper. He'd given her a stiff nod and a forced smile. It was a bitter cold greeting after last night's kiss.

"Okay, what's wrong?" Jade set down her tea and nailed PJ with sharp green eyes. "You haven't heard a word I've said."

"Uh-huh . . . Daniel's got an interview with the *Gazette* today . . . Ava's teething . . ." PJ searched for more and . . . nothing.

"That was five minutes ago."

Okay, so she was distracted. She'd gotten all of five hours of sleep after Cole's blatant rejection. "Got a lot on my mind, that's all."

Jade laced her fingers on the table, her rings clinking together. "The restaurant?"

"Not exactly."

"Well, what exactly?" Jade searched PJ's eyes.

PJ looked down at the wooden table. She drew a short thumbnail along a scratch in the wood surface. "I don't want to talk about it."

"There's a first."

PJ shot her a look.

"It's a guy," Jade said.

"What? No."

"You know, you always do that voice thing when you're lying."

"What voice thing?"

"That high-pitched finish. 'What? No,'" she mimicked, tossing her braid over her shoulder.

PJ pursed her lips.

"Is it Cole? 'Cause Madison's usually right about these things. She knew Daniel had feelings for me long before I did. Didn't even tell me, did I mention that?"

"Once or twice."

"Well, we're sisters. You'd think she could've mentioned it in passing."

"Because if she'd told you earlier you'd be so much happier now."

Now it was Jade who pursed her lips. "Fine. I'm married to the love of my life, and I have two precious daughters. I got my happily ever after, so sue me."

"All I'm saying."

"And now back to Cole . . ."

"I don't believe we were discussing him."

"You were about to tell me why he has you all hot and bothered."

"I'm not hot and bothered." Her pitch rose at the end of the sentence, darn it.

Jade lifted a brow and leaned back, waiting.

"Fine. He kissed me."

Jade leaned forward, a smile curling her lips. "Really?"

"And then he apologized."

Her sister's lips fell. "Oh."

PJ's stomach dropped all over again as his words climbed into her heart and set up camp. For all his encouragement, all his support and supposed belief in her, he'd sure jumped ship pretty quickly.

"Was it a nice kiss at least?"

"'Nice' doesn't really cover it. I lay awake all night alternating between reliving the kiss and cringing from his subsequent rejection. My emotions have been bouncing like a manic pinball from sheer bliss to supreme disappointment ever since."

"So what was the problem? Why did he apologize?"

"Apparently he thinks there's no point. We're competing for the house . . . one of us will steal the other's dream, blah, blah, blah."

"That's a good point."

PJ narrowed her eyes.

"Well, it is. Not necessarily insurmountable . . ."

"Obviously he doesn't agree. He made it pretty clear we're headed back to square one with our relationship." The image of his tight smile this morning made PJ's throat close up.

"If memory serves, that includes a lot of sexual tension and bickering."

"I can hardly wait. My life needs more stress."

"Did you tell him how you feel?"

"Of course not!"

"We wouldn't want to do that now, would we?"

"I think the kiss kind of spoke for itself. Although not so much for him, I guess. Can we talk about something else? Did you hear Ryan's buying the Avery house?"

"What's up with that anyway? I didn't know he was even in the market—and I'm only letting you change the subject because I love you."

"Remember how Abby used to talk about it? She loved the huge front porch and the big backyard with the tire swing."

Jade's face fell. "Why would he do that?"

"I think he's still hung up on her. He kind of snapped at me when I questioned him. I think she still keeps in touch with Amy at the paper. I wonder if I should—"

"Don't be a Madison."

PJ sighed. "You're right."

"She was just about the death of me with Daniel. I've never been so mad at her. Besides, I'm not so keen on Abby after she broke Ryan's heart like that."

PJ sipped her drink. She didn't know exactly what had happened between Ryan and Abby. She'd only been a teenager, too self-absorbed to pay much attention.

"Let's go dress shopping," Jade said.

"What do you need a dress for?"

"I don't. You do."

"Um, is there some upcoming event I'm unaware of?"

"We're having a girls' night out on Valentine's Day, Madison and us."

"How do you know I don't have a date?"

Jade gave a mirthless smile. "Daniel's going to be out of town and Beckett's visiting his dad. We were discussing it last night while you and your live-in hottie were busy making out." She blinked innocently.

"I have to work. I ran a major Valentine's Day campaign, and we're booked solid that night." And she desperately needed the income.

"We'll make it a late night then. You could skip out a little early, couldn't you? Let your crew clean up?"

"I guess so."

Jade drained her mug and grabbed her purse off her chair. "There's a new boutique in Louisville near that bakery you interned at. We're picking out something to show off those long, fabulous legs of yours, and I'm buying."

Chapter Twenty-Eight

ANOTHER ROUND OF SNOWSTORMS HIT AT THE END OF January. PJ tunneled from her mound of blankets to face the chilly air and cold floor. Judging by the overhead noise, school had been canceled for the second day in a row, and they were cooped up once again.

Only this time there would be no fun outing to the ice rink and Cappy's. This time she and Cole would keep to their respective floors, seeing each other only in passing. She wondered if the kids were driving him crazy yet. They'd been loud overhead yesterday, and Shaundra seemed to be working out her dance routine 24/7.

When she heard the mail arrive, PJ showered and dressed, then headed to the foyer. Upstairs, Zac's guitar screeched at high volume, Shaundra's country music blared, and someone, Josh, she presumed, was playing a solo game of Ping-Pong against the upright side of the table. The cacophony was getting on her nerves.

When she hit the foyer, her feet flew out from under her and she landed on the wood floor with a hard thunk.

Her backside protested. "Ow . . ."

Water soaked through her jeans. What in the world? She followed the wet trail from the rug to the stairs. Dad-blame it, if they were going to use the front door, could they at least wipe their feet?

She pulled upright, wincing at the pain, and wiped up the water with a kitchen towel before gathering the mail.

She fanned through the stack. The phone bill, the electric bill . . . ugh. She didn't even want to open that one today. A credit card offer. A hand-addressed envelope. She glanced at the left-hand corner, and her stomach bottomed out.

The envelope trembled in her hand, the rest of the mail forgotten.

Why, after two months? Why couldn't he just leave her alone? The nerve of him. She'd ignored his calls and texts; she'd changed her number. Why couldn't he just go away? What was it with men? Always thinking they knew what she wanted.

She ripped the envelope in half, then did it again and again until there was a pile of shredded paper on the hostess stand.

"Hope that wasn't the electric bill." Cole stopped at the foot of the stairs in his coat. He looked like he'd just woken, his hair slightly rumpled, his face unshaven. His keys jingled in his hand.

She snapped her eyes away, scooping up the shredded letter and dumping it in the basket under the stand.

He pocketed his keys in his jeans. "That wasn't from—"

"Is there something you need, Cole?"

It was none of his business. He wanted distance; he was going to get it in spades. She cleared the rest of the trash from the stand. Two mint wrappers, a broken crayon, a chewed-on pencil.

"You okay?"

"Just peachy." She turned to him, steeling herself against the concern in his green eyes. "But I'd appreciate it if you'd tell the gang to dry their feet so they don't tramp dirty slush through my foyer, and if they could maybe keep the noise down to a less deafening decibel level, that would be dandy."

His jaw tightened. "Anything else?"

"A little help around here would be nice. The walks need shoveled, and I've done it the last three snowfalls."

"I'll get right on it."

"Thank you."

"You're welcome." He pushed past her, out the door, and a minute later she heard the scraping of the shovel on the walk.

~

Cole undid the top button of his shirt and set his church bulletin on the table. He opened the fridge and surveyed the contents, wondering what he could pull together for lunch. The heavenly aromas of Belgian waffles and bacon wafted up from the restaurant, teasing him.

The week had dragged. Who was he kidding? Every day since their kiss had dragged. It didn't seem possible it had been less than a week since he'd held her in his arms. He frowned as he remembered their discussion on bills earlier this morning. She'd hardly looked at him. Her sunny disposition had been replaced by storm-clouded eyes. Big, dark, angry ones. It was hard to believe now she'd ever let him close enough to touch her, much less kiss her.

Well, that's what you wanted, Evans.

"Whatcha doing?" Shaundra reached around him for a can of diet soda.

"Figuring out lunch."

"I made a casserole last night—chicken tetrazzini. There's leftovers."

"Perfect." He grabbed the foil-covered dish. "Want some?"

"I had a late breakfast downstairs. Have you tasted PJ's quiche lorraine? Yum." She nodded toward the casserole. "You'll have to give me your honest opinion. I created it myself. Hey, PJ talked to me about culinary school. I wish I'd made up my mind sooner. It's too late for most of the scholarships."

He dished out a serving and started the microwave. "Well, you'll still get the $5,000 voucher from the government."

"That won't even cover a semester."

"There's always student loans. A lot of people do it that way."

"I know. And PJ said she'd help me with the applications and even write a recommendation. That's pretty cool of her."

"I'll write one too if you need another. And don't forget about the Pell Grant. I'll help you fill out the FAFSA."

"Thanks. PJ helped me with the recipe. She's teaching me about ingredients and what goes together and why. Zac said it was the best casserole he's ever had. He doesn't really like casseroles though, so that's probably not saying much."

"I'm sure I'll love it."

"Who do you think's going to win the house?"

His gut tightened as it always did when he thought about that.

"I don't know."

"I'm rooting for you. I want you to win, but I don't want PJ to lose either."

"Well, that's not the way it works."

"I know. So what do you think?" she asked as he took his first steamy bite.

"Wow. Very good."

"Really? You're not just saying that?"

"Very flavorful. Best meal I've had in weeks." Never mind that sandwiches and microwave dinners were her only competition.

She smiled wide. "I grated the Parmesan fresh."

"It's restaurant quality—really."

"Thanks! I can't wait to tell PJ you said that. She's showing me how to make crème brulee tonight. She sings when she cooks, did you know that?"

His lips twitched. "No, I didn't."

"She should definitely try out for American Idol."

"What?"

"She'd make it on TV for sure. She's like tone-deaf or something. She's so pretty though, don't you think?"

He made a noncommittal sound.

"She should have a boyfriend. There's this hot guy in her cooking class who keeps asking her out. I told her she should totally say yes."

His chest tightened at her words. "What guy?"

"Alec something. He's a fireman." She waved a hand in front of her face as if *she* were on fire.

"He's in her cooking class?"

"The bachelor one on Monday nights. Well, I gotta go to the store and get some stuff for tonight. See you!"

He wanted to call her back and pepper her with questions. Who was this Alec guy? Was PJ actually going out with him? Did she like him?

But there was one question he could only answer for himself: why did the thought of another man's interest leech the flavor right out of the casserole?

Sometime later a dull, repetitive thud sounded from outside, and Cole went to the window. The unseasonably mild temperatures had melted off the snow and warmed up the air. Josh and PJ were shooting around toward the basket Cole had attached to the front of the shed.

PJ sank a long shot, and Josh threw his arm over his head. When Josh made the same shot, PJ gave him a fist bump. She looked cute in her puffy white coat, her long denim-encased legs making short work of the court.

She put up another shot, which Josh proceeded to miss. PJ did a victory dance, making Josh shake his head, though a grin tugged at his lips. It was hard to believe this was the same boy who hadn't unpacked for a month. Cole knew better than to take responsibility for the change. They'd all played a part in making him feel like he belonged—even PJ.

He watched her as she playfully nudged the boy off the free-throw line. Maybe she couldn't hold a note or sit still for two seconds, but she had a soft heart and a generous spirit. All the more reason to stay far, far away.

Chapter Twenty-Nine

THE ANGRIER PJ WAS TOWARD COLE, THE LESS SHE'D WANT him. At least that's what she told herself as she tasted the soupe au pistou the following week.

"Nice touch with the cloves, Callie."

"Thank you, Chef."

"One sirloin, one meatloaf, and three salmon, all day," one of the servers called.

PJ pulled the filet from the oven. Perfect. She spooned on the béarnaise. "Callie, how's the rice coming?"

"One minute, Chef."

"Beth, tell the front to 86 the meatloaf special."

"Yes, Chef."

PJ put the sirloin into the oven and went to the walk-in for the salmon.

Where was it? She'd just bought it, had put it right here. "Callie, have you seen the salmon?"

"No, Chef."

"It's under the cod," Nate called. "Sorry, Chef, I moved it."

Everything was out of place. PJ put things back in order, working quickly. It wasn't busy, but they were short in the back because Ella was down with the flu.

"Chef!"

At the same instant that Callie shrieked, the fire alarm screeched.

PJ turned to see fire shooting up from a pan on the stovetop, halfway to the ceiling. Nate grabbed the extinguisher, but the flame had already caught on a nearby towel and spread up the wall. She couldn't believe how far it had gotten so quickly. Maybe the extinguisher would win, but maybe not. She couldn't take the chance.

"I'm going to empty the place," she called to Nate. "If you sense you're losing, get outside!" PJ dialed 911 as she dashed into the dining room, where patrons sat in a state of confusion.

"Get everyone out," she said quietly to the maitre d'. "Be quick and calm."

The operator answered, and she gave the address as she ran up the stairs. Were the kids home? Cole? Surely they would've come out at the deafening alarm. She threw open doors as she dashed down the hall, but the rooms were empty.

"Cole!" she called, flying up the attic stairs. She threw open his door, but his room was empty too. By the time she came downstairs, smoke had filled the now-empty dining room.

Nate and Callie spilled into the foyer, breathing into their whites.

PJ coughed. "Get outside." She darted past them toward the kitchen. She couldn't let her dream go up in smoke.

"Where you going?" Nate called, but there was no time to answer.

Pool at Cappy's had been a welcome distraction. Cole waved good-bye to Seth Murphy and got into the cold cab of his truck. Twice he'd nearly spilled about PJ, but he didn't know Seth that well. Besides, the guy was married to Layla, who was sister to Beckett, who was married to PJ's sister. He'd lived here long enough to know how things worked.

Besides, what was the point? Things were what they were. So he had feelings for PJ. Feelings that seemed to be growing despite the distance he'd put between them.

Just four months, Evans. Then it'll be over, one way or another.

Would it, though? What if he won? He'd get to keep the house, but he'd have to watch PJ move out. Where would she go? What would she do? Go back to the fudge shop? What about the loans she'd taken out?

Not your worry. He pulled from the parking lot, his head-lights cutting a path through the darkness.

You're going to have to sort all this out, God. Heaven knew he was at his wits' end.

He had to get a grip. He'd only known her nine months. Had only kissed her once. He couldn't be that far gone.

Could he?

It had only been ten days, and he already missed her wide smile and sparkling eyes. They hadn't been turned on him in a while. He hadn't seen much of her at all, which was kind of the point. But he missed her. He lay in bed aching to tell her about his day. His fingers itched to run through that silky hair of hers, and his lips tingled with want of her.

And all because of one kiss.

One kiss? Who was he kidding? She'd been getting under his

skin for months. He'd let himself get close to her, and look what had happened.

You're a real idiot, Evans.

She needed someone who'd protect her. Someone who'd be there for her, root for her, not someone who'd let her down.

Someone better than you.

He eased onto Main and turned the heat down. Up ahead, red lights strobed the neighborhood. His eyes caught on the red fire engine parked near their house, and his heart waged a violent battle with his ribs. He pushed the pedal, zooming past the cars parked along the curb.

People milled outside the Wishing House, huddled against the cold. Smoke billowed from the back, where the kitchen was.

PJ.

He pulled to the curb and jumped out, sprinting toward the yard. His eyes scanned the crowd. The kids were out for the night, but where was PJ?

He caught sight of Callie, Nate, and the kitchen crew. "Where's PJ?"

Nate shook his head. "She went back in."

He drilled Nate with a glare. "You let her?"

"It's not bad." Callie's hands fluttered around her face. "At least not yet. PJ's trying to put it out. The fire department just went in."

The wind nearly whipped away the last of her words as he rushed toward the house.

A middle-aged fireman stopped him at the porch steps. "Whoa, you can't go in there, buddy."

"PJ McKinley's in there."

The fireman faced him, legs spread. "I know. We'll get her out."

"This is my house."

"Step back, please."

Cole was just about to dart around the guy when a movement at the doorway caught his eyes.

PJ.

A fireman carried her. Her face was covered in soot, her clothes wet.

Cole shrugged out of his coat, tried to get to her, but the paunchy guard grabbed his arm. Cole stiffened, waiting impatiently until the other fireman and PJ neared.

PJ coughed twice. "Let me down, Alec."

"Are you okay?" Cole set his coat around her shoulders as her feet hit the ground.

"I'm fine. The kids aren't home. Everyone's out." She looked back at the house, her eyes watering. "But the house . . ."

"We'll have it out in no time," Alec said. "It's almost out already."

She coughed. "Are you sure?"

"I don't care about the house," Cole said. "Are you sure you're okay?"

"She needs the EMTs," Alec said. "Step aside."

Cole let them go. Thank God she was okay. Thank God. The adrenaline surge drained away, leaving him weak and shaky.

PJ hunched against dawn's chill as she climbed the porch steps. Ryan had heard about the fire first last night, being a volunteer, and news had spread quickly through her family. She'd received one frantic call after another until her parents had arrived to make sure she was okay.

She had spent the night at their house, though she hadn't slept. From the empty curb, she assumed Cole and the kids had found somewhere else to stay also.

She unlocked the door and stepped inside, coughing. The acrid smell of smoke filled her lungs and made her eyes water. Her heart beat into her throat as she went through the dining room and toward the kitchen, Alec's words late last night ringing in her mind. *They got it out. It's just the kitchen.*

Just the kitchen. Only the heart of her restaurant. She went through the door, letting it swing shut behind her.

She stopped, her breath leaving in a rush. Water was everywhere, puddled on the floor, on the prep tables. Soot climbed the ceramic tiles on the wall behind her stove and clung to the plates stacked above it. The painted ceiling was blistered and peeling. A wire whisk, grotesquely distorted, lay on the wet floor in front of the sink. Her eyes went back to the charred stovetop where she'd been working. Ruined.

What a mess. Her eyes stung, this time not from the smoke. How long would it take to get back up and running? It would be at least a week before she could get a new stove. Thank God for insurance! Without it she'd have lost everything, including the house. As it was, the time it would take to fix this would be a killer. She thought of the lost revenue and fought back panic.

Valentine's Day. She'd never have the kitchen in order by next weekend. She couldn't even imagine the thick smell of smoke dissipating by then. She couldn't afford this; the business was barely hanging on as it was. She hadn't paid herself in three weeks, and she'd been counting on next weekend to help carry her into spring. Plus the money she'd spent on the Valentine's promo would be wasted.

Why is this happening, God? Why can't I do anything right?

Now her numbers would look bad, and Mrs. Simmons would think she was irresponsible. She'd almost burned down the woman's ancestral home!

PJ's eyes swept the charred kitchen as water seeped into her tennis shoes. Maybe her family was right. The breath left her body as the realization swept through her. She was going to lose the house, lose her dream, and it was nobody's fault but her own.

She heard someone entering the house out front, the rattling of bags and voices.

"Open the windows, Zac, then clear the tables. Shaundra, start taking the curtains down."

"What about me?"

"Grab the wet vac from the back of the truck, then gather the linens. Make a pile by the door. We'll hit the Quick Spin later."

PJ left the kitchen and found Cole in the entry setting down an armload of bags. "What are you doing?"

He straightened. "How's the kitchen look?"

"Like someone detonated a bomb." She took in the bags of supplies. It wasn't even seven o'clock yet. "Where'd you get all this?"

"We spent the night at Seth's. He opened up the store for us." Cole began unbagging stuff: gloves, TSP, scrub brushes. "He gave me the rundown on cleanup. If we go at it, we should have you opened up by next weekend."

She swallowed against the hard lump in her throat. He was up at dawn—all of them were—to help her. Despite the tension between them. Despite their rivalry. Despite the fact that she'd been moody and a little hateful toward him lately.

"Why are you doing this?"

He looked up from where he squatted on the floor, his face softening.

Just then Josh barged through the front door with the wet vac.

"Hey, PJ." He set it down. "Sorry about your kitchen. Major bummer."

"Thanks for your help. I—" She swallowed against the tremble in her voice. "I really appreciate it." Her eyes swept over Cole, including him.

"No prob. Where should I put this?"

"I'll take it," PJ said. With a shaky smile she pulled the wet vac toward the kitchen. Maybe she'd get through this after all.

Chapter Thirty

THE NEXT SATURDAY COLE WOKE LATE AND GOT READY FOR a run. They'd finished the cleanup yesterday, and PJ's new stove had been installed. Her insurance company had been very responsive. She'd insisted on cooking a feast for the household last night: scallops in a butter sauce, chicken cordon bleu, mashed potatoes, and asparagus. For dessert she'd whipped up a cheesecake with a thick graham cracker crust and berry topping. He was still full.

Cole pulled on a pair of sweats. Everything had been put on hold for PJ this week, but she'd be open tonight, had called to confirm the reservations. Seeing her wide smile and sparkling eyes yesterday had been worth all the effort.

He'd kept the boundaries in place all week, despite their proximity. But it hadn't been easy. Smelling her sweet flower scent. Watching her laugh with the kids and blink back tears when Shaundra hugged her.

Her family had helped too. Her folks were nice enough, but he sensed that her mother disapproved of him. Maybe it was just that he stood in the way of PJ's dream, or maybe she still thought he'd tried to sabotage her daughter. He wasn't sure how much PJ had told them.

The doorbell rang as he was tying his shoes. He traipsed downstairs, figuring PJ would beat him to the door. But then he remembered she was helping Ryan move into his new home, never mind the hectic week she'd had.

A pimply teenager stood on the porch with a vase full of red roses, his breath fogging up the space between them. A Flowers on Main van was running at the curb where PJ's car was usually parked.

"Delivery for PJ McKinley."

A hollow feeling opened up inside. He eyed the flowers with distaste.

"She home?" The kid looked over Cole's shoulder, a little too eager to see a woman several years his senior.

"No, but I'll see that she gets them."

"You sure? I was hoping to talk to her."

"Get in line." Cole took the vase and closed the door.

The cloying scent of roses filled his nose. Red roses. Obvious and unoriginal. He eyed a plain white envelope sticking up from the bunch, wondering if they were from firefighter Alec. Was she going out with him then?

And if Alec was so interested, where'd he been all week while PJ scrambled to get her kitchen back in order?

But maybe it was someone else. What did Cole know about her personal life? It wasn't as if they'd had any heart-to-hearts lately—his idea. Looking at the bouquet, he wondered if he'd made a mistake. If he should've thrown aside his fears and taken the plunge.

No. He should be glad she had someone's eye. She deserved that. She deserved to be cared for and cherished. Deserved flowers for Valentine's Day or for no reason at all.

He carried the roses through the kitchen into PJ's room, fighting the urge to dump them into the garbage despite the pep talk he'd given himself. Her room was empty, as he'd suspected. He set the vase on her bureau and made himself leave the house. He had last night's dinner—and a whole new worry—to run off.

PJ slipped her feet into the black boots and zipped them up, then gave herself a once-over in the mirror. Her new red dress swept over her form, ending just past midthigh. She adjusted the black belt and added a touch of lipstick.

The restaurant was starting to empty after a busy dinner hour, and Callie and Nate had promised her they had it under control.

She'd been ready to cancel on her sisters after the crazy week, but they'd insisted she needed a night out more than ever now. Maybe they were right, she thought, her gaze catching on the flowers in the trash basket.

When she'd returned from Ryan's she'd found them on her dresser. Her heart had caught in her chest. It wasn't thoughts of Alec that had sent hope spiraling through her. And it sure hadn't been thoughts of Keaton.

But the words on the card were seared into her brain. *I miss you. Please call me, PJ. Please. Love, Keaton*

The man she didn't want wouldn't leave her alone, and the man she wanted didn't want her. She definitely needed a girls' night out.

She grabbed her peacoat and left the room, running smack into Cole in the hall. He caught her by the shoulders.

"Oh."

"Sorry."

He stepped back, his eyes sweeping over her. They lingered on her legs in a way that made PJ glad she'd chosen the heeled boots.

"You're headed out," he said.

She shouldered her purse. "Yeah. Callie and Nate have everything covered. They'll lock up."

"You look . . ." His Adam's apple bobbed. "Nice."

She met his eyes. They were the color of moss and twice as soft. "Thanks."

He shoved his hands into his jean pockets. "Did you, ah, find the flowers?"

"I did."

"They arrived while you were out this morning . . . I figured you'd see them if I put them on your dresser."

"Thank you."

She couldn't seem to look away. Or think of anything to say. She just breathed, and even that was labored. Her mind went back to the kiss they'd shared, to the feel of his arms, the taste of his lips. Her pulse jumped.

She had to stop this. "I—I should go."

He slowly stepped aside, giving her a wistful smile. "Yeah, well . . . you don't want to be late."

"See you later."

"Bye."

She brushed past him and out the back door, not bothering with her coat. She was already hot enough to heat a house.

Chapter Thirty-One

FEBRUARY DRAGGED INTO MARCH. THE RESTAURANT WAS so slow, PJ was down to a skeleton crew. She feared her employees wouldn't hang around until tourist season arrived. Her best server had already quit, needing more hours. PJ couldn't blame her.

In early March another letter arrived from Keaton. This time she skipped the theatrics and threw the envelope in the trash. If he didn't hear from her, eventually he'd give up and throw his energies into his marriage. Wouldn't he?

In mid-March, PJ finally agreed to a date with Alec. She might as well—Cole showed no signs of interest. Each tight smile and polite reply widened the crack in her heart.

Alec took her to a movie at the Rialto, then they finished the night at Cappy's, where they watched the first of the March Madness games. He was a sports enthusiast and nice enough. If his eyes weren't quite the right shade of green, if he was missing a cleft in his chin, if he was a little too lanky, that wasn't his fault.

So when he asked her out again the next weekend, she agreed.

Cole delivered a quick left jab to the boxing bag, followed by a right cross. He inhaled the dank shed air and exhaled heavily, his breath fogging in front of him.

He couldn't believe PJ was out with that guy again. What did this Alec have that was so appealing? So he was a firefighter. He had weenie arms and a cowlick that stuck up high enough to perch a crow.

He wondered what they were doing now. Where he'd taken her. If the creep was going to help himself to a good-night kiss when he walked her to the door.

He thought he heard a car in the alley and stopped, listening.

The sound of the motor grew louder. He caught the swinging bag between his gloves, stopping the rhythmic creak. The car's engine faded as it passed.

He delivered another cross punch, imagining Alec's head as the recipient, then followed with a left jab just for the fun of it. He should finish up here. It wasn't taking his mind off her anyway, and he sure didn't want to witness whatever would happen on the porch.

He pulled his gloves off and went inside, looking for another distraction. The kids usually hung around watching TV or playing Ping-Pong on Sunday nights, but tonight Zac and Shaundra were out, and Josh had turned in early.

After a quick shower Cole dressed in a pair of sweats and a T-shirt. He decided to call Lizzy, but he got voicemail and didn't leave a message. That was happening a lot lately. Must be busy with her new boyfriend—she seemed pretty infatuated with him. Or maybe she was sinking into herself the way she did when she was troubled. Maybe he should visit her again. But he couldn't drive that far without staying overnight. And besides, she'd be coming here to live in just a month. He was counting the days.

He eased back on his sofa and flipped on the TV. Notre Dame was playing Xavier in the second round. The basketball game was ticking toward its final minutes, but Cole was watching the clock more closely than the TV.

What were they doing on a Sunday night anyway? The sidewalks rolled up at five. Maybe he'd taken her to Louisville or Cincinnati. Or maybe he'd taken her to his house.

Ah, heck no.

He jumped up from the couch and paced the living room, tormented by thoughts of Alec's hands in places they had no right being. She'd worn her fitted jeans tonight with the tall black boots that made her legs go on forever. He'd seen them leaving, had seen Alec tuck her into the passenger side of his crappy Nissan.

So help him, if he touched her . . .

Maybe she wanted him to touch her. Maybe she wanted his lips on hers just the way Cole's had been. The thought stopped him in his tracks. She was going out with him, after all. It was their second or third date. He'd probably kissed her already. He clenched his jaw.

And here you stand, wishing it were you.

A car's engine sounded outside, perking his ears. He muted the game in time to hear the engine shut off. A car door slammed, then a moment later another. Finally. He checked the time. Ten forty-seven.

He looked toward the window. No. He was not going to

watch. If Alec touched her, he'd come undone and for what? Something he could never have?

He unmuted the TV and forced himself to perch on the recliner, his elbows digging into his knees. A controversial call was being replayed, but Cole couldn't focus enough to figure it out. Not with Alec and PJ on the porch, practically right under his window, doing God knew what. He muted the game again and listened for the car to start, knowing it was too soon but hoping anyway.

What was it about the woman that had gotten so deeply under his skin? He couldn't seem to get her off his mind for ten seconds straight. He felt her eyes on him sometimes, and it was all he could do to keep from grabbing her and pulling her into his arms. Lately when he talked to her in passing, a look of hurt would come over her face, making her eyes dim. Pain unfurled in his chest at the thought.

He didn't want to be the one hurting her. He wanted to be the one making her smile. The one making her laugh. The one making her eyes sparkle.

Instead he was upstairs alone while someone else did those things. What was taking so flipping long anyway? He tossed the remote and paced the living room, entertaining thoughts of going outside and interrupting whatever was happening on the porch. But what excuse could he have for going outside so late?

Besides, if PJ wanted this, wanted Alec, who was he to stand in her way? The woman had a right to go out with whomever she wanted, to kiss whomever she wanted.

Several long minutes later, the car started up. *Finally.* Cole's breath left in a rush. He crashed on the sofa, feeling all his energy drain away. The game had ended, and the Notre Dame coach was being interviewed.

Cole turned off the TV and listened for sounds below, but all was quiet. Maybe she'd headed to bed. The front door slammed shut and footsteps sounded on the stairs. He recognized the every-other-stair leap of Zac. A door shut down the hall.

A few minutes later Shaundra came in, barely making curfew, and chatted with him awhile before retiring to her room.

He should get to bed. He had to be up early, had a dozen windows to install tomorrow, and it was going to take his crew all day. But as tired as his body felt, his mind was still spinning with thoughts of PJ.

His eyes drifted across the room to the threshold where they'd stood almost two months ago. Two months, and he could still remember the smell of her skin, the feel of her silky hair, the taste of her sweet lips. His heart hammered at the memory. How could he miss something so badly that he'd only had once?

He inhaled deeply, a new smell catching his attention. Chocolate. She was baking. The restaurant was closed the next three days, so there could be only one reason for her late-night baking: she was stressed. He wondered if things had gone badly with Alec tonight. The thought lifted him, and he immediately chided himself.

He inhaled again. Just breathing in her chocolate masterpiece made him feel closer to her.

But not close enough. He closed his eyes and imagined her in the kitchen, her long legs making quick work of the space, her capable hands moving quickly and efficiently. An apron would be hugging her slim waist, and she'd have thrown her hair up in a messy knot, exposing the long column of her neck.

He squeezed the pillow in his fist. Muted sounds filtered up from the kitchen. She was probably taking the cake from the oven. She'd wait until morning to frost it, then she'd probably give it away.

She was probably cleaning up now. He wondered if she felt better. If baking had eased her mind. He wanted to go ask. He wanted to see her. He wanted to pull her into his arms and kiss her. His body ached with the want.

Before he could talk himself out of it, he tossed the pillow aside and left the room. His feet took the stairs quickly, driven by his need. He padded through the darkened dining room and pushed open the kitchen door.

A batch of cupcakes cooled on a wire rack, but that wasn't what held his attention. PJ's back was to him. He'd been right about the apron, wrong about her hair. It flowed down her back in a cascade of brown silk, begging to be touched.

She hand-dried a bowl and placed it on a high shelf, her long, lean body stretching, then dried her hands on the dish towel. She flipped off the lights, reached for the tie of her apron, and pivoted to the oven, where a lone dim bulb burned.

At the sight of him in the doorway, she stopped short.

PJ pressed her hand to her chest and sank back against the counter. "Cole."

What was he doing in here? The question caught in her throat at the look in his eyes. She felt the heat of his gaze from across the room. Those green eyes pulled her in and held her captive.

A shadow flickered across his jaw as his eyes burned into her. "I can't stop thinking about you."

Her breath hitched at the husky timbre of his voice. At the words.

He advanced slowly, purposefully. His eyes, locked on hers, were filled with longing.

"Is that so?" Was that her breathy voice? She gripped the edge of the counter before she could do something stupid like pulling him into her arms and kissing his neck.

"Yeah, that's so."

He stopped when he was close enough to make her body hum, and cradled her face in his hands. Then his lips were on hers. Not slow like last time, but deliberate, full of want.

Finally.

PJ slipped her arms around his broad shoulders, sinking her fingers into his hair. Finally.

This was what she wanted. Not Alec. Not Keaton. Just Cole.

He tasted faintly of mint. His clean, manly smell filled her lungs. His shirt was as soft as butter under her roving hands, contrasting pleasantly with the iron strength just beneath.

He ended the kiss.

A whimper escaped her throat.

Holding her eyes, he pulled the apron over her head and lifted her easily onto the counter, making them even. And then his lips were on hers again, his arms pulling her closer.

Her whole body sighed into him. The stubble of his jaw scratched the softness of her palm. The heat of his hands burned through her thin sweater. The softness of his lips opened her cracked heart all the way, filling it with something heady and delicious.

He ended the kiss, and his eyes opened lazily. Their breaths came raggedly. A battle waged inside between her heart and ribs. She couldn't bring herself to care who won.

Now that he was a few inches away, her brain neurons stirred to life. What had happened? What had changed? Why was he kissing her now like a starving man at an all-you-can-eat buffet when two months ago he'd shut her down cold? She was reluctant to ask, but needed to know this wouldn't end like last time, with an apology, rejection, and weeks of heartache.

Her hand slipped down his neck and rested there. "I—I thought this was a bad idea."

His fingers burrowed into the hair at her nape, and his thumb moved along her jaw. Every cell purred to life.

"I can't seem to help myself."

She wanted to close the three-inch gap, but his rejection was still fresh in her mind. Her heart couldn't take another apology. Another two months of distance.

Her eyes dropped to his lips, still damp and slightly swollen. So soft.

"Why are you going out with Alec?"

"I'm not."

"He just brought you home."

"I told him I couldn't go out with him again."

His eyes closed briefly. "Why not?"

Did she dare put her heart on the line? She wanted this more than she could say, more than she could believe. He'd wormed his way into her heart, quickly, deeply. But some things were worth the risk.

"He's not you."

Something flared in his eyes. He drank her in, scrolling her face, his gaze stopping on her lips.

He kissed her again, soft and gentle this time, savoring her mouth before kissing each corner of her lips, her cheeks, her forehead.

He leaned against her. "He didn't kiss you tonight?"

She forked her fingers through the hair at his nape, loving the feel of it. "No. Just a hug."

He growled.

She held back a smile. "I've never heard that sound from a human. I kind of like it."

"You'll hear it again if his hands come anywhere near you."

He cradled her face, giving her a long look that softened over the seconds. For all his masculine features, he had the longest eyelashes. They mesmerized her as he blinked.

Worry clouded his eyes. "I know we haven't even had our first date, but I don't want to share you."

Her heart sighed. "I don't want you to."

Another long, slow kiss later, they parted. PJ's heart hammered, her breaths came quickly. What he did to her . . .

"I can't get enough of you," he said, seemingly reading her mind.

"Kind of lucky we live in the same house then."

The house. She hadn't meant to bring it up. What would happen if she won? She wasn't about to ask. Not now when things were finally heading the right direction. When their love was as fresh and fragile as a newborn.

Either he didn't notice the mention, or he let it pass. "It's getting late. I have to be up early."

He lifted her from the counter, then set a soft kiss on her lips. "I want to take you on a date next weekend."

"I think that can be arranged."

He rewarded her with a slow, crooked smile. "Night, Sunshine."

"Night." Even as PJ went to her room and changed into her pajamas, her feet still hadn't touched the ground. She wasn't sure they ever would.

Chapter Thirty-Two

PJ SAID GOOD-BYE TO HER CLASS AS SHE STEPPED OUT ONTO the porch. The day had been unseasonably warm, and even now, as darkness swallowed the landscape and crickets chirped to life, the temperature was mild enough for short sleeves.

She sank onto the swing, giving a final wave. Class had gone well, but she'd been eager for it to end. When she'd awakened this morning Cole had already left for work, and she was in class when he returned.

He hadn't called or texted, and she feared he'd changed his mind. That he regretted the kiss. That second thoughts had crowded out the emotions so plain on his face last night.

She should take him a plate of the beef Bourguignon they'd made in class. But he'd been home long enough to grab dinner, and maybe she wouldn't be welcomed.

The screen door creaked open, and he slipped outside. He was silhouetted by the porch light, and his expression was a mystery.

"Hey," he said, walking toward her.

She wished she could read him better, but it was dark, and the one-word greeting gave little away.

She made room for him on the swing. "Hey."

Her heart rate sped as he eased down beside her, as his thigh pressed against hers. He stretched his arm across the back of the swing.

"Long day," he said.

"Oh yeah? Why's that?"

He gave her a long look, then leaned closer, bringing his warmth and manly smell with him. "'Cause I couldn't wait to do this again."

His lips touched hers softly, tentatively, a butterfly's wings. A touch so gentle yet it shattered her.

His arm tightened around her, and her heart did a slow roll. How had she made it all day without this? All these years? She hadn't known what a kiss was until Cole. It was a starlit sky on a summer night. It was a glass of iced tea after a long run. It was a warm, soft bed at the end of a trying day.

He kissed her cheek, her jaw, that sensitive spot on her neck. Every molecule of air left PJ's lungs, and she didn't even miss it.

"You smell so good," he whispered, taking a long second to nuzzle that space between her neck and shoulder. "It was the first thing I noticed about you."

Her breath caught in her throat at the feel of his lips. "The first thing?"

"My eyes were closed. Someone knocked me out cold."

"You're never going to let that go, are you?"

She felt his smile against her skin. "It's too much fun to remind you."

Thinking of their introduction reminded her of their circumstances. She didn't want to think about it, but she already felt so invested in this, in him. She had to be smart this time around. Go in with eyes wide open.

"We should probably talk, don't you think? I mean, given our situation?"

He groaned, lifting his head. His nose brushed her cheek, making a shiver dance up her spine.

"If I win the house," she said, "will you leave Chapel Springs?"

He sighed, drawing circles on her arm. "Probably."

She swallowed hard. "There are other houses . . . Maybe you could find something else here."

"Real estate isn't cheap here, Sunshine. You know that. It's the same reason you won't rush out to buy a building if I win. The overhead would eat all your profits."

He was right. Real estate in tourist towns didn't come cheap. There were other communities where he could score a better deal and have a chance of making it. She didn't really have that option. Her dream was here, in Chapel Springs. It was home, the place she wanted to sink down roots, marry someday, raise a family.

He tucked her hair behind her ear. "I don't want to think about this right now. This is all so new, and you know what? I've wanted you for so long, I just want to enjoy you."

Warmth curled through her at his words. He was right. There was plenty of time for this. They didn't have to plan everything out. Things would work out as they were supposed to. *Please, God.*

She snuggled into his side, and he tightened his arm around her, setting a kiss on top of her head. The swing squeaked rhythmically as he set it in motion.

She wanted to enjoy him, too, while it lasted.

She frowned as the last phrase formed in her mind. Then she pushed it away, sinking into the warmth of Cole's embrace.

Chapter Thirty-Three

THE LAST WEEKEND OF MARCH MARKED THE TASTE OF Spring Festival and the beginning of tourist season. PJ had a booth, featuring her wild berry cheesecake and blueberry cobbler. She'd closed the restaurant for the weekend, knowing the booth would be more profitable and hoping the treats would tempt people to try out The Grille.

The weather was cooperating on the festival's first day, offering clear, sunny skies and temperatures in the sixties. Booths from local eateries lined the river walk, and it teemed with neighbors and tourists alike. A local band played country music on the riverfront stage, and people milled on the lawn, snacking on food and catching up with their neighbors. The smell of grilling hamburgers fragranced the air.

PJ handed two bowls of steaming cobbler to a customer and rang him up while Shaundra sliced a fresh cheesecake behind her. Callie and Nate were coming to relieve them soon, and Cole was meeting her here at seven, ten minutes away. Tonight was their first date.

PJ had slipped away half an hour earlier to touch up her hair and makeup and change into fresh clothes. Just thinking about tonight made her stomach do a flip-flop. They'd decided to walk around town, eat festival food, and catch the main band at nine o'clock.

When the line was finally gone, PJ helped Shaundra with the pies and restocked the forks and plates.

"This place is hopping," Shaundra said.

"I hope we made enough cheesecake. I thought the cobbler would be more popular, with the cooler temperatures."

"We may run out of both before it's over. My feet are killing me."

PJ checked her watch. "Callie and Nate will be here soon."

Shaundra finished plating the pies and covering them with wrap. "And then it's date time." She waggled her brows.

"How'd you know about that?"

"I have my ways." Shaundra unwrapped a package of napkins and stacked them by the plates, a mysterious look on her face. "Okay, fine, Cole told me. He couldn't decide what to wear. Had all his shirts out last night, scowling at them."

He was worried about what to wear? A smile crept over PJ's face.

"Yeah, sweet, right? He's a little rigid with the rules, like curfew and stuff, but he's a good man. You guys make the cutest couple. Oh, customer."

PJ turned with a ready smile and nearly dropped the big cobbler spoon on the trampled grass. Keaton stood on the other side of the table in a button-down and khakis.

A hopeful smile curved his lips. "Hello, PJ."

Her heart thundered. Not like it used to. She didn't want him here. The flop of hair over his forehead didn't seem boyish anymore. It barely moved in the breeze, like it had been sprayed in place.

His smile faltered.

"Hi. You want some cobbler? It's blueberry, served warm with a crunchy oat and pecan crumble topping. Or there's cheesecake, freshly made with a thick graham cracker crust and topped with blueberries, strawberries, and raspberries."

His forehead furrowed.

"Or not." She clamped her lips shut.

"I didn't come for dessert. We need to talk."

"How'd you find me?"

He shrugged. "Small town. Everyone's proud of their local chef." His lips curled up. "So am I."

She felt Shaundra's appraisal and checked her watch. Cole would be here in six minutes. "This isn't a good time."

His mouth tightened. "There doesn't seem to be a good time, PJ. I just need ten minutes. After all we meant to each other, it's the least you could do."

After all your lies, I owe you nothing. She pursed her lips to hold back the words. Upsetting him would serve no purpose.

"Five minutes." Maybe she could have him on his way before Cole arrived. She pulled off her plastic gloves and edged out of the booth. "I'll be right back, Shaundra."

"I got it covered."

Feeling Shaundra's eyes, PJ led him behind the booth to a vacant area near a dogwood tree, avoiding an empty bench just yards away. No reason for him to get comfortable. She turned, crossing her arms.

He stopped and tucked his hands into his pockets. "You changed your phone number."

"You wouldn't leave me alone."

"Why do you think that is, PJ?"

She looked into the deep blue eyes she used to think were striking. Now they just seemed cool and calculating.

"You should be trying to save your marriage, Keaton. You have a little boy who needs you and a wife who—"

"I don't love her. You don't know how it is. We haven't had a real marriage in years. She doesn't talk to me like you or look at me the way you do. Our marriage was over a long time ago."

"A marriage is over when divorce papers are signed, and I hope you won't let that happen. I don't belong in the middle of this, Keaton."

He set his hand on her arm. "You belong wherever I am."

She stepped back, letting his hand fall, bumping the trunk of the tree. "That's not true. It's over, Keaton. You need to move on and leave me alone. I'm trying to get on with my life, and I don't want you sending me letters and flowers and showing up at—"

He took both her arms. "You don't mean that. Don't you remember how things were between us? I love you, PJ. I can't stand being apart from you anymore."

She closed her eyes. "Stop, Keaton."

"Why, because you still feel the same way?"

Nice wasn't working. She drilled him with a look and spoke firmly. "What we had is over. You need to go home and leave me alone. Please. I don't want you here." She turned to go.

He grabbed her arm. "She doesn't even love me. She just wants the lifestyle I provide."

"That isn't my concern." She tried to pull away, but his grip tightened like manacles.

Suddenly he was wrenched backward. He didn't let go, and PJ stumbled forward.

Cole's nostrils flared. "Get your hands off her."

"You again. This is none of your business, pal."

"She's my business, and I'm not asking again."

Keaton's eyes swung to PJ. "Is this your new boyfriend? You've already found a replacement, is that what this is about?" His hand tightened painfully on her arm. "Is it?"

Cole grabbed Keaton and swung, planting his fist in Keaton's face. PJ stumbled backward into the tree.

Keaton caught his balance. His face darkened. A trickle of blood ran from his nose, and he wiped it with the back of his hand.

The crowd around them stilled, watching.

"I'm just talking to her. This has nothing to do with you." Keaton walked toward her.

Cole stepped between them. "She doesn't want to talk to you."

"Get out of my way." Keaton tried to edge around him.

Cole shoved him hard. Keaton staggered backward, colliding with a trash barrel, and Cole surged forward.

PJ grabbed his arm. "Cole, no. That's enough."

He stopped. His jaw flexed, and he glared at Keaton. "Stay away from her."

An ugly look came over Keaton's face as he pulled to his feet. He pointed at Cole. "I'm pressing charges, pal. You don't know who you're dealing with."

Cole's arm flexed under PJ's hands.

Sheriff Simmons approached from between the booths. "All right, that's enough."

Keaton walked toward PJ again, and Cole tore his arm loose from PJ's grasp and shoved him back.

"That's enough, I said."

Cole got in the passenger side of PJ's car. After being hauled away in front of half the town yesterday, he'd had the pleasure of a full night in jail while he waited for the bank to open.

He'd been searched, charged, printed, and locked in a cell. He needed a shower and a shave, but what he really wanted was his dignity back.

He could feel PJ's eyes on him as she started the car, but he couldn't bring himself to meet her gaze.

"Are you okay?"

"I'm fine."

"I'm so sorry this happened."

"You have nothing to be sorry about."

She pulled from the lot and turned onto the street. "I hated leaving you there all night. The kids were worried about you."

"I've slept in worse places."

"Zac remembered to take the garbage out last night, and they were all up and out the door on time this morning."

"Good."

The streets were already crowded for day two of the festival. They stopped in front of a busy crosswalk. It was hard to believe people were still eating funnel cakes and taking riverboat rides.

His disorderly conduct charges had probably made today's *Gazette*. The other half of the town would soon know about his arrest. Worse yet, Mrs. Simmons would find out, since her nephew was the one cuffing him. No one would think him fit to run a home for young adults after this.

"Are you mad at me?" PJ asked in a tiny voice.

At the sight of her watery brown eyes, his heart softened. "Why would I be mad at you, Sunshine? You didn't do a thing."

"But Keaton—"

"Is responsible for his own actions. Just like I'm responsible for mine."

And that's why his bank account was completely wiped out for bail money. Why he'd plead guilty in front of a judge in a few weeks. He could only hope he'd escape with a fine.

"I'm going to talk to Keaton about dropping charges."

His eyes snapped to hers. "No, you're not."

"You were only defending me, and now you're in trouble. It's not fair."

It sure hadn't felt fair when he was being stuffed into the back of the sheriff's cruiser while a smirking Keaton looked on.

"Did he bother you any more last night? Is he gone?" That was all he'd thought about while tossing on the cot all night.

"He's at a hotel in Scottsburg. After I take you home, I'm going to talk to him. I think I can get him to drop—"

"No, PJ. I don't want you near him. And definitely not alone with him in some hotel room."

"Well, I don't want you having a record and doing jail time or paying a fine for defending me."

"You're not going there alone. I'd be happy to come along, but I'm pretty sure I'd end up right back in jail."

She turned onto their road and traffic thinned out, allowing a quicker pace. "You don't know Keaton. His dad is a lawyer. He has contacts. You don't need a stiff fine or a criminal record. I'll just call him."

The thought of PJ even talking to the jerk again made his stomach tighten. He didn't like the way the guy had grabbed

PJ, didn't like the possessive way he'd stared her down or the creepy way he'd stalked toward her.

PJ pulled to the curb in front of the house and shut off the engine. When she reached for the handle, he took her wrist gently.

His eyes climbed her arm to the finger-sized bruises, and his jaw knotted. He wished he'd put his full weight behind the first punch. What else was the guy capable of?

"You need to get a restraining order."

Something passed over her face, and then it was gone. "I think he might leave me alone now. I was pretty blunt with him last night after you left."

And Cole remembered how blunt Keaton had been with PJ. "Don't call him, don't go see him." He brushed his thumb across her pulse, glorying in the shiver that passed over her. "Promise me."

Her eyes held his, the wavering clear on her features. Finally she exhaled, her lips turning up at the corners. "All right."

His breath whooshed quietly from his body.

"Thank you for coming to my rescue," she said.

"My pleasure."

"I'm sorry about our date."

He tipped a smile. "There'll be plenty of others."

"Promise?"

More than anything he wanted to put the past fourteen hours from his mind. Wanted to focus on his kids and PJ. Especially PJ.

He kissed the inside of her wrist and threaded his fingers through hers. "Promise."

Chapter Thirty-Four

THE WEEK RUSHED PAST IN A FLURRY OF MEALS AND CLASSES.
Keaton hadn't tried to contact her again, and PJ thought he'd
finally gotten the message.

She and Cole found quiet moments on the porch or in the
living room upstairs. Sometimes they played Ping-Pong with
the kids, and one night they played basketball with Josh and
Shaundra. PJ lived for their quiet talks and lingering kisses. It
grew harder each evening to say good night.

They finally had their first date a week later. She wore the
red dress Jade had bought her for Valentine's Day with the
heeled black boots. When Cole's eyes swept over her, they flared
appreciatively.

"I like you in a dress. I didn't say so last time since you were
obviously headed out on a date, but your legs were made to be
shown. And those boots . . ."

PJ's skin heated under his appraisal. "It wasn't a date. I went
out with my sisters."

Cole gave a mirthless smile. "I fretted all night for nothing?"

"Pretty much."

He took her hands, pulling her close, and put them behind
her back the way he liked to do.

"Well, you're all mine tonight," he whispered into her ear. "And I'm going to enjoy every minute."

He took her to an outdoor concert at Waterfront Park in Louisville. They had a picnic on the lawn and danced to slow country ballads. PJ wanted the night to go on forever. The look in his eyes as they moved, swaying to the music, mesmerized her. The tender way he held her made her feel cherished and protected.

She told him stories from her childhood and, when she managed to shut her mouth for ten seconds straight, Cole opened up about his foster family. He told her about Greg and Becky and Lizzy, who'd be joining their household in two weeks.

His love for Lizzy, for Josh and Zac and Shaundra, shone through in the warmth of his voice when he talked about them. Cole might be quiet, sometimes guarded, but when he opened his heart to someone, he threw it wide open and loved generously.

He held PJ's hand on the ride home, and by the time he walked her to her bedroom door, it was well after midnight. The house was quiet, the kids were above in bed, and only the light from the foyer spilled into the short hallway.

She leaned against her closed door. His eyes scrolled over her face, and her heart did a slow roll. His lips had grazed her cheek as they'd danced. They'd skimmed her temple and glided along her neck, but he hadn't kissed her all night, and she thought she might crawl right out of her skin if he didn't do so and fast.

"Thank you for tonight," she said. "I had a great time. I hope I didn't talk too much. I talk when I'm nervous."

"I hadn't noticed."

She gave him a look.

He set his hands at her waist. "Why were you nervous?"

She slid hers up his thick biceps, stopping at the collar of his button-up. "It was our first date." She bit the inside of her lip. "And I kind of like you." More than like, truth be told. No need to scare him off, though. She'd probably already said too much.

His eyes warmed. "I like you too. A lot." He leaned forward, ever so slowly, and dropped a lingering kiss to her mouth.

A curl of warmth unfurled inside as he came back for seconds. They'd been dancing around this moment all night, but it had been worth the wait. If only she could suspend time, live here in the moment for an eternity or two. Forget the time that ticked away too quickly toward the June 1 deadline.

His hand found the small of her back as his body pressed hers.

His shoulders were solid and muscled under her palms. The hair at his nape was feather soft on her fingers. His lips were firm and pliant against hers. Heat pooled in her stomach. She didn't want the kiss to end. That would mean their date was over and the night had ended.

A moment later he drew away, his eyes at half-mast. "Good night."

"Night."

"I'll meet you in the backyard at nine?" They'd agreed to clean out the flower beds in the morning.

"I'll be there."

He kissed her forehead. "Sleep well."

She was still trembling from the kiss after he disappeared from view. Sleep was a long way off.

By noon they'd raked away winter's dead leaves and weeded the beds. Red and orange tulips sprouted proudly in clusters, their heavy heads bowed. Daffodils proliferated throughout the landscaping, adding splashes of sunshine yellow.

The sun climbed over the rooftop, hitting their backs with an intensity uncommon so early in spring. PJ had long ago pulled her hair into a ponytail and removed the hoodie that covered her Girl Chefs Rule T-shirt.

Despite the hard work, she'd enjoyed her morning with Cole. He didn't seem to mind her chatter as they worked. He often tugged her ponytail or brushed a streak of dirt from her cheek as he passed. She liked that he was always touching her. It made her feel connected. She didn't even mind when he teased her about her singing or went over an area she'd already done.

She finished trimming the hedges while he went to pick up mulch. The landscaping was sorely in need of a fresh covering, and Seth was letting them have it at cost.

She finished the hedges, made a couple club sandwiches, and set one of the patio tables. She'd just sunk onto the front porch step with a glass of iced tea when Cole pulled up to the curb with a bed full of rich brown mulch.

He got out, lowered the tailgate, and tossed her a smile that curled her toes. "I see how it goes when I'm gone."

"Hey, I made us lunch."

"All is forgiven." Abandoning the mulch, he joined her on the porch.

He practically inhaled the sandwiches and chips. She reheated apple dumplings left over from yesterday's brunch, then they went back to work in the yard.

An hour later a bead of sweat trickled down her back. Her back ached, her arms burned, and since when was it eighty degrees in April?

"I'm starting to wish for winter again," she said. "I'm about ready to call it a day."

Cole lowered the full wheelbarrow to rest nearby. "Then you'd have a half-empty restaurant and be fretting over money."

A retort was stolen from her lips when he whipped off his shirt. A sheen of sweat covered his muscled torso. His biceps bulged as he lifted the wheelbarrow and dumped the load.

Maybe another hour or two.

They worked in companionable silence, PJ stealing glances when he wasn't looking. She caught sight of the scar on his shoulder as he turned toward her, and she remembered wondering about it months ago. About four inches long, it ran down the front of his shoulder toward his heart.

He dumped the last load under a nearby shrub and grabbed a rake to help her spread it.

"How'd you get the scar?" She nodded her chin toward his shoulder when they stopped for a water break.

Something flashed in his eyes, and she wondered if she shouldn't have asked. She doubted it was from a fall from a tire swing or a best friend's dare.

He lowered the water bottle and capped it. "The car accident— something flying loose. Never did find out what it was."

She hadn't realized he'd been in the car too. "The one that took your family?"

His jaw flexed. "Yeah."

She'd thought maybe he'd been abused in foster care. This was almost worse. A constant reminder of the day he lost his family. The day he'd become the sole survivor at the tender age of twelve.

"How'd it happen?" she asked softly. "The accident . . ."

He picked up the rake and worked mulch around the base of a dogwood tree. "I don't like talking about it."

"Sometimes it helps."

His muscles flexed as he pulled the rake. A drop of sweat ran down his temple.

She remembered how painful it had been when her brother had died. "I know what it's like to lose someone you love."

His eyes bounced off hers. "I know you do."

"It's worse when it happens suddenly, I think. There's no time for good-byes, no time to say, 'Hey, I know I'm a pain in the butt sometimes, but I really love you.' I hope Michael knew that."

"I'm sure he did."

"Was it like that for you?"

He reached for another pile, spreading. "Not exactly."

"I can't even imagine losing my whole family. It's probably why you're so strong. You've survived so much."

"I'm no hero, PJ."

"You are to me."

He gave a wry laugh, shook his head.

"You don't give yourself enough credit. What you've been through would've broken most people. And here you are, all these years later, not only thriving but helping others."

His jaw flexed. "Stop."

"It's true. I had no idea how good I had it growing up until I met you. I see these kids you're helping, what they've been through, and it makes me thankful. It makes me want to give back too. You inspire me."

He stopped suddenly and impaled her with a look. "It was my

fault, all right? I don't deserve your admiration. I don't deserve anything." He reached for another pile, spreading the mulch fast and furiously.

"What do you mean, your fault?"

He kept working, his eyes fixed on the ground, as he jabbed at the mulch. The rake caught on a root, and he yanked until it turned loose.

PJ set a hand on his sweat-slickened arm. "What happened?"

His arm flinched under her touch. He stopped, breathing heavily. His chest rose and fell rapidly. His eyes were pinned to the ground.

She longed to soothe away his pain. To bring peace to his tormented soul. "What is it, Cole? You can tell me anything." She wondered if he'd ever talked about it with anyone or if he'd kept it bottled up inside all this time.

He swallowed. "Two weeks before the accident, I found out my dad was having an affair." He stopped. His nostrils flared.

She squeezed his arm, waiting patiently for him to continue.

"I walked in on him and another woman—he never saw me."

"Did your mom know?"

Cole shook his head. He started raking again, and her hand fell.

"We were taking a long trip to visit my mom's friend. I didn't want to go. My dad was driving, and I was arguing with my mom, irritated with Noelle. It was all so stupid. So selfish."

Her heart ached at the pain on his face.

"I was mad at my mom, and I wanted to hurt her. I told her about the other woman. My dad glared at me in the rearview mirror. I can still see that look. My mom started questioning him, and they argued. I don't remember what happened after that. I guess Dad took his eyes off the road for a minute. He went over the center line—at least that's what they told me. There was another car coming over the hill."

An ache opened up inside. "That's awful. I'm so sorry."

His hand tightened on the rake. "I'm the one who's sorry. If it weren't for me, they'd still be alive."

"You were only twelve."

He shook his head, continuing to pull and spread the mulch in quick, angry movements. "My sister . . . I was supposed to protect her."

She grabbed his arm, stopping him. She waited until he looked at her. His eyes were haunted, the skin over his face stretched taut.

She wanted to go back in time and wrap her arms around his twelve-year-old shoulders and tell him it wasn't his fault. He'd had fifteen years of heaping blame on himself, and her words felt as futile as a drop of water on a raging fire.

She took his face and turned it toward her. "Maybe no one's ever told you, but it wasn't your fault, Cole. You were a child. Accidents happen, and sometimes nobody's to blame."

He stared back, something flickering in his eyes. Denial, maybe. Reluctance to believe.

"If the same thing had happened to Zac or Josh, what would you tell them?"

His eyes darted away. She tightened her grip on his face until he looked at her again.

"What would you tell them?"

He blinked twice, those long lashes, so boyish, fluttering over his pain-stricken eyes. He swallowed hard.

"You'd tell them it wasn't their fault. Because it wouldn't have been. You were a child, and you did a childish thing. That doesn't make you at fault. Your family loved you. They wouldn't want you drowning in guilt."

Her hand fell away as he went back to work. PJ wondered if anything she'd said was making a dent in that stubborn heart of his. *God, please help him. What a terrible burden to live with all these years. Heal him deep inside. Release him.*

She knew what guilt felt like. Her relationship with Keaton had her drowning in it. Only all these months later was she finally starting to see that it was Keaton who was to blame. Her only crime had been naïveté.

"I guess we've both been blaming ourselves for something that wasn't our fault," she said.

The only response was a quick glance and a tight smile. He didn't believe it yet, but she prayed he would in time.

Chapter Thirty-Five

THE SMELL OF GRILLING BURGERS WAFTED THROUGH PJ's parents' backyard the following Friday. Twilight had fallen, and the white twinkle lights in the landscaping were like a thousand fireflies lighting the night. A mild breeze brushed PJ's arms as she folded them on the picnic table.

Her dad manned the grill while Grandpa stood nearby. They were no doubt talking about the early planting and the likely yield from this year's corn harvest.

Her eyes drifted to the court, where Ryan and Cole had teamed up against Beckett and Daniel. Cole had been reluctant to come. PJ wondered if it was too early to bring him here, but she sensed he needed family. Needed a place to be accepted, a place to call home.

The week had been rough on him, with the notice of his arrest in the newspaper. The grapevine had been even more effective at spreading the word, and she'd received concerned calls from all of her family. She'd dodged the specifics about Keaton. But Cole had been notified today that Keaton was dropping the charges. Maybe his dad didn't want the publicity, or maybe Keaton didn't want his wife to know he'd been here. PJ didn't care so long as Cole was off the hook.

"Okay, so what exactly happened Sunday?" Madison set Ava

down, and the little girl toddled to her grandma, arms up. "Your ex-boyfriend came to see you at your booth, and Cole was there? Did he get jealous or something?"

"There are so many rumors," Jade said. "It's hard to know fact from fiction."

"Cole was defending me. Keaton wouldn't leave me alone."

Mom scooped up Ava. "Keaton's such a nice young man. I'm sure he didn't mean any harm."

"He's from Indianapolis?" Jade asked.

"You remember," Madison said. "She was dating him last spring, and they broke up before graduation."

"Why was he in Chapel Springs?" Mom asked.

PJ shrugged. "I guess he wants another chance."

"And you're not interested?" Mom asked.

"Mom, I'm with Cole now." If her mom knew about Keaton's marriage, that would put an end to all this, but PJ would rather serve Spam and Velveeta sandwiches at The Grille than tell her.

"Honey, if Keaton was only talking to you, then why did Cole feel he had to get violent? I'm a little concerned about his reaction."

"Mom, Keaton's been calling and texting me for months—harassing me. Remember when I changed my number back in December?"

"That's the reason?" Jade picked up Mia and handed her a Cheerio.

"He's written letters and sent me flowers and just wouldn't leave me alone. Cole knew I was upset about it."

"Well, maybe he's pressing too hard," Mom said. "But Cole's the one who got arrested."

"The charges have been dropped."

"Has he talked much about his childhood?" Madison asked. "Some of those kids have pretty dark backgrounds."

PJ shot her a look.

"Well, they do."

Madison smelled Ava's diaper and wrinkled her nose. "Ugh, I think this one needs to be changed."

"And some of them are just victims of their circumstances," PJ said.

The guys on the court high-fived each other as the game came to an end.

"Cole's been nothing but good to me. He's a good man."

"Oh, honey, we're not saying he's not. We're just concerned about you. His first reaction was violence. Doesn't that at least put up a red flag?"

PJ stood, gathering Ava from Madison's arms. "I'll change her."

She needed a few minutes to herself. She wished for once they'd just believe in her. They'd be quick to understand Cole's reaction if they knew how Keaton had deceived her—but it would only reinforce their notion of her naïveté.

Cole passed the hamburger platter to PJ's brother and started on the potato salad. Good cooking ran in the family, apparently. He'd already helped himself to seconds.

The chatter was loud and happy with at least four conversations going on at once, broken by "Pass the potatoes, please" and "Would you hand me the salt?" The twins added liveliness, squealing and laughing from their high chairs.

He'd been worried about their reception of him after last weekend's unfortunate event. He'd been snubbed by a bank teller and warily eyed by a grocery store clerk. But PJ's family seemed friendly enough. He still sensed some resistance on her mother's part, but maybe that was just the way Mrs. McKinley was toward all her children's suitors in the beginning. He would earn her trust. PJ was worth fighting for.

At the beginning of the meal, they'd quizzed PJ on the restaurant's performance. When she gave an honest report, Ryan offered to look over her financials to see where she was falling short. Her dad had brought up the kitchen fire twice, a sore spot for PJ since she'd been working the stovetop where it started. Her mom subtly questioned her expensive Valentine's ads in the *Gazette*, never mind that it had been a very profitable weekend for the restaurant.

PJ's smile had grown tighter with each question. Cole knew they meant well. It was obvious they loved her and wanted her to succeed, but they had no idea how demoralizing their quizzing was. Each dig at her self-confidence wounded him. Twice he nearly said something, but then PJ squeezed his leg and he bit his tongue.

Besides, after Mrs. Simmons had called him this week, he didn't think she had anything to worry about. Word of his arrest had spread all the way to Colorado. She'd asked for the details and seemed to be reserving judgment, but he was no fool. He was supposed to be a role model for the foster kids. A bright light in the community. And even though the charges had been dropped, his arrest would remain on his record. Still, he couldn't bring himself to regret standing up for PJ.

His feelings for her had grown exponentially the past several weeks. She smoothed out his jagged edges. She was his first thought in the morning and his last thought before bed. The one he wanted to spend every free minute with. The one he wanted to pull into his arms and never let go of. He was beginning to wonder what he'd done before she'd come into his life, waving a ceramic planter and singing off-key.

"She's got you all twisted up, eh, boy?" PJ's grandpa said.

Cole realized he'd been staring at the man's granddaughter, probably with the moony eyes of a grade-schooler high on his first crush.

"Stop that, Grandpa." A delicate flush bloomed on PJ's cheeks.

"Young love . . . It was just like that for your grandma and me."

"That's not true," Madison said. "You weren't even in love when you married."

"Their love grew out of friendship," PJ told Cole, then she fixed a look on her grandpa. *"After* the wedding bells."

"And then she had me all twisted up—like I said."

Cole shifted on the bench. He wasn't even used to having these feelings, much less discussing them at a table full of the woman's family.

"How's the new house working out, Ryan?" Beckett asked. He finished off his burger, wiping his chin with his checkered napkin.

Cole wanted to hug the guy.

"All unpacked."

Madison shot him a look.

"Okay, mostly unpacked."

"His walls are as barren as a desert." Madison poked her husband in the side. "Like someone else I used to know. And he still has sheets up on the windows."

"That sounds familiar." Jade traded a look with Daniel.

"Honey, I said I'd help you with all that. I'll come over Sunday and see what we can do. There are a lot of walls to fill up in that big old house."

"Thanks, Mom."

"You know what you need, Ry?" Madison said. "A dog. There's this cute basset hound at the shelter, two years old, had all his shots, and he has the sweetest chocolate brown eyes."

"I love basset hounds," PJ said. "Those big floppy ears. You should definitely get him, Ry."

"Or a cat," Jade said. "He could always get a cat. Our neighbor's just had a litter. You want one?"

"He's allergic to cats, remember?" Mrs. McKinley said.

"Oh yeah." Jade pressed her lips together. A snicker squeaked out anyway.

"Yeah, yeah, laugh it up," Ryan said.

"What is it?" Cole asked.

Beckett shrugged, the only other one who seemed not to be in on the joke.

Mom gave Jade a disapproving look. "When he was eight or nine, he had a crush on the little girl across the street—"

"Tallulah Franklin," Madison said.

"She was a pretty little redhead, and Ryan was head over heels."

"Mom sent him over with a pie, and he thought he'd impress her by teaching her cat a trick. Only by the time he got home, his face was beet red."

"He had an awful rash all over his face and chest, and his eyes were so swollen, poor guy."

"She said he looked like a Play-Doh head, and the name kind

of caught on," Madison said. "He never went back, and that was the end of the Ryan and Tallulah saga."

Ryan frowned. "Thanks for the recap. I don't want a dog or a cat. I'm not home enough to take care of a pet." His eyes swiveled around the table. "So don't be getting any cute ideas for my birthday."

"How about a bird?" Mom said.

"Or a bunny," Jade said. "They have cute little twitchy noses."

Ryan scowled. "No pets."

PJ's mom set her napkin on her empty plate. "So, Cole, tell us a little about you. What was life like before Chapel Springs?"

Ryan looked heavenward. "Thank You."

"I was working in Fort Wayne for a home improvement company for the past several years."

"He was a crew manager," PJ pitched in. "That's how he knew so much about renovation."

"How'd you get into construction?" Mr. McKinley asked.

"My foster father did home improvement on the side. I worked with him during the summers."

"Did you have any foster brothers or sisters?" Mrs. McKinley asked.

"I did. Mostly they came and went, but I've stayed close with one of them."

"Her name's Lizzy," PJ said. "She's coming to live at the house in a week when she turns eighteen."

"Oh, that's great," Madison said. "It's terrific what you're doing for those kids."

The table grew quiet. No doubt everyone was remembering that he was out to steal PJ's dream.

Finally Daniel dropped his napkin on his plate and wrapped his arm around Jade. "I'm stuffed. The food was great, as always."

"Hey, Mom," PJ said. "Can I get Grandma's potato salad recipe? I want to add it to the Sunday brunch."

"Sure, honey. It's in my recipe book over the stove. She'd be tickled pink to know it was being served in your restaurant."

PJ squeezed Cole's leg. "Be right back."

"The copy machine's out of black ink," Dad called after her. "There's a cartridge in the overhead cabinet."

The rest of the family headed to the court for a game of HORSE while Mrs. McKinley began gathering the dishes.

Cole opted out of the game and stood to help her. He had some trust to earn, and there was no time like the present.

"Oh, honey, you don't have to do that."

"Least I can do, since I didn't pitch in with the cooking. Trust me, you don't want that."

Her wide smile reminded him of PJ's, but that's where the similarities ended. PJ had dark straight hair while her mom's was short and blond. Her mom's eyes were ice blue, not warm chocolate brown, and PJ was tall and slim like her dad while her mom was average height and a little thicker.

He followed Mrs. McKinley into the house with an armful of dishes. They unloaded them and returned for the rest. Darkness had fallen, and the lights lit up the small court. The game of HORSE had already gotten competitive, and a playful argument ensued.

As they gathered the dishes, the air between him and Mrs. McKinley seemed to become charged. He was beginning to wish he'd skipped out on cleanup like the others.

"It seems as if you've had a lot of misfortune in your lifetime, Cole. It takes a strong person to overcome such difficulties."

Cole gave a tight smile. "We play the hand we're dealt. Not much else we can do."

Mrs. McKinley scooped up the silverware, her movements slowing down.

He got the feeling she was stalling.

"You seem like a really nice young man . . ."

Cole clenched his teeth as he set the lid on a casserole dish and pulled it toward him. "But . . ."

Mrs. McKinley gave a you-got-me smile and made a big deal out of stacking the remaining plates just so. "PJ's our baby, as I'm sure you know, and we couldn't love her more . . ."

Cole refused to bail her out. He straightened with the Crock-Pot in his arms and met her gaze head-on.

"But she hasn't always made the best decisions, particularly regarding young men. Oh my, some of the boys she brought home in high school!" She gave a little laugh that strained his last nerves.

"At first her dad and I thought she was going through a rebellious phase. I mean, her first boyfriend got expelled from school for drug use, her second was constantly getting in fights at school, the next one had another girlfriend, and on and on. Each one seemed worse than the last. I guess she saw some salvageable quality in each one of them. Or maybe she thought she could fix them, I don't know."

Cole followed her to the house. "And you think I'm just another in a long line of poor choices."

She turned on the first porch step, their gazes level. "I

have no qualms with you, honey. I know you've been through a lot." Her gaze darted to the ground, then back to him. "But PJ needs someone stable. Someone who can be the voice of reason. Someone levelheaded." Her eyes bored into his.

She was referring to his arrest. He wondered for the dozenth time if he should've just kept his fists to himself. "I was defending PJ on Sunday. I'm not going to stand by while some guy manhandles her."

"We met Keaton once before when we visited her at college. He seemed like a very nice young man, and as I recall from my conversations with PJ last spring, he had his act together. Graduated from college with honors and had a nice steady job. She was happy with him. He treated her well."

Except for the wife and little kid, he was quite the catch. But Cole couldn't say that, now, could he? It was PJ's secret to tell. Besides, it would only reinforce what her mom said about her poor judgment. Warmth climbed Cole's neck, and he locked his teeth together.

"I really thought they'd end up together, and I just think, you know, maybe she'd give him another chance, if she were available. It's obvious he's still interested in her."

"That's PJ's decision."

"You're right, it is." She gave him a look that made it clear he was standing in the way of that.

PJ burst through the door, waving a paper. "Got it!"

"Oh, good, you got the ink replaced. I never can figure out how to do that."

PJ folded the paper and stuffed it in her pocket, then took the Crock-Pot from Cole. "You go play. I'll finish this up with Mom. It sounds like they need a referee."

Cole agreed, eager to part ways with Mrs. McKinley and forget all the ugly thoughts she'd planted in his head.

"You okay?" PJ asked after her mom slipped into the house.

"I'm fine." He set a kiss on her perfect lips. "Go help your mom."

Chapter Thirty-Six

SOMETHING WAS WRONG WITH COLE. HE'D SEEMED distracted and less affectionate the last couple days. When PJ quizzed him about it, he said he was tired or anxious for Lizzy's arrival, but she couldn't help but think it was something more.

Maybe something had happened at the farmhouse. But other than the awkward questioning at the table, her family had behaved. She was glad. He needed people, needed family, more than he even knew.

But it was Sunday, and once again she was seeking him out. She found him upstairs, making the second bed in Shaundra's room.

"Knock-knock," she said.

The smile he turned on her made her insides melt. "Hey, Sunshine."

Her spirits buoyed. "Getting things ready for Lizzy?"

"Yeah. I found this bedding at the thrift store. What do you think? Something a teenaged girl would like?"

It was turquoise and yellow with giant daisies. "It's perfect. She's going to love it. I can't wait to meet her."

He straightened, the smile falling as he took in the room. A twin bed hugged each wall with one nightstand and a narrow walkway between them. A small bureau was against the opposite wall.

"It's kind of small for two, isn't it?" he said.

"No smaller than the room I shared with Jade. They'll make do. Shaundra will be a great roommate, and it's not like she'll be here much longer."

She'd decided to go straight to culinary school, starting with the summer session at Vincennes. She'd even scored a decent scholarship.

"That's true."

But then he'd be filling Shaundra's spot soon after—if he won the house. That June 1 deadline was closing in.

Cole had gone quiet, and she wondered if his thoughts were traveling the same path. They hadn't discussed what would happen. At this point, PJ didn't want to talk about it. She didn't even want to think about it.

Cole gave the porch swing a push and settled his arm around PJ. When she cuddled into his side, he tucked her head under his chin. Her hair smelled like Italian food with just a hint of the sweet flowery notes underneath.

She shivered against the chill in the evening air, and he rubbed her bare arms. She was telling him about a student in tonight's class who'd mixed up the basil and oregano, ruining her pesto.

As he listened to the lilt of her voice, his mind replayed Mrs. McKinley's words, as it had so often the past four days. Was he just another in a long line of losers? Was PJ better off without him?

She wasn't better off with Keaton. He knew that even if her mom didn't. But was he going to fail her like he had his family, his sister? Was he only going to hurt her in the end?

His phone vibrated in his pocket, and he smiled when he checked the screen. Lizzy.

"Mind if I take this? It's Lizzy."

"Not at all." PJ pulled away, a sweet smile curving her lips. She'd helped him put the finishing touches on Lizzy's room. It was all ready for her arrival at the end of the week.

"Hey, Lizzy-Lou."

Silence greeted him. Then a sniffle sounded.

"Lizzy?"

"Cole, this is Becky." Her voice was thick with tears.

Dread snaked down his spine. "What's wrong?"

"Is someone there with you?"

The sharp blade of panic cut through him. "Yes, what happened, Becky?"

"Honey, I don't know how to tell you this . . ."

He stiffened, meeting PJ's eyes. Fear flooded through him. "Is Lizzy okay?"

More sniffles. "No, honey. No, she's not. She—Greg and I came home this evening and . . . she was on the floor in her bedroom. She took Greg's pills he had left over from his surgery—all of them." Becky broke down.

PJ set her hand on his thigh, and he realized it was stuttering up and down. "Is she okay? Did they pump her stomach?"

"She—she was already gone when we got home. We called 911, but there was nothing they could do. Oh, why did I leave her alone tonight? We took the kids out for pizza, and we invited her along, but she said she had homework . . ."

She was gone? Lizzy was gone? His eyes burned, his breath felt stuffed into his lungs. His heart pummeled his chest, making an ache big enough to swallow him whole.

"That boy broke up with her yesterday. She was so upset, but this morning she seemed better, and I never dreamed—" Becky sobbed into the phone.

"Is she okay?" PJ whispered.

Cole tried to remember their last conversation. Just a few days ago. She'd seemed less excited about coming, but he thought she was just sad about leaving Braden. They hadn't been seeing each other long, though. And she mentioned that Braden could move to Chapel Springs when he graduated in June.

But now she wasn't coming. She'd never be coming. She was gone.

"Honey, are you there? Are you okay? I know how close you two were . . ."

"I'm here." Was that his flat voice? "I—I have to go."

"We'll let you know about the arrangements. Are you okay? Are you coming home?"

He swallowed hard. "Yeah. Yeah, I will. I just—I have to go."

He didn't wait for her to say good-bye. He turned off the phone, letting his hand fall to his lap. This couldn't be happening. Lizzy couldn't be gone.

PJ took his hand. "Cole? Talk to me."

He watched the hanging basket of flowers across the porch sway in the wind. He tried to remember the last time he'd seen Lizzy. He'd gone back to Fort Wayne to see her and get the rest of his things just before the kids came. She'd been crying, but he'd told her he was doing this for her and that in less than a year she'd be coming to live with him.

She'd looked up at him with those haunted blue eyes, those wire frames as crooked as always. "Promise?" she'd said.

"I promise. I'm going to take care of you."

His gut tightened painfully at the memory. He struggled to draw a breath.

"Cole?"

He turned to PJ. A rock had lodged in his throat. He tried to swallow it away. "She's dead."

PJ gasped. "Oh no." She palmed his face. "I'm so sorry."

He had to do something. He jumped up and paced across the porch. "I should go. I have to go help Becky."

"Becky?"

"Our foster mom."

"I'll go with you."

Music blared from the upstairs window, and he remembered the kids. A funeral would be a few days away. He couldn't be gone that long. He squeezed the back of his neck.

"What am I thinking? I can't leave the kids."

"I'll stay with them. Or go with you—whatever you want. My family can help."

She's gone. She's gone, and I didn't protect her. I promised, and I let her down.

Just like Noelle.

Just like Mom and Dad.

"Cole? You want me to ask my mom to come stay? I can close the restaurant for a few days."

At the mention of her mom, he shook his head. "No. I'd feel better if you stayed with the kids. You can keep the restaurant open. I should go pack."

He entered the house and went numbly up the stairs. He

didn't know PJ had followed until he was in his bedroom, grabbing his empty duffel bag.

"You can't go tonight. It's late, and it's a long drive. There's nothing you can do till morning anyway."

She was right. It would be after midnight by the time he arrived in Fort Wayne. He set the duffel bag on the bed and dropped beside it.

The mattress dipped as PJ sank down beside him. She put her arm around him. He felt her gaze on him. He wanted to lay his head in her lap and bawl his eyes out, but something stopped him. Something dammed up the tears and held his arms frozen to his sides.

"What can I do? Can I get you anything?"

"Promise?" she asked.

"Yeah, I promise. I'm going to take care of you."

The backs of his eyes burned.

"You want to talk?"

He stood, needing distance and not knowing why. "No, I just—I think I need to be alone," he squeezed out.

He didn't look back at her, didn't want to see the hurt he knew would be on her face.

"Are you sure? I can—I can stay with you, just hold you, if you want."

He gave her his best shot at a smile, but it fizzled before it even started. "I'm sure. I just—I need some time."

Chapter Thirty-Seven

THE DAY OF THE FUNERAL WAS BLEAK AND OVERCAST. A SMALL group clustered around Lizzy's casket. The pastor's words droned on, but Cole didn't hear anything he said. He stood with Greg and Becky, their extended family, and their three current foster children. Lizzy's mom, a druggie who'd shown little interest in her daughter while she lived, hadn't bothered to show for her funeral. Braden, the guy she'd been so distraught over, hadn't come either.

Cole felt something deep and black building as he stared at the small spray of roses on the casket. He'd chosen white ones dipped in turquoise, Lizzy's favorite color. The casket was the cheapest model available, but it was white with pink lining, and he thought she would've liked it.

When the funeral was over, they returned to the house. It had been ominously quiet the past three days. Greg's eyes were continually bloodshot as he helped with the kids. Becky sobbed quietly in her room several times a day. When they returned to the house, they sent the kids to their rooms to play, checked on Cole, and disappeared into their own bedroom.

Cole stared out the kitchen window into the backyard as the dark clouds finally let loose, pummeling the ground with rain. He thought of Lizzy's casket sitting at the grave site and wondered if it had been lowered into the ground.

Everywhere he looked, memories of her played like a ghostly hologram. Tugging him from bed on Saturday mornings. *"Dit up, Cole! Watch cartoons now!"* Shrieking with glee as he pushed her on the swing set out back. Struggling through math homework, her elbow on the table, head on her fist. *"I can't do it! I'm too stupid!"*

Too many memories.

And not enough.

Why, God? I should've been here. I should've figured out a way to take her with me. I should've known something was wrong. I let her down.

His phone vibrated with an incoming call. Probably PJ. She'd texted or called a couple times every day, but he'd only responded twice. He was too overwrought to deal with his feelings for her. Too tired after three nights of little sleep.

And he knew that the dark thing that had been rising inside him had everything to do with her. As much as he needed to leave this house, escape the memories, he could only dread his return to Chapel Springs.

PJ would be there, and the darkness building up in him reminded him that he didn't deserve her. Didn't deserve her love—if that's what she felt for him. He destroyed the people he loved. He wasn't worthy of someone like PJ.

The phone stopped buzzing, and he released a heavy sigh.

PJ. The kids. The house. Lizzy. It all spun in his mind like clutter caught in a tornado. He didn't know what to do about any of it. But one thing was for sure. He wasn't going to figure it out from here.

Chapter Thirty-Eight

THE RESTAURANT WAS SLAMMED DESPITE THE THUNDER-storm. One of PJ's servers was a no-show. Shaundra had filled in for a while, but she'd had to leave at seven.

"Chef, we're in the weeds out here," one of her servers called from the window. "Any chance of more help?"

PJ turned from the stove. "Already tried. Sorry. Hang in there. Rush is almost over."

"Two steamed scallops, on the fly," another server called.

"Mussels are done," called someone from the hot line. "Drop the calamari."

Callie returned from her restroom break, joining the line as though she'd never left. A few minutes later she brought over a bowl of mushrooms. "I think Cole's back."

He'd texted earlier today that he was coming home tonight, but PJ had thought he'd hunt her down when he arrived. Of course she'd been busy, and he probably hadn't wanted to interrupt.

"Why do you say that?"

"I think I saw his truck out back. And the shed light's on."

He was definitely home then. No one else went out there. She wanted to drop everything and go to him, but she couldn't leave while the kitchen was buried.

PJ sautéed the mushrooms and dropped the calamari. She

wondered how long he'd been back. She was dying to get her arms around him. She hated that he'd gone through this alone.

Not alone, PJ.

He'd had his foster parents. Still, she'd hated being apart from him while he was hurting. He hadn't communicated much while he'd been gone, but he'd been busy with funeral arrangements and, no doubt, grieving—which he seemed to prefer doing alone.

She wondered if that was because he'd never had much choice. Maybe he'd just learned to suck up his pain and deal. She hated that for him. Everyone deserved the comfort of a loving family.

Twenty minutes later things had slowed down. PJ pulled off her apron. "Taking five," she called.

"Take your time," her sous chef said. "It's under control."

She checked with the maitre d' before she left and resolved a problem with the credit card machine. The front was clearing out, and her servers didn't seem so frazzled.

She went out the back door, dashing through the rain toward the shed. She probably looked like heck in her dirtied whites and ponytail. She probably smelled like garlic and onion, too, but she couldn't help the excitement that built inside at the thought of seeing Cole again. Four days without him was four too many.

The door squawked quietly on its hinges as she pulled it open. Cole's sharp jabs thwacked the punching bag. His feet shuffled on the cement floor, and his back muscles bulged under his black T-shirt. The light from the bare overhead bulbs glinted off his dark hair. He delivered another series of punches.

Mercy, she'd missed him.

She covered the distance between them and, between punches, slipped her arms around him.

He started, stiffening.

"It's just me. You are a sight for sore eyes." PJ flattened her hands against his taut stomach. His back was warm and solid against her cheek, his shirt slightly damp. "When did you get here? You should've popped in to say hi."

He pulled off his gloves. "Haven't been here long."

She listened to his deep voice rumble in his chest.

He smelled like the soap he used, something earthy and musky. She inhaled deeply. Delicious. She realized he hadn't turned in her arms, wasn't touching her at all.

He stepped away. "I'm sweaty."

"I'm wet from the rain."

"Kitchen must be busy." He was looking everywhere but at her. "Lots of cars out there."

Why were they talking about the restaurant when they had so much catching up to do? "How'd the funeral go? You didn't say much in your texts."

He shrugged, tossing his gloves on the concrete floor. "Fine."

She couldn't imagine a funeral for an eighteen-year-old ever going fine. She looked at him closely, noting the dark circles and a vacant look in his eyes that she'd never seen before.

Fingers of dread crept up her spine. She'd only intended to share a quick hug and a kiss or two and save the rest for later. But she suddenly felt the need to stay with him.

"How'd the kids do?" he asked. "Anything come up while I was gone?"

"No, they were great. Concerned about you. They're really pretty self-sufficient these days."

"That's the plan. Thanks for your help."

"No problem. You must be so tired. And hungry. Come

inside, and I'll make you something. Tonight's special is a sea-food medley in a tomato-butter sauce—something new I tried. You'll love it."

He wiped the sheen from his face with the tail of his shirt. "I ate on the way home. Thanks, though."

Thunder cracked, so close the building rattled. Rain pummeled the roof. He looked toward the door, his jaw clenching.

"You okay?"

"It's pouring."

They spoke at the same time.

His eyes ricocheted off her. "I'm fine. Just tired, like you said."

She took in his rigid stance, hands pocketed in his basketball shorts. "It seems like more than that."

He gave her a tight smile. Outside the rain picked up, growing even louder. "You should probably get back to the kitchen. We can catch up later."

The fingers of dread tightened around her spine. "What's going on, Cole?"

His sigh seemed to come from his feet. "It's been a long day, PJ."

"Has something changed?" She winced. *Of course something's changed, PJ. Lizzy died.* "I mean, I know something's changed. I meant, between us? Are we okay?"

He palmed the back of his neck. "I really don't want to do this right now."

She stepped closer. "Did I do something wrong?"

"No."

"Talk to me."

"It's nothing that can't wait until closing."

"Just tell me."

"You're in the middle of supper."

"*Tell me.*"

"Fine. I can't do this," he blurted, then pressed his lips together like he wished he could call back the words.

PJ wished he could too. Wished she would've been more patient. Wished she'd just kissed him, made him forget whatever was eating him up.

"Can't do what?" She hated how small and weak she sounded.

"Can't we just table this for now?"

"This conversation, you mean?"

"Let it go, PJ."

"This? Us? That's what you can't do?" *Please, no. Tell me I'm wrong. Tell me you're tired and cranky and didn't mean it the way it sounded.* She longed for him to take her in his arms and press a kiss to her forehead like he'd done before and tell her there was nothing to worry about.

Instead he turned, palming the back of his neck. Several long seconds passed. Seconds filled with thudding heartbeats and shallow breaths.

When he finally turned to face her, the hard look in his eyes made her wish he hadn't.

"I did a lot of thinking while I was gone." His voice was smooth and calm. "I think we need to cool things off."

"Cool things off . . ."

Thunder struck outside. Inside.

"This isn't going to work between us."

"You're just . . . grieving. You've had a traumatic week, and you're upset, understandably so. Take a few days and—"

"It's not that."

Her eyes burned and a lump swelled in her throat. "Why are you doing this?" Her voice wobbled. "What happened?"

Something flickered in his eyes before he looked away, his jaw going rock hard. "Nothing happened. I told you, I had a few days to think, got a fresh perspective. We're not good for each other, PJ. This isn't going to work. We just need to finish our time here and go our separate ways."

She didn't know who this person was. This stranger standing here without an ounce of warmth in his face, in his voice. She didn't want to know him. She wanted her Cole to come back. The one who couldn't let her pass without a touch, the one who caressed her face with heartbreaking tenderness, the one who held her so tightly she felt safe and cherished.

What had happened? She swallowed against the knot in her throat, forced back the tears that threatened. Was there someone else? Someone back home he'd never told her about? A relationship he'd rekindled?

Jealousy burned in her gut. "Is there someone else?"

His eyes darted to hers. "No."

She saw no signs of deceit in his face, in his posture. But then, she'd seen no signs of deceit in Keaton either, and he'd lied to her for months.

Maybe her family was right. Maybe she did have poor judgment. Maybe she did make bad decisions. Maybe she wouldn't know a good man if he fell at her feet.

She gave a wry laugh, remembering that Cole *had* fallen at her feet, the very first time she'd met him. She had a compelling urge to repeat the scenario.

So they were back to this? The past four weeks meant nothing to him?

She lifted her chin, meeting his gaze. "Whatever you say, Cole. I have work to do."

She brushed past him, hit the door with a force that knocked it back on its hinges. She strode toward the house, barely feeling the shards of rain. Barely feeling the pain rising up to choke her.

~

The shed door clanked against the wall and rain pelted in. It took everything in Cole not to follow her. The sheen in her eyes had about killed him. He'd ached to take her in his arms and kiss away the pain. To tell her he didn't mean any of it.

Instead he knotted his fists and forced his feet to hold their ground. She might hate him now, but this was better for her in the long run. His breaths came heavily, doing nothing to ease the ache in his chest.

How could she think there was someone else? Didn't she know he was dying inside at the thought of hurting her? That he hated himself for letting things get this far when he'd known all along who he was, what he deserved?

The blackness rose from deep inside, closing in like a thick fog. His breaths accelerated, the heaviness crushing down on his shoulders. He advanced on the punching bag and delivered a bare-fisted jab. Then another and another, until the ache in his hands matched the one in his heart.

Chapter Thirty-Nine

PJ DRAGGED HERSELF OUT OF BED THE NEXT MORNING. She'd tossed and turned all night, the bite of anger edging out any trace of weariness. Why did it seem like Cole was always making the calls? *We need to take a step back . . . We need to cool things off . . .* Didn't her feelings matter?

As she slipped into her jacket in the foyer, Cole came down the stairs. Every nerve ending was aware of him. Of the familiar rhythm of his footfalls, of the way his keys jingled in his pocket, of the clean morning scent that wrapped around him.

His steps faltered when he saw her. He gave a tight smile, his eyes as distant as the rising sun. "Good morning."

She hardly had time to respond as he skirted around her, heading to the back door. A moment later the door shut and then his truck started.

Her body deflated like a punctured balloon. Somehow in all her tossing and turning, she'd convinced herself that his decision had been a response to losing Lizzy. That he was tired and hurt, and that he'd change his mind once he slept on it.

But all that hope sputtered out of her body now.

She went to the early service and sat with her family, stretching a fake smile across her face. When she returned home she helped her staff ready for the brunch. The day passed with agonizing slowness, anger building with each passing hour. She slept badly that night and spent the next day cooking up a storm of food she ended up giving away to a single mother from church.

The next days passed in a flurry of cooking and classes. Cole worked until dark and slipped into the house unseen. They were strangers again, except now she felt his absence keenly.

A week went by, then two. When the anger faded she wished for it back because pain had come to take its place.

Cole had been in a funk since Lizzy died. Even the kids had noticed. They tried to distract him with offers of basketball or Ping-Pong. He went through the motions, but he missed Lizzy so much he felt dead inside. He couldn't remember feeling so lost since the car accident that took his family. Some nights he woke, his breathing ragged, his thoughts racing.

Then there was PJ. Everything in him longed to take the two flights of stairs, wake her with a tender kiss, and tell her he was sorry. That he was wrong.

But he wasn't wrong. This was the right thing for her. She'd get over him eventually, move on, find someone worthy of her. Someone who could protect her, someone who wouldn't let her down. He was doing what was best for her because that's what you did when you loved someone. And he did. So much.

He just had to get through this. *Help me, God. Help me let her go.*

While he installed windows he let his mind wander a few months into the future, making plans. If she won the house, he'd go back to Fort Wayne, get a job. The kids would be self-sufficient by then. He'd blown through his savings but he could start over. Get more benefactors. He could do this again some-where else someday.

And fail them, like you failed Lizzy?

He shook the thought away. If he won the house, he'd go through the applications he'd received, narrow it down. Take four kids immediately while he renovated the downstairs, made the dining room into more bedrooms. He'd need a few more sponsors, but he could speak at some of the area churches and try to rally more support.

But the thought of undoing all of PJ's hard work, the thought of stealing her dream, felt like a blow to the solar plexus. If she lost, she'd feel like a failure in front of her family. Maybe even deep inside. It would only reinforce the things she believed about herself—things that weren't true.

To top it off, he'd have to see her around town. He'd run into her at the grocery or at Cappy's. Eventually she'd start dating another man, get serious, and he'd see them together, holding hands, gazing into each other's eyes. He'd watch her give her heart to someone else, watch her start a life with someone else.

He could hardly bear the thought. But he didn't know what else to do.

The answer came a couple weeks before presentation day in the middle of the night. His eyes flew open, and he knew what he had to do. Loving PJ meant letting go. Letting go of his dream, letting go of her. Completely. He'd leave her with her dream intact. This was her home, where her family lived, where she belonged. He was the outsider. He could go anywhere.

Later that day he was still working out the details when Zac barreled into the living room.

"I got the job!" he said.

Josh turned from the sink full of dishes and gave him a wet high five. "Congrats, bro."

Cole shook Zac's hand and pulled him in for a man hug. "Knew you could do it." After interning at a local garage, he'd scored a full-time job as a mechanic at the local Buick dealer.

"They want me to start right after school ends."

"Perfect."

Josh had gotten a promotion the week before. When school ended in two weeks, he'd be the assistant manager in the produce department. After scouring the newspaper for an apartment to share, he and Zac had found a place they could afford. They were moving out the last week of May. Shaundra was moving out a few days earlier to settle in at Vincennes for the summer session.

He watched Zac grab something from the fridge, watched Josh scrubbing a pan, and took a moment to appreciate all they'd accomplished over the past eight months. They weren't kids anymore. They were young adults, and in two weeks' time they'd be out on their own. Moving on with their lives.

He tried to feel good about that. But thoughts of Lizzy smothered his pride before it had a chance to swell. He shook the thoughts from his head. He didn't want to think about Lizzy.

He settled on the couch and flicked on the TV, losing himself in a Reds game. An hour later the boys had turned in for the night. He flipped off the game and leaned forward, elbows planted on his knees. He needed to go to bed. He had to be up early. But his bed had become a place of torture where he thought endlessly of PJ and every intimate moment they'd shared.

Even though the restaurant was closed now, delicious smells wafted upstairs. It seemed cooking was all PJ did lately, and these days she wasn't offering any samples.

He hadn't seen her in days, had arranged it so their paths didn't cross. It was better that way. Better for her. Never mind that he lay in bed trying to remember the sweet flower smell of her. Trying to remember the silky texture of her hair on his fingers, the satiny softness of her skin.

Living with her was a new kind of hell. In just two weeks he'd be leaving her for good, and it would get easier. At least that's what he told himself.

Chapter Forty

PJ CROUCHED DOWN, SCANNING THE BOOKSHELVES IN HER room for the cookbook. Where was her copy of *Gourmet*? She wanted to make coq au vin for the weekend special, and the recipe she'd just experimented with didn't measure up.

By the time the sauce had properly thickened, the chicken was overcooked. *Gourmet* had a recipe for making the sauce, then cooking the chicken in it. She'd made it once in culinary school, and it had been a big hit. The meat was flambéed in cognac and the sauce thickened with beurre manié. The dish was rich and savory, and the chicken far more tender than the recipe she'd tried.

She frowned at her bookshelves. Where was it? The thought of losing all those great recipes, recipes she'd tweaked and honed, with notes jotted in the margins, made her want to cry.

She thought back, trying to remember the last time she'd used it . . . with Shaundra! And she'd asked to borrow it to make copies.

Shaundra was still at work, but the book was probably in her room. She hoped. She'd just run up and get it. Cole was surely in bed. She checked her watch. It was getting late, but she could sleep in tomorrow. Besides, it wasn't like she'd been sleeping anyway.

She should be working on her presentation for Mrs. Simmons instead of experimenting with recipes. She had only two weeks left and hours yet to go before she was ready. But she didn't even want to think about that tonight.

She left her room, pausing in the foyer to listen. All was quiet upstairs. No footsteps or TV or wailing guitars. The lights were out.

PJ crept up the stairs and tiptoed down the hall. In the bathroom a pool of light spilled across the sink from the night-light. The floor creaked as she passed the boys' door. The living room was dark and quiet.

Shaundra's door was cracked. PJ tapped quietly just in case, then eased the door open and flipped on the lamp. Her eyes swept the tidy room. Lizzy's unused bed was still covered with the turquoise daisy blanket. Sadness swept over her, threatening to take her under.

No. She wasn't going there tonight. Wasn't going to think about Lizzy or Cole or how she never saw him anymore even though they lived under the same roof. It was disgraceful how many hours she could spend thinking about someone she didn't see. Someone who didn't want her.

She pushed the thought away, slipping into the room as she scanned it. There. On the nightstand. Whew! After grabbing the copy of *Gourmet*, she shut off the light and turned to pull the door, cringing at the squeak.

When she turned, a body blocked her path. She sucked in a breath before she recognized the shadowed form. She set her hand on her heart.

"Cole. You scared me."

"Thought you were Shaundra."

They spoke simultaneously.

"I was just—getting the newspaper," he said.

PJ held up the book, her heart hammering. "My cookbook. Shaundra borrowed it. I'm making coq au vin for Friday, but my recipe isn't right, the chicken was overcooked, and I thought I'd—"

Shut it, PJ! She clamped her lips closed.

She felt his eyes on her in the dark, heard him draw a deep, quiet breath, as if he were breathing her in.

She stilled. Even her breath seemed to freeze in her lungs. Did he miss her? Did he regret breaking up? Did he lie awake at night too, remembering their kisses?

"Cole . . ."

"I should get to bed . . . Good night." He took the steps to the attic, seemingly forgetting about the newspaper.

PJ's breath escaped, his sudden departure leaving her drained and tired.

Chapter Forty-One

THE NEXT DAY PJ WAS RESTLESS. SHE KEPT REVIEWING THE moment in the hallway and wondering if she'd imagined the breath he'd drawn. She must've. He was the one who'd broken up with her. If he missed her he wouldn't be working all hours, hiding upstairs, and sneaking breaths of her.

She worked on her presentation most of the morning. Mrs. Simmons had sent them an e-mail explaining the information they should include and how the day would work. They would meet at the town hall and give their presentations to the board. Cole would go first, opposite of last time. Mrs. Simmons would announce the winner the next day. She'd arranged for an interview with the *Gazette* for the winner and a feature in *Southern Indiana*.

PJ's numbers looked very promising. She had all the right things on paper. The restaurant, while slow in the winter, had picked back up. She'd gotten endorsements from several VIPs, including the mayor, and was including Maeve Daughtry's glowing review. She also had a newspaper article on local job growth that had mentioned her restaurant.

On the B & B front she had quotes from the tourist board about the community's need for additional lodging. She had a very compelling case, with facts and figures to back it up.

So why did she feel so down? Why did the thought of winning the house no longer excite her as it once had? Why did she still feel empty inside even though she'd done exactly what she'd set out to accomplish?

She was tired of mulling this over. She closed her laptop and set it on her nightstand.

Ten minutes later she entered her mom's antique shop. The bell tinkled in welcome, and the familiar musty smell of Grandma's Attic assaulted her.

Her mom slipped from her office, her face lighting up. "PJ, what a lovely surprise."

PJ hugged her. "Hi, Mom."

Mom returned the embrace, then ran her hands across PJ's shoulders and down her arms. "You're losing weight. Are you eating?"

"I'm a chef, Mom, of course I'm eating." Just maybe not enough.

"Come to my office. I was just having lunch."

Her mom's office was more like a turn-of-the-century sitting room, complete with wingback chairs and fireplace. A Turkish rug cushioned the wood floor. PJ perched on the edge of the rose-colored sofa across from her mother.

Mom pushed half her chicken salad sandwich across the coffee table. "Eat."

PJ wasn't hungry, but she knew better than to argue. "This is tasty," she said after taking a bite. "Grapes, almonds . . . nice flavor." She'd add some curry and a pinch of salt. Less celery.

"It's Deb Tackett's recipe—she brought it to the last Rotary meeting."

"Nice. Store been busy?"

"Not too bad. I finally sold that French armoire, the one in the front by the old telephone booth?"

"That green monstrosity?"

Mom pursed her lips. "It was just waiting for the right buyer. And I made a nice profit. How about you? How are you feeling? Is your anxiety better?"

"I haven't had an attack in weeks. My lab work came back normal at my last checkup. Dr. Lewis said my thyroid has stabilized."

"That's great, honey. And you won't have any more episodes?"

She shrugged. "I have to get regular lab work to keep an eye on it, but he seemed encouraged."

"I haven't seen you in over a week. The restaurant must be busy."

"It has been. If we weren't so close to the deadline, I'd have hired more help a few weeks ago."

She took another bite of her sandwich. As it was, she could hardly expect people to apply when there was a fifty-fifty shot of losing their job come June 1. She was days away from possibly losing everything she'd worked the last year for. At the thought, she waited for the anxiety to kick in, but it never arrived. Not even when she reminded herself of the loan.

Her thoughts turned to Cole instead, and she wondered how he was faring. She wondered if he'd selected his next round of kids, just in case. She wondered who they were and where they'd come from—what would happen to them if Cole lost the house.

"Speaking of the deadline," Mom said, "how's your presentation coming along?"

And there it was. How did her mom manage to know exactly what was bugging her?

PJ set down the remainder of the sandwich and wiped her

mouth with a napkin. "I think I've made a really strong case. I'm turning a profit, the community response has been great, and everyone knows we need more housing around here."

"But . . ."

The smile slid from PJ's face. What was wrong with her? This was everything she wanted. She'd barely made it through the winter, but in the future she'd have a full tourist season of profitability to carry her through. And a B & B would be more lucrative than the restaurant.

"I don't know, Mom. Something's missing."

"From the proposal?"

If only it were that easy. Her eyes darted to her mother. "From me."

Mom set down her sandwich and tilted her head, her blue eyes questioning.

"I wanted this so badly a year ago. And the more I worked at it, the more I wanted it. I wanted to prove that I could do it, you know? To the family. And maybe to myself too."

"To us?"

PJ sighed. "I know you all love me, Mom, but everyone's always second-guessing me and thinking I need help and can't do it on my own, and I guess I just wanted to prove that I was capable. I was so busy trying to prove myself when I got out of school that I lost perspective. It's been all about that and not about what I want."

"You don't want the restaurant and B & B?"

"Yes, I do. I do want it." But at the expense of Cole's dream? "I worked hard, and the restaurant is really viable. I have a good shot at winning, and I still . . . I just thought I'd feel differently. I don't like the way I feel about myself. Like I'm not capable, despite the evidence to the contrary."

Mom covered PJ's hand. "Oh, honey, I'm so sorry. I never meant to make you feel that way. I guess . . . you're our baby . . . we want to take care of you. We never meant to make you doubt yourself. Of course you're capable. God made you a bright, competent young woman."

"I don't feel that way."

"Feelings can be misleading. Remember that scripture . . . the heart is deceitful above all things? If your heart's telling you you're not capable, it's lying. What's God telling you?"

PJ made a face. "Honestly? I haven't asked in a while. I've been too busy trying to make a success of myself."

Mom squeezed her hand. "Well, it's never too late. We all have thorns, you know."

"Thorns?"

"Those things that rise up around us, strangling us. Thorns don't keep a seed from sprouting, but they'll keep it from producing fruit. You have so many good things ahead of you, PJ."

"But I've made so many bad decisions." Like Keaton and virtually every boy she'd dated before him. Had the house been a mistake too?

Mom squeezed her hand. "We all make bad decisions sometimes. Cut that thorn away, and see how God nourishes your life."

Chapter Forty-Two

PJ KNOCKED ON RYAN'S DOOR, BALANCING HER WILD BERRY cheesecake on her other hand. She'd finished her proposal last night, but she still felt disquiet in her soul. Tomorrow was the big day.

She'd been praying hard over the last week since she'd talked with her mom, getting back to her devotions. She had a feeling her self-doubt wasn't going away overnight, but it was time to put things in her life back in order. Get back on track. She had new clarity about that.

About the house, not so much.

Ryan swung the door open.

"I come bearing edible gifts."

"In that case, come on in."

She ducked under his arm. "How was work?"

"Not bad."

She took in the room on her way to the kitchen. "Hey, the living room is looking great. I didn't think you'd have enough things to fill it out."

"Everything I own is in this room except my bed."

She set the cheesecake and topping on the butcher-block island and scanned the room. The kitchen floor had been under construction when they'd moved him in, so she hadn't seen this room. Marble counters topped the rustic blue cabinets. A small window over the farm sink overlooked the backyard. It was old and quaint and lacked the little touches like curtains and cookie jars and dish towels, but she immediately thought of Abby. His ex-wife would've loved it.

"Thanks for the cheesecake."

Her eyes swept over the range and she gasped. "A Wedgewood! A white vintage Wedgewood double oven with a gas stovetop and six burners! What a beauty."

"It probably doesn't even work."

Her head snapped around. "You mean you don't know? You've been here three months! Didn't I teach you anything in class?"

"What can I say? I'm a bachelor, and that thing is ancient." He gestured to the microwave and toaster. "Those are the only appliances I'll ever need."

PJ patted the glossy range. "Shhh. He didn't mean it, baby."

Ryan rummaged through a drawer, coming up with a knife. "I'm going to slice this sucker. Want some?"

"No thanks."

When he had his slice they retired to the back porch. It was smaller than the one at the Wishing House, but the Adirondack chairs were a nice touch. "These new?"

"Yeah."

The yard was big and shaded by thick oak trees. Somewhere nearby, the buzz of a mower droned. She inhaled the smell of freshly cut grass. "You need some flowers back here, maybe a hanging basket."

"I have about as much skill there as you." He forked a strawberry. "So what are you doing over here? Besides trying to fatten me up."

PJ shrugged. "Zac and Josh moved out on Friday, and Shaundra moved to Vincennes on Sunday. The house is too quiet." Next door a couple picnicked with their two small children. "Are the neighbors nice?"

He glanced up at the little family, his face going sad. "Yeah, they're great." His eyes shifted to the tire swing, then back to his plate.

She wanted to ask him about Abby, but last time hadn't gone too well. "You doing okay?" she asked instead. "You seem kind of . . . down."

"I know what you mean about a quiet house. You were right, what you said a few months ago. It gets a little lonely around here." He scraped up a bit of cheesecake and dragged it through the sauce. "But I'll be fine. I have work to keep myself busy . . . football . . . the fire department . . . reality shows."

She wanted so much more than that for him. He was a good man, and he had so much love to give. "You should go out more. I could set you up with one of my friends . . . I was just talking to—"

"No. No more blind dates. My last one . . ." He shuddered, then finished off the last of the cheesecake and set the plate aside. "You were right about something else."

"Wow, two things in one day."

The wind rustled his dark hair as he looked out over the yard. She knew he was thinking about Abby, and as much as she wanted to ask, patience was key with Ryan. He'd tell her when he was ready, and not a second before.

"I'm not over her," he said finally. "I've tried to date other women, but . . . they're just not Abby, you know? I miss her."

"I'm sorry, Ryan."

"I have a lot of regrets. I should've done things differently. Should've tried harder, loved her better. She deserved that."

"Sometimes it just doesn't work out, no matter how hard you try." Heartbreak was bittersweet. She was learning that for herself.

"Maybe."

"Do you ever, you know, think of trying again, with Abby?"

He breathed a laugh. Crossed his arms. She could tell by the look on his face he thought about it all the time.

"You know what the last thing she said to me was?" He looked at PJ. "She said, 'It's over this time, Ryan. Don't call me, don't text me, don't even look at me. We're done.' And then she moved two hundred miles away just to make sure."

The sheen in his eyes nearly broke her heart. "I'm sorry, Ryan." She wished there were something she could do. Something she could say. But she couldn't heal Ryan's heart. She couldn't even heal her own.

He sat back in his chair, drew a deep breath, and seemed to shake off some of the melancholy. "So . . . what happened with you and Cole? Madison just said things didn't work out."

That's pretty much the explanation PJ had given to everyone. She shrugged and told him about Lizzy's death and Cole's change of heart upon his return. Then she told him about the accident that had taken his family.

"I don't know, Ryan. He's lost so much, and he blames himself for his family's death."

"That's a lot of weight to carry."

She remembered the look on Cole's face when he'd told her about the accident, those haunted eyes, and wondered if he blamed himself for Lizzy's death too. For not being there, for not knowing.

"Maybe that's part of the reason he started that house," he said.

"What do you mean?"

"Maybe he's trying to make up for what he thinks he did. Sometimes guilt makes people do things so they can compensate for past mistakes. Maybe every time he saves a kid, it's like he's saving his family. A do-over."

The explanation pulled a curtain from PJ's eyes. A do-over. Was that what Cole was doing? "Oh my gosh."

"Sometimes I can be right too."

"He couldn't save his family, but he can save others. Is that even healthy?"

"I don't see why not, as long as he comes to realize he wasn't at fault to begin with."

"I told him it wasn't his fault." She thought of her own issues with self-doubt. Just because people told her she was capable didn't mean her heart believed it. "But it's not that easy, is it?"

"It's a start."

She had a fresh understanding now about believing things that weren't true. She'd done the same thing. The lies they'd each told themselves had wreaked havoc inside. *Lord, show him the truth. Show* me *the truth.*

Her heart wrenched to think of the self-blame he'd lived with all these years. She wanted to tell him over and over it wasn't his fault until he believed it. She wanted to take him in her arms and soothe away the pain. But she didn't have that right anymore.

"Do you love him?"

Her heart clenched. She yearned for his touch. She wanted what was best for him.

She thought of tomorrow and all the changes it would bring.

One of them would be moving from the house. The thought of Cole leaving Chapel Springs stole her breath. The thought of taking his dream made her ache all over.

"Hey." Ryan nudged her foot with the toe of his tennis shoe. "If you do, don't let him walk out of your life. If there's anything I've learned through all this with Abby, it's that regret makes a very poor companion."

Ryan understood her misery. Alone in this big house. Would that be her, one week from now? "I know what you mean about missing Abby. I miss Cole so much—and we still live in the same house."

"Until tomorrow."

Yes, everything would change tomorrow. She thought of her presentation on her laptop, all her i's dotted, all her t's crossed. She had a strong chance of winning. A strong chance of taking away Cole's dream—his do-over.

Her stomach knotted at the thought. Could she do that? Did she even want to? What would that do to him? And so soon after losing Lizzy?

A bright light flashed on in her mind, providing sharp clarity. She did love Cole. So much. And if she loved him, she couldn't take away something he needed so badly.

If she loved him, she'd sacrifice her own desires for him.

She popped to her feet. "I have to go." She rushed past Ryan and into the house.

"What'd I say?" Ryan called.

She threw a hand in the air. "I'll talk to you later. There's something I have to do."

Chapter Forty-Three

PJ ENTERED THE TOWN HALL ON TREMBLING LEGS. SHE HAD practiced her presentation all morning. Because of a scheduling conflict with a board member, Cole's presentation had ended over an hour ago.

She sat in the lobby, cradling her laptop. Her leg bounced up and down. *Settle down, PJ.* She had to make this happen for Cole. Surely Mrs. Simmons would see what a treasure Crossroads was. How badly these kids needed his help. Just look at what he'd done with Zac, Josh, and Shaundra in nine months.

The door opened, and Mrs. Simmons greeted her with a delicate embrace. "PJ, dear, how lovely to see you."

"You're looking well, Mrs. Simmons."

"Oh, the Colorado climate agrees with me. And all those great-grandchildren are keeping me young. Come in, come in, the board is all here. Snowball too. I just can't bear to leave her more than a few days."

PJ followed the shuffling woman into the large open hall, her heels echoing on the wood floor. Snowball sat regally on the end of the table, her tail flicking silently.

"There's been a change of plans, dear, if you want to just set your things down a minute."

Change of plans? PJ greeted the board, who sat behind the

long table as before. After shaking their hands, she set her laptop and note cards on the small table they'd provided. There were two empty easels up front, and a white screen was pulled down against the brick wall in readiness.

Mrs. Simmons lowered herself to the padded chair, folding her bejeweled hands on the table. "As you know, Mr. Evans was in earlier for his presentation. The board and I were astonished to hear that he wishes to withdraw from the competition."

PJ's mouth went slack. "What?"

"He didn't discuss this with you, I presume?"

He quit? PJ's words got stuck in her throat. She shook her head.

"He no longer wishes to stay in Chapel Springs—for personal reasons, he said."

PJ shrank inside. Shriveled up and died. Living in separate houses wasn't enough, apparently. He wanted to live in separate towns.

"This was a most unexpected development. We've heard nothing but good things about Crossroads and the children under his care. And despite Mr. Evans's unfortunate encounter with the law awhile back, we believe him to be an upstanding citizen and a capable young man."

PJ nodded.

"The board and I have discussed this turn of events. We've also heard many wonderful things about your restaurant, and of course your reports have been encouraging, especially during the warm months. You've recovered nicely from the off-season and are turning a lovely profit. We've reviewed your previous presentation regarding the bed-and-breakfast and agree that the community would benefit from extra lodging.

"To sum it up, dear, we believe in you and your vision, and therefore we're thrilled to award the Wishing House to you. Congratulations!"

The board members beamed at her, applauding.

PJ forced a smile to her face. This wasn't supposed to happen. This wasn't what she wanted. What about Cole? What about Crossroads?

But Cole had quit. Was leaving her.

The board members approached, shaking her hand, congratulating her. PJ worked to keep the smile on her face, mumbled words of gratitude that didn't register in her brain. Mrs. Simmons patted her on the back like a proud mother hen, then notified her that the closing date on the house was scheduled in thirty days. When the woman was finished, she gathered her belongings and filed out the back with the rest of the board.

PJ left the building. Her mind spun as she got in her car and headed toward home. What the heck had just happened?

Why had Cole quit? Was it really to escape her? Was it too late to change things? To talk him out of it? Why would he do this? She knew how much helping those kids meant to him. He needed to do this. Wouldn't be able to do it anywhere else, not now that he'd spent all his resources on Crossroads.

She had to change his mind. Had to tell him she was dropping out, that the house was his. She'd fix this. Tell him he didn't have to go. That she would leave. The board would understand. If they didn't, she'd give her presentation and convince them of it.

She pulled to the curb and dashed toward the house, taking the porch steps two at a time. She entered the quiet house.

She leaped up the stairs, flipping on a light as she raced down the hallway. "Cole!"

Her heart raced faster than her feet. She'd been trembling all morning, at the thought of her presentation and now in anticipation of seeing Cole, of having a real conversation—something they hadn't shared in weeks.

Her legs quaked as she jogged up the attic steps. She knocked on the door. "Cole, it's me."

She drew in a breath, trying to calm herself. She could fix this. It wasn't too late. She just had to convince Cole to stay and convince the board to change their minds. If she quit, what other choice would they have?

She knocked again, becoming aware that all was still on the other side of the door. Not a sound of movement inside.

"Cole?" She turned the doorknob.

His room slowly came into view. Her lips parted. Dread sucked the air from her lungs, leaving them hollow and aching. Her heart fought for release.

His bed, his furniture, his makeshift nightstand and piles of clothes. All of it was gone.

Chapter Forty-Four

He'd left her. He'd packed up his things and split. Couldn't get away from her fast enough. He hadn't even said good-bye. The realization was a punch in the gut. PJ closed the door and went numbly down the stairs. The adrenaline rush left her limbs weak and shaky.

She reviewed the past few weeks for any hint she might've missed. Things had been awkward. He'd avoided her, of course. Had he really been so miserable here with her that he'd had to forfeit his dream? That he'd had to leave town the moment he had the opportunity?

Her phone vibrated in her pocket, and PJ grabbed for it. Her heart sank when she saw it was her mom. She was no doubt curious how the presentation had gone—PJ hadn't told anyone what she'd planned. Or maybe Mom had heard via the grapevine that PJ had been awarded the house and was calling to congratulate her.

When the phone stopped buzzing, she turned it on and called Josh. "Hey, Josh, this is PJ," she said when he answered. "Have you heard from Cole today?"

"Yeah, he stopped by the grocery store when I was on break and said he was leaving town. Wished me luck. Told me to call him if I needed anything."

"Did he—did he say why?" PJ swallowed hard.

"Naw, not really. I'm really bummed he's shutting down Crossroads. Tried to talk him out of it."

When she got off the phone, she sank onto a step and dialed again. When Zac had gotten home from work, he'd found a note from Cole on his door telling him good-bye.

Officially at a new low, PJ hung up.

A note. She sat up straight, hope blooming. Maybe he'd left her a note. She popped to her feet and dashed to her room, flinging open the bedroom door. Her eyes scanned the dresser where he'd left the vase of flowers on Valentine's Day. They darted to her armoire, to her nightstand, and across her unmade bed.

Her spirits sank as hope came crashing down. Not even a note.

Cole turned off the radio. The on-air bickering over a baseball team was wearing on his nerves. People calling in, ragging on the coach, complaining about the record. These people needed to get a life.

By now the board had granted PJ the house. She had her dream. Her proof that she was capable. Her family would support her, the community would get behind her, and PJ would start believing in herself.

He'd already arranged for his own new start. He'd gotten his job installing windows back. He'd stay at Greg and Becky's until he found an apartment. No matter how he tried to convince himself otherwise, his new life sounded bleak.

The miles between him and Chapel Springs, between him

and PJ, stretched with each second. He felt more hollow by the moment, but he told himself it would get better. Time healed all wounds. Eventually he'd go two seconds without thinking of her, then two minutes, two hours. In time he'd go a whole day without thinking of her. Without aching for her. Right?

Please, God.

He thought of all he'd left behind. Crossroads, Zac, and Josh. He'd miss those guys. He already missed Shaundra.

He was sad for those four kids he'd chosen from the many applications he'd received. Kids who wouldn't have the same opportunity Zac, Josh, and Shaundra had been given. A weight settled heavily in his chest. There would be another house someday. Other kids. He wasn't giving up.

He said a prayer for those four kids, that God would provide a safe place for them and for all the kids he hadn't chosen.

Out of nowhere PJ cannonballed into his mind, with her chocolate brown eyes and her wide smile. It had been weeks since he'd seen that smile. He allowed himself the luxury of remembering the feel of those sweet lips on his, the feel of her silky hair in his fingers. He could hardly stand the thought of not seeing her, not touching her or holding her. The last several weeks had been so hard, but he had a feeling the "hard" had only begun. The ache opened wide, nearly swallowing him, and he tightened his grip on the steering wheel.

I miss her, God.

A sign ahead proclaimed Fort Wayne ninety-two miles away. He clenched his jaw and pressed harder on the gas pedal. The sooner he arrived, the sooner he could put PJ and everything from Chapel Springs behind him.

Chapter Forty-Five

PJ PUT UP A SHOT. IT BOUNCED OFF THE RIM AND RIGHT into Beckett's hands. He made a lay-up, despite Madison's over-the-back. The game-winning shot.

Madison poked her husband in the ribs. "Lucky shot."

Beckett high-fived PJ. "And we win again."

"No thanks to me." She was off her game tonight. "I'm going to sit the next one out." She left the concrete pad as teams reorganized, following the flagstones across the lawn toward the new swing set.

In the distance the sunset silhouetted the cornfields on the horizon. Dusk had settled in, blanketing her parents' backyard with evening light. The landscaping lights twinkled against the encroaching darkness, and the oscillating buzz of katydids called from the nearby woods.

Mom was pushing Mia in the toddler swing. A tiny purple barrette clasped a shock of brown hair at the top of the baby's head.

"P-Day!" the toddler said as PJ approached, her chubby legs kicking happily.

"Hi, baby girl." PJ took the low swing beside her, her long legs folded awkwardly.

"Sing!"

"Are you swinging? Is Grammy pushing you?"

"Sing!"

"She does love to swing," Mom said.

"Where's Ava?"

"Dad took her inside so Jade and Daniel could take a walk. Beautiful night."

"It is."

The noise of the basketball game filtered over: the ball slapping the concrete, shoes grinding against loose gravel, playful teasing. The familiar sounds of family and home should've been comforting. Instead PJ felt nothing but discontent.

She straightened her cramped legs and clasped the cool metal links in her palms. If she were honest, she'd felt nothing but discontent for three weeks. Ever since she'd won the house. The irony wasn't lost on her.

Keeping the restaurant open had been easy enough. Her employees were grateful to have their jobs. She'd even hired another line cook and another server. She'd been busy, the restaurant was flourishing, and the upstairs remained untouched.

"You've been quiet lately. Everything okay with the restaurant?"

PJ forced a smile. She'd been doing that a lot lately. "Business is great. Couldn't be better. My new line cook is good. He worked at the Candlelight Café for seven years."

Mom gave Mia a push. "And the B & B? How are your plans coming along?"

She was supposed to get another loan. The rooms needed nicer furnishings, and she needed to hire a housekeeper and someone to answer the phone and handle check-ins during restaurant hours. She needed to order a new sign, set a grand opening date, and work on some marketing plans.

She'd done none of it. She'd gone upstairs exactly twice. The first time she'd noticed Cole had left the furniture in the kids' rooms, the living room. The second time she'd planned to make a list of things she needed. She'd planned to make the living room and dining room into a suite. But she'd taken one step into the kitchen and remembered all Cole's hard work. He'd done it with his own two hands. Installed shelving, painted, laid flooring. And now she was going to come in and undo all his hard work?

She'd stared at the doorway, remembering their first kiss while a lump swelled in her throat. What she'd give if she could turn back time and undo everything. But what would she do differently? She didn't even understand what had gone wrong. Maybe she'd scared him away, clung too hard.

"PJ?"

She blinked. "Um, sorry. I—what were we talking about?"

Mom gave her a sympathetic look. "The B & B. I have a new girl helping out part time at the store. I could take a few days off next week and help you paint or polish floors, whatever you need."

"I haven't really done anything with the upstairs yet."

"Are you waiting for the closing?"

A mere six days, and the house would be in her name. "I guess so."

"Dad and I saw the article in *Southern Indiana* this week. Beautiful shots of the restaurant and of you in your whites."

"Thanks." The feature had been well written. It all looked so good in black and white. Sounded so perfect. Local girl wins dream home. Woohoo.

"Honey, what's wrong? I thought you'd be ecstatic about winning. You worked so hard, and you did it. But I don't think

I've ever seen you so unhappy and withdrawn. Is it too much? Are you overwhelmed?"

"No, Mom, I'm not overwhelmed."

"What is it then?"

She hadn't told her family how it had all gone down. Maybe she'd needed them to believe that she'd earned the house. That she'd won it on her own and not because Cole had forfeited. Somehow that didn't matter anymore. All that mattered was she was lost without Cole and worried about how he was faring after losing both his dream and Lizzy.

"Down," Mia said.

Mom lifted Mia from the swing and set her on the ground. She toddled toward the pink push car, her short legs working fast.

"I didn't exactly win the house, Mom."

"What do you mean?"

"He quit. Cole forfeited, so they gave the house to me."

Mom leaned against the swing's A-frame, appearing to digest the information. A playful dispute broke out on the court.

"Is that what's bothering you? You don't feel like you earned it?"

PJ shook her head, looking at her mom. "The presentation I prepared—it wasn't for me. I was going to make the case that Cole should have the house. That Crossroads should stay open and expand."

Mom's eyes widened. "Why?"

"Because he was doing a worthy thing. Because those kids need help. Because he knew how to make a difference in their lives. Because he needs—so badly—to help others, Mom. His family died in a car accident, and he feels responsible for their deaths. It wasn't his fault, he was only twelve, but all these years he's carried that guilt. I think Crossroads was his do-over, his chance to save those kids. And I couldn't stand the thought of him losing that."

"Did he tell you that—that it's his do-over?"

"I don't even think he's aware of what he's doing."

Mom's face softened. Her eyes homed in on PJ, and she gave her a knowing look. "You love him."

The certainty of her mom's tone sank deep down inside PJ, opening spaces that had been closed for years. Seeping into crevices she didn't know existed, filling her with its weighty truth.

"Yeah," she whispered, her eyes burning. "I do."

She did love him. Loved the way he gave so much of himself, loved the way he protected her, the way he touched her, so tenderly, the way he looked at her, his green eyes as deep and fathomless as the ocean.

"I know I've made bad choices in the past. I've picked some real losers, more than you even know about . . ." She met Mom's gaze. "But Cole's not one of them. He's a good man, Mom. He's special. He's—he's perfect for me. Only he doesn't want me."

She gave herself a straitjacket hug. "I don't even know what happened. One minute we were together and everything was fine, and the next he's breaking up with me, saying we're not good for each other."

Something shifted in her mom's face. Her eyes clouded.

"I don't understand why he broke up with me. I don't understand why he needed miles between us so badly that he gave up his dream. All I know is the house is too quiet. My arms are too empty, and my heart is in a million pieces."

Mom's eyes glassed over, and some unidentified emotion scurried across her face. "Oh, PJ. I'm so sorry."

Mia's startled cry carried across the lawn, and Mom rushed toward her. The baby was stuck inside the car. Mom scooped her from the coupe and soothed her with quiet words, brushing the tears from Mia's chubby cheeks.

When the baby was pacified, Mom walked toward the house with Mia on her hip. She gestured for PJ to come along. "Let's go see how your dad's doing with Ava."

PJ numbly tagged behind. She'd thought she'd feel better once she unloaded her burden, but it turned out that the same heavy weight that had followed her there still sat squarely on her shoulders.

Chapter Forty-Six

COLE PULLED INTO HIS APARTMENT LOT AND PARKED HIS truck in the empty space assigned him. The sun had set behind his building, washing it with gray in the waning light. He left his truck and skirted a couple kids coloring the sidewalk with chalk.

Somewhere in the building a baby cried. The smells of Mexican food filtered from someone's apartment, making his stomach growl. All he wanted was a plate of food, a shower, and his bed.

He'd been working dawn to dusk for three weeks. His hands were calloused and his body ached, but at least he was keeping busy. Getting tired enough that sleep crept up on him at night no matter how troubled he felt inside.

Becky and Greg had dragged him to their counselor the minute he'd returned to town. Somehow they'd talked him into going twice a week. It was hard. Painful. But the counselor was patient, and Cole was sorting out some things. Things about Lizzy. Things about his family.

He opened the main door and trudged up the stairs. The building smelled like a mixture of mold and cigarette smoke instead of fresh flowers and haute cuisine. The brown carpet was faded and frayed, the iron handrails chipped and cold to the touch. The stairs didn't creak faintly under his feet, and the rail was too skinny to fill the curvature of his palm.

He took the second set of steps, fishing his keys from his pocket. A woman sat on the floor by his door.

Cole stopped at the top. What was she doing here? "Mrs. McKinley . . ."

"Cole." Her head came off the wall as she straightened, meeting his gaze. Her knees were pulled up, her arms folded on them. She looked more like a little girl than a fiftysomething mother and grandmother.

She stood, brushing her hair behind her ear in a movement so like PJ it made him ache inside.

PJ. A chilling thought flittered through his brain, snagging hard. "Is PJ—is she okay?"

"Yes, yes, she's fine. It's nothing like that." The woman gave a sheepish smile. "She doesn't even know I'm here."

He regarded her for a long minute, trying to fathom why she'd made the long drive.

"Can I come inside? Just for a minute?"

He immediately thought of the barren state of his apartment, of last night's dishes left in the sink. But curiosity prevailed. "Ah, sure."

He let them in and gestured to the sofa. He remembered her tidy farmhouse and wished he could vaporize the ball of socks, the empty coffee mug, the junk mail scattered across the coffee table.

"Can I get you anything?" He thought of the paltry selection in his fridge. He couldn't remember his last grocery run. "Water? Coffee?"

She perched on the edge of the couch. "No, thank you. I

went out for a bite while I waited for you. There's a nice little diner just down the street."

He took the other end of the sofa as an uncomfortable silence thickened the air between them.

"How'd you find me?"

"We moms have our ways." She fiddled with her purse strap, winding it around her small hand as she took in the apartment.

"How is she? PJ?" His heart thumped hard in anticipation of her answer. For a sliver of news that might satisfy his hunger.

"Not so good, if you want to know the truth. You up and left without so much as a good-bye." Her tone softened the harsh words.

"I'd have thought you'd be pleased about that."

Her eyes squeezed in a wince, and she looked down at her lap. "You're very direct."

"I see no need to beat around the bush."

She met his gaze. "You're right. I did want you out of PJ's life. I looked at what I knew of you and filed you with all her loser ex-boyfriends. That was wrong of me. I shouldn't have judged you, shouldn't have butted in, and I'm sorry for that."

"You came all the way here for that?"

"I told you in person you were wrong for her. Least I can do is admit I was wrong face-to-face."

He gave her props for going the extra mile. "I appreciate that. But you were right about some of it." He wasn't good for PJ. She deserved so much more.

"No, I don't think I was."

He wasn't going to argue. There was no point. He leaned forward, his elbows digging into his knees, wishing she'd leave before he said something stupid. Before he begged her for more news of PJ. Something good. Something to warm him up. Something he could take with him to bed at night.

"She's in love with you, you know."

His heart constricted painfully. He rubbed at the spot as if he could soothe it. Hope rose, and he squashed it down firmly. He didn't dare look at her. She was a perceptive woman, and his feelings for PJ were hovering way too close to the surface.

"She thinks you left because of her. That you couldn't get away from her soon enough."

He ached inside at the thought. He never wanted to hurt her. It was better this way. She'd get over it. Get over him. Better he let her down now than later when she was all in.

"I know I'm being a nosy mom again, but I don't think she's right. I think you took to heart the things I said. That perhaps I added to the erroneous things you already believed about yourself, and I'm so sorry for that."

He'd barely begun scratching the surface of that in counseling. Just thinking about it made anxiety worm through him. He sure didn't want to discuss it with PJ's mom.

"I'm sure PJ must've told you we lost a son . . . Michael. Nothing can prepare you for something like that. The depth of grief, the overwhelming darkness . . ." She gave Cole a penetrating look. "The guilt . . ."

He looked away, clenching his jaw.

"I know all about guilt. You don't lose a teenaged son and not ask yourself the questions. Why did I let him go swimming? Why wasn't I there with him? What kind of mother am I? The guilt can eat you alive."

"What did you do?"

"I wallowed in it. For a while. I screamed at God and begged for answers until my voice was gone. Cried more tears than I knew I had. But I had countless friends who prayed with me and for me and held me up when I didn't think I could take another breath.

"Eventually the darkness lifted, and I came to realize I had three other children who needed me. A husband who was hurting too. I remembered that God loved me enough to give me seventeen years with Michael, loved me enough to give him a home much better than the one he had here. Loved me enough to give me assurance that I'd be with him again someday. There's beautiful peace in that."

But what about the guilt? What about the wretched unworthiness that lived down deep inside, that swallowed him alive?

"But the guilt," she said. "That took awhile. We think we're in control of things, and moms are probably especially bad about that. We think if we do the right thing everything will work out for the best, and our kids will be healthy and safe.

"But God has a plan, and even though we don't understand the why of it, we can remember that He loved us enough to send His Son to die for us. He settled His love right there, on the cross, and anything else that happens, I can trust Him to know what's best. Not understand it. Not take responsibility for it. Just trust." She gave him a wry smile. "Easier said than done, I know."

Her words opened something inside him. Something light and freeing. Someone else had been through the fire and come out the other side. He knew God loved him, but trusting was hard. And the guilt was buried so deeply he didn't know how to dig it out.

"Just let go of it, Cole. God doesn't want you carrying around that guilt. He doesn't want you alone and miserable. He made you for better things. We've only got one life. One chance. Don't waste it."

Cole felt a burning behind his eyes and blinked it away. He thought of those applications he'd tossed in the trash, those kids who needed him. He thought of PJ. Did she really love him? He couldn't speak. His throat was swollen and raw.

"I love my kids—every one of them. I'm still trying to do my best by them, even though I can't control their lives, and when I see one of them hurting needlessly . . ." She gave a sheepish smile. "Well, I'm a mom." She hitched her purse on her shoulder. "I should let you get back to your evening. You've had a long day, and I have a long drive back."

He stood numbly and walked her to the door. "Thanks for coming all this way, Mrs. McKinley."

"Think about what I said. You're a good man, Cole. I'd hate to see you miss all the great things God has in store for you." She opened the door and turned to him. "And, Cole . . . it's Mama Jo." She patted his cheek gently then pulled the door closed.

Chapter Forty-Seven

PJ FLIPPED OFF THE LIGHTS AND MADE SURE THE EXTERIOR lights were on. It was early to retire, but she was out of things to do. Her cooking class had been canceled at the last minute. The ladies of the Rotary had a fund-raising event tomorrow morning and needed extra time for final preparations.

PJ changed into her pajamas, settled into bed, and flipped on the TV, needing the sound of voices filling the house. She spotted her laptop on the nightstand. She should work on a website for the B & B. The closing was only three days away. She should be nearly ready to open; instead, the upstairs remained untouched.

She stayed busy enough through the day, or tried to. But nighttime came and memories charged in like unwelcome guests, making themselves at home in her brain. She indulged them until tears spilled down her cheeks and soaked into her pillow.

Enough of that. You have to stop this, PJ. He's gone. He doesn't love you. You have to move on.

But her heart sang a different tune. Her heart wondered if he thought about her sometimes too. If he missed her touch. If he lay in bed thinking of what could have been.

But he was the one who left.

She really had to stop this. She plugged in her cell and started channel surfing. Nothing was on Monday nights, nothing that would occupy her mind.

A scratch at the window made her jump. Stupid branch. Every time it was windy, the scratching spooked her. She needed to trim the tree.

Had she locked the front door? She'd unbolted it earlier for her class. Normally it wasn't a big deal, but since her trouble with Keaton she'd been diligent, especially now that she was alone in the house.

Heaving a sigh, she pulled herself from her comfy bed and padded from her room. The wood planking was cool, and bits of dirt stuck to her bare feet, reminding her it was time to sweep.

She walked through the kitchen, startling when the dishwasher changed cycles. She was jumpy tonight, for no good reason.

The house smelled faintly of garlic and thyme from the roasted chateaubriand she'd experimented with earlier. The beef had turned out tender and flavorful. If she added it to the menu, it would be her most expensive dish—a culinary treat for special occasions.

The exterior lights filtered through the leaded transom window, guiding her to the foyer. A shuffling noise sounded on the porch. It was only a squirrel or the wind.

The doorknob clicked.

Her heart hammered, pounding up in her ears. Thoughts raced. Keaton. No phone. No help. She reached for something, anything—an umbrella left by a customer weeks ago. She pulled it from the stand and cocked it back as the door swung open. A large shadow entered boldly. She closed her eyes and swung the umbrella like a bat, the wooden handle connecting.

"Ow!"

The umbrella flew from her hands, clattering across the floor. A squeak escaped her throat as she turned to run.

Then the voice registered in her brain.

She stopped midturn, palming her chest. "Cole?" she whispered into the darkness.

"Why do you keep hitting me?" His voice was disgruntled.

Her breath left her body in an epic sigh. She flipped on a light.

He palmed his forehead, blinking against the brightness.

"Omigosh. Are you okay?" She pulled his hand away, wincing at the angry red knot already rising at his temple. "I'm so sorry. I thought—what are you doing here?"

He rubbed his head, glowering. "Second-guessing myself."

She pushed the door shut and urged him to the steps. "Sit down. I'll be right back."

She retrieved the cold compress she kept on hand for burns and made her way back to the foyer. The man had probably come for his things, and she'd walloped him upside the head. Again.

Way to go, PJ. If you can't talk him into loving you, maybe you can beat him into it.

When she returned, she sat on the step above him, putting her even with him, and pressed the compress gently to his temple.

He flinched. "That's quite a swing you have there," he said, sounding a little less peeved.

"I'm sorry. I wasn't expecting anyone."

"I thought you had a class tonight."

"It was canceled." He must've planned to slip in while she was busy, take whatever he'd come for, and leave without having to see her.

He shifted, and his stubble scraped against the palm of her free hand.

She snatched it back. "You didn't have to sneak in."

"I wasn't."

"You thought I was busy, and you were going to slip upstairs and take your things. That's not necessary. You can have whatever you came for."

He gave her a penetrating look, something shifting in his eyes. "I hope so."

Did he think she was going to put up a fight? That she'd claim his things just because he'd left them behind? Didn't he know her better than that by now?

"Help yourself." She took his hand, pressed it against the cold pack, and stood.

He dropped the compress and bolted to his feet, blocking her way. His eyes locked onto hers. Green, familiar, and so close.

Her insides fluttered. He didn't even have to touch her to draw a response. He stirred so much with just a look. Always had, from the very beginning. How lame was she?

"What if I came for you?"

For her? Her heart turned over in her chest. A seed of hope sprouted inside her, but she was afraid to believe. She'd been burnt too many times before.

"What?" she asked.

"What if I want another chance?"

"You left." Her voice cracked, and she swallowed against the tightening in her throat. "You just up and left without even saying good-bye."

His eyes softened as he laid his palm against her cheek. "I'm sorry I hurt you. I was wrong. I thought I could let you go. Thought you'd be better off without me—and maybe you would.

But I can't do it. I'm done trying. I know I've got a lot of stuff to work out. But I want to work it out here, with you. I want to be the man you deserve." His voice was as thick as honey, his eyes as solemn as she'd ever seen them. "Give me another chance."

Her eyes prickled with tears. She couldn't speak past the lump in her throat.

"Please don't say no." His eyes scrolled over her face, pleading. His thumb teased her lower lip.

She drew in the scent of him. Clean. Musky. All man. She missed that smell so much. Missed the husky texture of his voice, the gentle comfort of his touch.

"Going once . . ."

She was helpless to speak at the look in his eyes. There was no need for words anyway. Words were overrated.

"Going twice." His breath feathered her lips as he drew near.

Her insides went to liquid. She couldn't think of anything she wanted more than his lips on hers. She strained toward him as he neared.

His lips met hers, brushing softly. Once. Twice. She felt it clear to her bare toes.

"Gone," he whispered against her lips.

She *was* gone. Completely, totally, irrevocably gone.

He deepened the kiss, and she savored the familiar taste of him. He was everything she remembered. Was he really here? Wanting her? Needing her? If this was a dream, she hoped she never awakened.

He pulled her closer, drawing her into his embrace. She wound her arms around him, taking comfort in the solid strength of his shoulders. Her hand found the warm beat of his pulse at his neck and rested there.

A moment later his lips left hers. She held back the whimper that rose in her throat. Their breaths came raggedly.

His eyes burned into hers as his thumb stroked her cheek. "I am so gone over you, PJ. I love you. So much."

Her breath left on a deep sigh. "I love you too."

Her reward was the gentle upturn of his lips. "I missed you. I don't want to be without you. Ever. Again." He brushed her lips slowly, softly.

Warmth unfurled inside her as he moved his mouth across hers. She thought back to the beginning. She'd thought she'd known what she wanted. But all of her wishes were just falling stars, here one moment and gone the next. What mattered was right here, right in front of her.

When he drew away, she whispered, "I can't believe you're here."

He gave her a penetrating look, the kind that reached deep inside and settled low and sure. "I'm never letting you go again. You're stuck with me. I'll find a job. We'll make it work."

PJ had other ideas about that, but it wasn't the time.

"Promise?" she asked. Her eyes wandered over his beautiful face, taking in the familiar planes, the scruff on his jaw, the cleft in his chin. She met his gaze and saw forever in his eyes.

"Promise," he said.

Epilogue

THE DEED WAS DONE. LITERALLY.

PJ slipped inside the house, the folders clutched to her chest, and dashed up the stairs. She knew Cole was here, had seen his truck in the back lot.

He'd spent the past three nights upstairs on the living room sofa and the past three days looking for work. In between classes and cooking and planning, they'd found quiet moments. Cole had gone to see a local counselor yesterday, someone recommended by PJ's pastor. He was determined to work out his issues, and PJ was determined to be there for him as he did so.

There was no one else for her. She knew it with a certainty that grounded her. And the best thing? The feeling was mutual.

She practically skipped down the hallway and burst into the living room. Cole looked up from the newspaper, spread open on the dining room table.

"Whatcha doing?" Her voice crackled with energy. Her heartbeat was like a jackhammer in her chest.

He gave her an amused look. "Looking at the help wanted ads. What's got you so wound up?"

"I just closed on the house with Mrs. Simmons."

His brows shot up. "Oh, hey. Wow, why didn't you tell me?" He rose from his chair and embraced her. "Congratulations, baby. I'm so happy for you." His hands moved across her back, doing nothing to settle her.

"Thanks. It was a big day."

"Let's go out tonight." His voice rumbled low in her ear. "Celebrate."

"I like the way you think. We do have a lot to celebrate."

He took her hands in his and put them behind her back. "You'll have to put me to work up here while I'm still unemployed. I could add that wall, make this into a suite, like you wanted."

"Or I could just leave it like this."

"Well, yeah, but a B & B needs a suite, don't you think?"

"That's a good point." She pulled from his arms and reached for the folders she'd set on the table. "But before I go any further, there's some paperwork you need to sign." She opened the manila folder and set the pen on the top sheet, her hand trembling.

"Me? What for?" He took the pen and leaned over, bracing his hands beside the folder, his broad shoulders hovering over the table.

She watched his face. Watched while pensive lines furrowed his forehead as his eyes toggled across the page. His lips slackened as realization dawned.

"What?" His gaze darted to her, then back to the paper. He flipped the page, scanning it, then straightened. "No," he said firmly. "It's your house, PJ. You won it."

"You gave it up for me. And you know what? I was going to give it up for you too."

"What are you talking about?"

"I went to presentation day prepared to make a case for why you should have the house. Why Crossroads should stay open.

It was an easy sell because you made a difference in the lives of those kids, but I never had the chance to give it."

He dropped the pen. "I'm not taking your dream, PJ."

"You're not taking anything. I have my restaurant. That's all I want. Well, not *all* I want. I want you to have your dream too. I want those kids to have a safe place to go. I want us to do this together. You with Crossroads, me with my restaurant. Both of us living our dream under the same roof."

She pulled the second folder from beneath the manila one and opened it on the table.

His eyes fell to the rumpled pages, his face falling. "Where'd you get these?"

"I found them in the garbage after you left. Your Promising pile. Four kids who need a home . . ." She opened her arms wide. "And all this empty space just sitting here."

He swallowed, his eyes fixed on the papers, on the pictures of those kids.

"We should really do something about that, don't you think?"

He met her gaze. "I can't believe you'd do this."

"It's actually kind of selfish. I like having you under the same roof."

He gave a wry smile, rubbing the bruise at his temple. "I'm not sure it's safe."

PJ pursed her lips. "If you sign these papers, I will solemnly swear not to wield weighty umbrellas or ceramic pots or any other inanimate object as a weapon against you. So help me God."

He moved his hand over his jaw, his eyes turning serious. "This is a big decision, PJ."

"I've given it a lot of thought."

"Are you sure?"

She cupped his cheeks, loving the roughness of his jaw under her palm. "I couldn't be more sure. It was all I could do not to call those kids days ago."

He gave her a long look. Green eyes had never looked so warm. "You're an amazing woman, Sunshine. And I am one lucky man."

Smiling, she moved into his arms the same way Cole had moved into her heart.

Reading Group Guide

1. Which character did you most relate to? Why?
2. PJ found herself so busy with her new restaurant that she didn't make time for important things. Have you ever been too busy for God? For your family? How did this affect you and others?
3. PJ felt shame over her former relationship with Keaton, a married man. Discuss her feelings on this. Is it a sin to be tempted? Did PJ do anything wrong?
4. Cole spent years blaming himself for his family's accident. Was it his fault? Have you ever been in a situation where you blamed yourself for something you had no control over?
5. What did you like about the McKinley family? What did you dislike? Every family has its foibles. What do you love about your family? What annoys you?
6. Sometimes we absorb lies about ourselves that we come to believe as true. PJ's lie was "I'm not capable." Cole's was "I don't deserve love." Is there a lie that you believe about yourself? How has it affected the decisions you've made?
7. PJ and Cole both dealt with guilt and shame. Have you ever dealt with those feelings? How did you handle them?

8. What's the difference between guilt and shame? Should they be handled differently?

9. PJ's mom talked to her about the thorns in her life that kept her from growing. Do you have thorns in your life? What are they and what can you do about them?

10. Cole lost his family at a young age. The foster kids Cole took in had already faced traumatic events in their young lives. Sometimes bad things happen to good people. How is this consistent with a view of a loving and compassionate God?

Find the recipe for PJ's Wildberry Cheesecake at
www.DeniseHunterBooks.com

Acknowledgments

Writing a book is a team effort, and I'm so grateful for the fabulous team at HarperCollins Christian Fiction, led by publisher Daisy Hutton: Ansley Boatman, Katie Bond, Amanda Bostic, Karli Cajka, Laura Dickerson, Elizabeth Hudson, Jodi Hughes, Ami McConnell, Becky Monds, Becky Philpot, Kerri Potts, and Kristen Vasgaard.

Thanks especially to my editor, Ami McConnell. Woman, you are a wonder! I'm constantly astounded by your gift of insight. I don't know of a more talented line editor than LB Norton. You make me look much better than I am!

Author Colleen Coble is my first reader. Thank you, friend! I wouldn't want to do this writing thing without my buds and fellow authors Colleen Coble and Kristin Billerbeck. Love you, girls! This is my first finished book since the death of our dear friend Diann Hunt. She helped us brainstorm every book, including this one. I miss you and love you, Di!

I'm grateful to my agent, Karen Solem, who is able to somehow make sense of the legal garble of contracts and, even more amazing, help me understand it.

Kevin, my husband of twenty-five years, has been a wonderful support. Thank you, honey! To my sons, Justin, Chad, and Trevor: you make life an adventure! Love you all!

Acknowledgments

Lastly, thank you, friend, for letting me share this story with you. I wouldn't be doing this without you! I enjoy connecting with friends on my Facebook page, www.facebook.com /authordenisehunter. Please pop over and say hello. Visit my website at the link www.DeniseHunterBooks.com, or just drop me a note at Denise@DeniseHunterBooks.com. I'd love to hear from you!

Escape to the salty air of
Summer Harbor, Maine, in

Married 'til Monday

THOMAS NELSON
Since 1798

Three Small-Town Love Stories

by Denise Hunter from the Smitten series—available in a single collection!

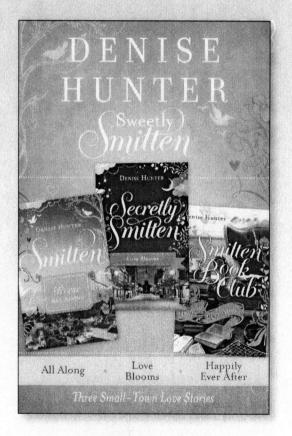

Available in e-book

About the Author

PHOTO BY AMBER ZIMMERMAN

Denise Hunter is the bestselling author of many novels, including *The Trouble with Cowboys* and *Barefoot Summer*. She lives in Indiana with her husband, Kevin, and their three sons.